THE GIRL ON THE BALCONY

DIANA WILKINSON

B
Boldwood

First published in Great Britain in 2025 by Boldwood Books Ltd.

Copyright © Diana Wilkinson, 2025

Cover Design by Aaron Munday

Cover Images: Shutterstock

The moral right of Diana Wilkinson to be identified as the author of this work has been asserted in accordance with the Copyright, Designs and Patents Act 1988.

All rights reserved. No part of this book may be reproduced in any form or by any electronic or mechanical means, including information storage and retrieval systems, without written permission from the author, except for the use of brief quotations in a book review. This book is a work of fiction and, except in the case of historical fact, any resemblance to actual persons, living or dead, is purely coincidental.

Every effort has been made to obtain the necessary permissions with reference to copyright material, both illustrative and quoted. We apologise for any omissions in this respect and will be pleased to make the appropriate acknowledgements in any future edition.

A CIP catalogue record for this book is available from the British Library.

Paperback ISBN 978-1-83603-325-7

Large Print ISBN 978-1-83603-326-4

Hardback ISBN 978-1-83603-324-0

Ebook ISBN 978-1-83603-327-1

Kindle ISBN 978-1-83603-328-8

Audio CD ISBN 978-1-83603-319-6

MP3 CD ISBN 978-1-83603-320-2

Digital audio download ISBN 978-1-83603-321-9

This book is printed on certified sustainable paper. Boldwood Books is dedicated to putting sustainability at the heart of our business. For more information please visit https://www.boldwoodbooks.com/about-us/sustainability/

Boldwood Books Ltd, 23 Bowerdean Street, London, SW6 3TN

www.boldwoodbooks.com

To James... a son in a million

PROLOGUE
TEDDY

I fiddle with my EarPods, tap my fingers on the drop-down table, and bob my head in time to imaginary music. The EarPods ran out of battery ages ago, so I've heard every word the woman across the aisle from me said. And holy shit. I'm pretty sure she just owned up to cold-blooded murder.

We're sitting near the front of the plane, heading for Luton airport, and suddenly I'm eavesdropping on her conversation. She's talking behind a very chubby hand, but my hearing is so acute I could hear a pin drop.

I take a large swig from my water bottle, not sure whether I want her to stop talking or to carry on. Either way, I keep my ears pricked but my eyes averted.

'He was such a bastard,' the lady tells the girl in seat 2A. She's having to lean across an empty seat between them to tell her story. 'But you know that, don't you?'

They seem to know each other, but the girl looks so shocked that I guess she's hearing this particular tale for the first time, how this woman masterminded her husband's death on a roof terrace in Marbella. The lady then announces that indoor cameras show footage of the girl inside the villa shortly before her husband's death.

I take a cursory glance round, and notice the girl is shaking like a leaf as she digests the words. I sneak another glance when the lady stops talking. She leans heavily into her seat with a smug, self-satisfied expression, before tucking into a mini box of Pringles. I'm sort of wondering if I might have been sleeping and dreamt the whole thing. But I'm far too wide awake.

Suddenly, the seatbelt signs go on, and the captain announces our descent.

'Hello.' I hear a voice. 'Don't you love flying?'

As I tug at my seatbelt, I don't immediately twig the lady is talking to me. I scoop out the EarPods, and slip them into their holder. Hopefully she'll not guess I overheard her conversation. About how she had someone trap her husband on the terrace in 40-degree heat, and deliberately didn't let him out.

'I don't mind it,' I say, aiming for nonchalant, but her directness immediately has me on edge.

'I'm Astrid, by the way. On my way to London. And you?'

'Stephen.' I blush, tongue-tied, and uneasy.

'I'm from Norway,' she says.

'Oh. I've never been but the fjords are on my bucket list.' I grab my bag to give my hands something to do.

'You like travelling?' she continues.

'Yes, it's my favourite pastime.'

'I've got a lovely villa in Marbella, and spend most summers there.' There's a glint in her eye that suggests she's imparting more than just the words. The plane buffets from side to side as it careers along the runway, giving me the opportunity to look away from her face. But her next words have me snapping my gaze right back. 'Maybe, Stephen, you should come and visit me at my villa?'

***

Wait till I tell Hayley. She'll never believe what's happened. That I was sitting beside a member of the Norwegian royal family, a woman who owned up to being a cold-blooded murderer. A fact she doesn't know I overheard.

I help Astrid carry her cabin bag into the arrivals hall, and as we're waiting by the luggage carousel, she repeats her offer, looking more serious this time.

'Stephen, I'm looking for a young man to help out around my villa, and act as an escort for me round Marbella. Maybe you'd be able to step in for a few months in between travels?'

She slumps down onto a seat, her face red and puffy.

At first I think she's joking, making polite conversation, but when she digs around in an enormous handbag and hands me a business card, I realise she might be deadly serious.

'I pay well,' she says, laughing so loudly that heads turn. She then asks for the business card back, and scribbles something on the back.

'How does that sound for a monthly salary?'

Is she for real? That's what bar work offers for a six-month slog. I'm lost for words.

Her luggage arrives, and I help her lift several large, very expensive-looking cases off the carousel.

'Maybe you can help me out to my taxi?' she asks. 'I need a strong young man like you in my life.'

I jump to it, the pound signs practically flashing in my eyes. 'Of course.'

'Just one thing. My offer only stands for a couple of days. Let me know by the end of the week, otherwise I'll have to find myself a new minder.'

Holy shit. What the heck is my girlfriend going to say?

1

JADE

I'm strolling along the main street in Fuente Alamo. Well, more skipping than strolling.

The Pedersens, the Danish couple I've just wined and dined, have all but signed on the dotted line. If they buy the townhouse, 4,000 euros commission will be in the bag. It could be a lifesaver, as my finances are in desperate need of a boost.

The greengrocers is brightly lit, with an amazing array of fruit and vegetables on display outside. You wouldn't think it was only February, and 9.30 at night. Spain is so unlike England, where everything shuts down for the day around 4 p.m.

I've had a couple of glasses of wine, money well spent, and I'm feeling on the reckless side of jovial. I'm on such a high, and for the first time in ages I've a spring in my step. I dip my fingers into the satsuma display, and pocket a couple.

I jump when a horn beeps, but the car passes. For a second I think it might be someone who saw me pocketing the oranges. I slow my pace, aiming for nonchalant, when I hear a wolf whistle. I turn my head, fearing it might be the shopkeeper calling me out. But there's no sign of anyone in the store.

'*Hola, senorita.*'

I freeze when I realise I'm the target of the greeting. I give a wan smile as two guys with lecherous expressions wink, and walk past.

By the time I reach the back street where I've parked my Fiat Punto, my celebratory glow has dulled. The side road is so dark, with no sign of life anywhere. All the activity in Fuente is centred on the main street, and everywhere else is spooky as hell. I need to get back to the resort, and to bed. I'm so exhausted, and will properly celebrate tomorrow when the Pedersens put down their deposit. That's the plan.

Once I've driven through the town, I hit the unmarked dirt track that leads back to the resort. The resort where I live and work, Campo de Golf.

The motorways in Spain are dimly lit, but this dirt track is on a whole new level. Even with the headlights on full I could be wearing a blindfold. It's as if I've been sucked into a black hole.

Worse still, the car is being tossed in the air every few metres by gaping potholes. An occasional oncoming vehicle teases me with bright lights before it shoots past. I can just about see the steering wheel.

Then, out of nowhere, a full beam approaches in my rear-view mirror. The light is blinding, and a monstrous vehicle is soon only centimetres from my bumper. If I hit the brakes it'll smash into me.

What are they doing? It can't be over the theft of a couple of satsumas. Really? Okay, I shouldn't have pocketed them as I walked past, but I was in such a good mood. I didn't think anyone would notice, or care.

There's nowhere for their car – what looks like a black 4X4 – to pass, as we're on a twisty section of the road. Yet I'm not convinced that's their aim. It feels like they're trying to force me into the ditch. My speedometer won't go any higher, having struggled to reach 80 kph, with a death-rattle clunking noise coming from under the bonnet.

The vehicle behind is now so close, it's actually started to nudge against my bumper. Holy shit. It's banging, metal on metal, and shunting me forward in the darkness. At least it's speeding me up, but what the hell. This isn't friendly dodgems. These guys mean business, whatever that business is. If I'd snapped up a crate of Rioja, I get why someone might come for me. But a couple of oranges? Maybe the guys tailing me are the shopkeepers. Or perhaps they're the two swarthy guys who whistled as they walked by.

Deep down, I'm scared it's someone else, someone from my past. But no one knows where I am now, so I try to dismiss the thought.

Anyway, whatever or whoever it is, does it really matter? From where I'm sitting, I've got two options. Carry on and let them crush my car to pulp, or pull over on to the barren unlit field and pray for them to drive past. If they stop and come for me, I could make a dash for it. I'm fit, fast. But it's impossible to see.

My heart is thrashing in my ribcage. I've no idea what to do. Surely, if their aim was to force me off the road, they'd blast the horn. Yet I'm starting to feel that isn't it. They're after my blood.

I'm forced to slow down as my car gasps for air. It appears to be giving up the ghost. I direct the wheel towards the side of the road, making a snap decision that ploughing into the adjacent field has the slight edge over being crushed to death.

It's then I see something moving in the field. It's huge, and seems to be heading this way. Likely a raging bull with razor-sharp horns, seeing as I'm in Spain. I look around, but I've run out of options. It's the field, or stay where I am and get crushed like scrap metal in a junkyard.

Suddenly it seems a good idea to roll down the window and hurl out the satsuma peel. I may as well lose the evidence, and play ditzy blonde. Turn their thoughts away from murder because that's what it feels like.

If they're professionals, or Spanish mafia, this could be it.

I have sudden flashbacks of Marbella. The heat, the terror, and the heart-stopping getaway. That dreadful premonition returns – that what's happening now might have something to do with what happened there.

I might not have been directly responsible for Isaac's death, but I wasn't innocent.

2

The Fiat chokes and splutters, and finally conks out. I can't even drive on to the field with the roving wildebeest. It's small comfort that I'm unlikely to get mauled to death, but I'm still shaking like a leaf.

My life flashes before me. It's crazy, but the thing I'm most worried about is getting back to feed the cat. I might be about to be bludgeoned to death, but all I can think about is the stray that wanders round each night.

Although I'm trembling head to toe, I'm unable to move. The making-a-run-for-it option is off the table, as I'm superglued to the spot. I close my eyes, and start counting down from 100 to try to calm my nerves. This usually works at the resort's mindfulness class, but for now, it's not doing its pitch.

The laser-sharp headlights are still searing through my back windscreen. The filthy glass of the Fiat suddenly seems gleaming. Instead of risking night blindness, I keep my eyes peeled ahead, in the direction of the dark unknown. I've no idea what to do next, except wait.

The men have killed their engine, and the silence is worse

than the roar of action. Their lights are still on, Gestapo-interrogation bright. A few minutes, and still nothing happens. They don't get out, keeping me sandwiched between them and the blackness. What are they doing? I'm too scared to look round, visions of a Kalashnikov pointed at my head.

Then all of a sudden, I hear their engine rev up again. If their aim is to shove my Punto another few miles along the dirt track, then what choice do I have? It's only about a mile to the resort entrance. I say a quick prayer, not sure who's listening, but I plead for these maniacs to move on.

Suddenly they're alongside, leering in through the driver's side window. The passenger leans across, makes an obscene gesture with a middle finger, and swivels a large slithery tongue in my direction. Both men are dark-skinned, and very hirsute. Hair straggles downwards from their heads, and thick beards complete the hardman look.

They're the sort of guys you really don't want to meet on a dark night. They're like characters from a slasher movie.

I look down at my feet, hoping if I don't react they might take off. It seems the wisest move considering I don't have a back-up plan.

After what seems like an eternity, the vehicle moves slowly away. I manage to read the registration, repeating the numbers and letters in my head. It's only when the car zooms off that I'm able to breathe again, and manage with damp shaky fingers to type the registration into my phone. This seems a positive move, although I've no idea why.

I just hope, whoever they are, they don't come after me again.

3

The Fiat manages to start again after a few attempts, and five minutes later, I'm rolling up to the resort. My heart is still racing, but thankfully it's calming down.

The illuminated sign for Campo de Golf which welcomes you to the resort is blinding. It could be lighting up an airstrip for incoming planes. The letters are big and bold, like those on an upmarket Vegas nightclub. It's never looked more inviting.

There's an opulence about the entrance façade, selling luxury to new arrivals. It certainly did its pitch when I looked round on a warm, sultry afternoon. The fierce Spanish heatwave had lingered, and by early October the weather was glorious. Not too hot, and certainly not too cold. I had no idea back then how bleak and desolate the golf resort would feel in the depths of winter. I now actively discourage prospective buyers from coming to look at properties until at least the end of March. It's still early February, and is dark by 6.30 p.m. when a grim desolation engulfs the place.

Both sides of the security kiosk are flanked by towering stone walls. Another set of blinding neon lights point back onto the walls themselves and highlight the gushing water feature. The oily-slick sales reps joke to clients that it looks a bit like the Trevi Fountain. They point it out, but don't linger. Certainly, no one is chucking coins into the murky water channel.

There's no sign of anyone in the security kiosk. Manned 24/7, the blurb says, the cost shared by all the residents (of which I'm one). Yet another thing they don't tell you before you sign your life away. Although I'm sneaky enough, now the boot's on the other foot, to also leave out this information when showing people around. If the sale is a definite *no-go*, I own up. I certainly don't want them loitering with another agent.

It's really tough being a sales agent. Especially in Spain where the competition for selling holiday homes is fierce. It was meant to be a whole new future setting up shop here. Managing, rather than selling, million-pound homes has quickly become my bread and butter. Sales are virtually non-existent in the winter, and it breaks my heart that, in order to make ends meet, I've had to rent out the little apartment I bought. I'm keeping everything crossed that by the summer I'll start earning serious money, and can move back in.

I drive past the empty kiosk. When Santiago, the security guard, is locked inside it, his head and shoulders look as if they're sitting on a serving platter. He is so uninspired by the job that he could be dead. Tonight, as usual, he's likely asleep in the cabin off to the right, preferring his own company. He's happy enough in the daytime, munching his way through tortilla chips.

It's still only ten o'clock, but I'm exhausted. It's been a busy day, and I'm so ready for bed. The yawns threaten to swallow me up. I drive slowly over the speed bumps, gritting my teeth when the suspension creaks and joins the death rattle. The scraping noise is like chalk on a blackboard. Oh for my warm duvet.

I pass the clubhouse, the hub of the golfing activity. In fact, the hub of activity for the whole resort. It's also enveloped in darkness, with only a couple of vehicles in the car park. Happy hour has long passed. Once I reach the roundabout, I slowly unwind. Nearly home. I hum as I do the sharp right on to the last stretch of road.

I'm staying on the second phase of the resort development. Phase 1 was built first, comprised of large detached villas, whereas Phase 2 is made up of small communities sited around communal pools.

The whole resort is pretty creepy in the dark, and the spookiness gets worse the further away you are from the clubhouse. A dull orange glow from dusky streetlamps doesn't help the ambience, rather upping the eerie feel. All around has the atmosphere of a very plush ghost town.

Up ahead I suddenly spot a random car, and slow down. Holy shit. It can't be.

No. No. No.

The car's parked outside number 66 where I'm staying. A large red people carrier, and it's directly alongside Avery Knowles's villa. The villa I've been staying in for the past two months.

Avery emailed this week to confirm he wouldn't be out until mid-May. It's only February. What the hell is he doing here now? And how the heck am I going to explain to him why all my worldly goods are strewn around his villa?

When I rented out my own apartment, I had to stay somewhere...

The last time I saw Avery was early November, a couple of weeks after I'd set up shop on the resort, and he was my first client. He was smitten with the villa, and paid up straightaway. I was euphoric, counting up in my head how much I might make from my new business. Turns out Avery was a random lucky introduction to the job.

Waking up in his king-sized bed after we'd agreed the deal, after a night of celebrations, with him next to me was mortifying. But afterwards, we managed to avoid each other with the stealth of ninjas. Not that anything happened between us. I've learnt my lesson where one-night stands are concerned. All we did was share a shedload of sangria and collapse fully clothed. Although how I managed to pass out, I've no idea. I still have no recollection of drinking that much, but with a sale in the bag, it wasn't the time to accuse him of date rape or of spiking my drinks. He might be a creep, but business is business.

Other than email communication regarding management and villa rentals, we don't keep in touch, and I haven't seen him in person since he signed on the dotted line. He's been a couple of times with golfing buddies, but I've managed to avoid face-to-face interaction.

Passing out on a new client's bed wasn't the sharpest move, but living in their property without permission is something else entirely. I hold a key for business purposes, not for free accommodation.

What the hell am I going to do?

I look in the mirror, wondering if I can turn round, in the vain hope he hasn't seen me. But it's too late. He's standing up ahead, in the middle of the road waving his arms in the air. He's seen me all right, his arms are criss-crossing frantically, as if he's directing a jumbo jet towards the terminal.

Shit. I've no choice but to face the music.

4

HAYLEY

Three months earlier

The front door creaks on its hinges. Teddy's home.

Waiting for him has been like waiting for a son to return from his gap year. Relief that he's safe is competing with a sense of dread. Mainly dread of what's in his travel bag. Tropical insects, caked underpants, a random tarantula or two. Who knows? My nightmares have been riddled with gruesome images.

It's not only the thought of the laundry, and sifting through maggot-infested clothes, but more the general upheaval. Life's been pretty tranquil for the past three months, and I've genuinely started to enjoy my own company.

'In here.' My yell competes with the clattering of a holdall. I suspect it's much heavier than when he left, owing to the carved elephants, incense burners, and multiple market-cheap pashminas. These are going to make him millions apparently, as they were only a snip in Vietnam's Ben Thanh market.

My WhatsApp was so clogged with travel-blog updates that I

ended up deleting the lot. No doubt there'll be more treasures in his bag once I'm brave enough to unzip it.

'Scrivens. Come here.'

He wanders in, arms thrown wide.

I'm still Scrivens, and he's still Teddy. They're student monikers from seven years ago. We're like Ant and Dec, a stuck-at-the-hip partnership. Well, we were.

He's still travelling. Still looking for the next big thing. Still living the life of a student, unaccepting that adulthood comes with responsibilities. That includes earning money. That's my role. Mum/girlfriend/breadwinner rolled into one. He was certainly quick to pick up on the advantages of a doormat partner.

He wraps his octopus-tentacle arms around me and I brace against the stench. He smells as if he's been sleeping on a rubbish tip.

'Oh my God. You stink.'

I flap my hand up and down, turn my head sideways, and breathe out the rancid fumes.

'Charming.'

He unlatches the tentacles, runs his rough skeletal fingers (complete with dirty raggedy nails and skin like desiccated coconut) over his beard. He's like a Yeti. His facial hair covers his features, and the only skin showing on his face is cheekbones, and the bags under his eyes.

Teddy is still at the pretty-cute stage of manhood. He's got boyish features, despite the Yeti look, and has the emotional maturity of a ten-year-old. I fell for his vulnerability, but he's become increasingly selfish, milking my mothering instincts for all they're worth.

'Are you hungry?' I step backwards, distancing myself from the smell.

'Starving.' His eyes light up.

'I've got chicken casserole in the oven.'

'Heaven. I haven't eaten properly in days.' A second's silence. 'Make that months.' His cheeky grin doesn't weave its once-guaranteed magic.

'Money run out?' I aim for wide-eyed curiosity as he doesn't look in any fit state to be dumped. Not on an empty stomach, and definitely not before he's had a shower. Goodness knows when he last washed.

'You're a star. Yay. It's great to be home.'

He's like a kid back from boarding school, despite the fact he's twenty-seven.

He slopes off into the bedroom. Five seconds later he pokes his head and shoulders back round the door. He's ripped off the smelly T-shirt, displaying his six-pack, but doing so has exacerbated the putrid odours.

I could do with a clothes peg on my nose.

'Scrivens. Wait till you hear what I have to tell you.' His eyes are now even more wide-eyed than mine were a few minutes ago. They're agog with excitement. Perhaps he's got marijuana in his backpack. He seems high on something.

'Oh? You were robbed at gunpoint in the Amazon jungle? Mugged in Hanoi? Don't tell me.'

'No. Better than that. You'll never believe it.'

He's like a little kid hiding a spider in its fist. *Look, Mummy, what I've got here.*

'Why not shower, and then tell me all about it.'

'Will do.'

Soon the bathroom door is closed, and when I hear him whistle I cringe.

5

Apart from a lingering overkill of facial hair, there's a hint of my old boyfriend when he reappears. My soon-to-be ex-boyfriend. At least he smells better, slathered in Lynx cologne.

Lucky he didn't get lost in the jungle, because search teams would have had trouble identifying him. His passport photo, taken only a couple of years ago, could be of a completely different person. It shows a fresh-faced young man with wavy hair and a baby-smooth complexion. His skin is now weathered, his brow wrinkled and fine lines leak from his eyes.

My heart thuds in my chest. I'm really going to do it, on the umpteenth time of trying. I'm going to tell him it's all over, and this time there'll be no going back.

'Hmm. Smells great. Come here, Scrivens. God, I've missed you.'

As I stand and stir the casserole, he zooms in for a hug, offering up a slobbery kiss, before picking up a fork and scooping out a mouthful.

When I smack his hand away, he moves to the table and folds

his long legs underneath him. I'm not sure he's picking up on my mood, as he blows heartily on the forkful to cool it down.

'How've you been, Scrivens? You go first.'

'I'm okay. Still trying to make ends meet. You know how it is.'

'No big scoop yet?'

I lift the casserole onto the table, then sit down and lean back in my chair.

His fork swoops in again, and this time a piece of chicken catapults on to the floor.

'Can't you wait?'

'Sorry. I'm starving.' He's like a salivating dog, but slaps his own wrist this time.

Perhaps if he wasn't ageing backwards, regressing to teenage ways, I might have second thoughts. But he's only been home half an hour, and is already driving me nuts.

'No. No big scoop yet. Car thefts. Break-ins. Marital bust-ups. Usual boring stuff, but it pays the bills.'

With this comment, I give him a stony stare. Teddy hasn't contributed a penny to anything in the past three months.

'I will get my act together. Actually, I've got exciting news. Wait till you hear this.'

6

Holy shit. Once Teddy gets into his story, I'm riveted. I'm devouring every word. This could be it. The scoop, the one that will crack open my career. Who knows? If I can get an exclusive covered by the US media, I might even win the Pulitzer Prize.

I don't tell Teddy this, of course. I'll need his help on the case, as he's my way in to the heart of the story. But I know Teddy. If he thought my involvement might ruin his chances of a once-in-a-lifetime opportunity (with lots of money involved), he'd likely find a way to cut me out. Maybe this is my means of getting something back for the last seven years. This could be the story that finally puts me on the map as an award-winning journalist.

I'd never do Teddy any harm, we've been together too long, but perhaps without letting on, I can finally milk something from our relationship. I'll no longer be dumping him tonight. No way. He's been given a stay of execution a while longer.

When he gets up from the table, he suddenly notices the futon I unfolded earlier, anticipating that once I told him we were history, he'd be so pissed off he wouldn't care where he slept.

'Oh, you've unfolded the futon? Why's that?'

'Lauren stayed over,' I lie.

I'll warn my sister in the morning to back up my story.

'For an awful moment I thought it was for me.' He laughs, a boyish snigger, while flicking lanky locks off his face.

His eyes are black-ringed like a panda's, and he's having trouble keeping a lid on the yawns. Hopefully, he'll be too exhausted to make a move tonight.

'I'm knackered. Let's crash out, and I'll help with the clearing up tomorrow,' he suggests, heading towards the bedroom.

'You go on. I'll be ten minutes.'

'Okay, Scrivens. I love you.'

He doesn't respond when I say nothing, which confirms he must be knackered, and moments later he's snoring like a foghorn.

My mind is racing with what he's told me. Tomorrow I'll try to research what I can to support his story. This really could be front-page news. Here and across the world. A Netflix series even. My mind is buzzing with potential.

The one thing about Teddy that I would trust with my life is his hearing. It never lets him down, even when I mumble swearwords under my breath. That's why I believe him now. His whole tale is down to what he overheard, and what he wasn't meant to hear.

Some woman owned up that she masterminded a murder.

When I finally crawl into bed, I kiss the top of his sleeping head, and whisper, 'Glad you're back, Teddy bear.'

When something jumps out of his hair, I scream. Looks as if he's also brought home a bloody load of nits.

7

JADE

I park up, and slink slowly out of the car. Avery is soon right next to me, his hands stuffed deep in his pockets, and giving me daggers. Although it's been less than three months since I saw him, he seems to have put on a shedload of weight, and lost an even greater shedload of hair. I can't remember if his hair was thinning when I last saw him, but he's hard to recognise now his head is close-shaven and he's sporting a stubbly beard. Even in the dull foggy lighting, he's still white and pasty.

'Avery,' I say.

I'd like to say what a nice surprise, but it's a bloody awful surprise.

'Right, Jade. What the hell is going on?'

He sweeps his arm towards the front porch. My clothes, shoes, toiletries, even my embarrassing Victorian button-up dressing gown are lying higgledy-piggledy on the step. There's a box alongside containing what looks like my Nespresso machine and Aeroccino frother.

'I can explain.'

No. I can't explain without getting in deeper shit. If I tell him

I've only been staying in his villa for a couple of days, I doubt he'll buy it. How the heck can I own up to two months? Why did I bring so much stuff? If I'd just brought an overnight bag, it wouldn't look so bad. I should have left more in the office.

From inside the villa I see a woman watching us. She's staring out the kitchen window, and from how still she is, she could be a mannequin's bust. All I can see are her head and shoulders. She's like a ghost haloed by the under-cabinet strip lights. They're still flickering, despite Avery asking me to put new ones in. It's on my mammoth to-do list of maintenance chores.

'Go ahead. This had better be good.'

'I rented my own place out last month. I'll pay you rental, I promise. Peak season rates?'

I actually rented my own place out shortly after he bought his villa, around three months ago, but I've got to give it my best shot. It's a vain hope that the shorter the length of time I've been squatting might lessen the gravity of the crime.

If I wasn't able to afford living on the resort before, this will wipe me out. I don't need to fall out with Avery. He's a paying client, and very pally with the other owners in Las Colinas community. Twenty properties in all, and I manage eight of them. I can't afford to lose any more clients.

'You swore to me that you never rent out properties without telling the owners. But living in them, rent free, yourself? You've got to be kidding me,' he hisses, now so close up that an expulsion of spit hits my cheek.

Avery is a creep, but I've made such an effort to be nice to him. My first client and all that. I've tried hard to be pleasant, but I'm going to have trouble getting out of this mess. He's glowering at me as if I've robbed him at knifepoint.

The lady from the window appears suddenly by the front door. She's tall and willowy, dressed for summer in a floaty white dress. She's barefoot, and her toes are so long I think of the aye-aye, a species of lemur. It's the animal with the world's largest toes. I'm a quiz nerd, with a mental hard drive packed with random trivia. Whatever, she's got to be freezing as the temperature is Arctic cold.

'Avery. Don't stress. No harm done,' she says in a calming tone, wandering out on tiptoe to join us. She's at least a head taller than Avery.

'Crystal, go back inside. You'll catch your death.' He's crocodile snappy, which I suspect is down to me. He swats her away with a slap on the arm, and she rubs a palm across a reddening clump of goosebumps.

'Ouch. That hurt,' she says, but holds her ground.

If she expects an apology, she'll have a long wait. His narrowed eyes are concentrated in my direction.

He's never mentioned a girlfriend before. The villa was bought in his name, so I'd assumed there was no wife either. I've had him down as a bachelor, but then I'm a pretty lousy judge of character. I vaguely remember a lady with him when I first showed the villa, but don't recall seeing her again. She certainly wasn't around when the deal was agreed. And there's never been any obvious sign of a woman's presence in the villa when I've cleaned the property after his golfing trips.

Crystal watches us, but doesn't go back inside. Instead, she extends milky-smooth fingers which must be the longest I've ever seen.

'Hi. You must be Jade. I'm Avery's partner, Crystal.'

'Oh, hi.' I'm tongue-tied, not sure if I'm more embarrassed at being caught red-handed, or because I've discovered Avery is in a relationship. Also, Crystal doesn't look the sort of girlfriend I'd have imagined for him. He claims to be sporty. Golf, tennis, padel, running, cycling. You name it, he's claimed he does it. From the way he speaks, sport seems to be an obsessive hobby. But judging by his unfit appearance, I suspect it's all talk.

Avery is wearing a Campo de Golf polo shirt. Navy blue with gold edging and the resort's palm tree logo. Beige chinos are straining at the seams, and although he's dressed for golf, I suspect he'd be more at home in a pub than on the fairway. A pitted beer belly strains over his waistband.

'Avery. Leave it for now.' Crystal speaks calmly, her demeanour in complete contrast to his. The woman looks as if a puff of wind would blow her over.

'Here. Let me help with your stuff,' she says, turning to me.

She picks her way cautiously over the cold terracotta tiles towards my stash of discarded possessions.

'Thanks.'

I shuffle round Avery, keeping my head bowed in shame. Thank goodness for Crystal. Avery has no intention of lifting a finger to help, although I can't say I blame him. I can almost see steam coming out of his nostrils. How could I have been so stupid? I was desperate, and it was a last resort, but what the hell am I going to do now?

I shovel up my clothes in both hands, mortified when a pair of lacy knickers escapes. Crystal giggles, bends and picks them up.

'You won't want to leave these behind.'

Jeez, they're my sexy red ones, the ones with a ribbon that rides up between the buttocks.

'Thanks.'

Crystal winks as we load the lot into my already chock-a-block Fiat trunk.

'Can I have the keys back, please.' Avery's voice pierces the silence, as he extends an open palm. I scrabble round in my bag, hands shaking, and panic when I can't find them. I couldn't have lost them, could I?

When I finally pull them out, Avery steps forward, and snatches them off me. He tosses them in the air before tucking them into his straining chino pocket.

After he's stormed off, Crystal lingers. I want to cry, mortified at having been caught in the number one sin of Spanish property agents.

Somehow, I hold it together.

Crystal pats me on the shoulder. Sisterhood over *spousehood*. 'Don't worry. He'll have calmed down in the morning. He's just tired after the journey.'

'Thanks. I'm really sorry.'

'I know.'

How does she know? She has no idea.

I've now lost over 100 euros a month maintenance income, and goodness knows how much more when Avery spreads the word around the community that I'm not to be trusted. With my own flat rented out, little money left in the bank, I've no idea what to do next.

I'm now officially homeless.

8

How could I have been so stupid?

Once back in the car, the sobs erupt. Tears stream down my cheeks as I wind my way back towards the clubhouse. I take a left turn, cruise past the half-built hotel, and head for the Spanish Village. When I get to my office, I'll have to decide what to do, and where I can crash out tonight. It might have to be the office floor.

I drive past a random security guard strolling along the pavement with what looks like an unmotivated Rottweiler on a long leash. The guy might recognise my car, but I doubt that's the reason he doesn't give me a second glance. He looks consumed by apathy. Even if he suspected I was an illegal immigrant wielding a Samurai sword, I doubt he'd bat an eyelid. Even the dog looks bored out of its skull.

I park up near my office. There must be room for at least fifty cars, but apart from two others, mine is the only one. You could build a whole city on the empty car parks around the resort. There must be at least 100 spaces for every property.

As I wander towards my office, I look up at the second-floor apartments above the vacant shopping units across the way. The one on the end, the corner apartment with the wrap-around balcony, is dimly lit. A smoky light attached to the outer wall provides the only sign of life for miles around.

For most of the day, this particular apartment has the benefit of the full force of the sun, owing to its position. This is my apartment, the one now rented out to Gabby Rackham, an aspiring artist apparently on a sabbatical.

She arrived in Spain shortly after I'd set up shop, with the intention of honing her talents by painting golf courses and vistas of rolling hills. There's nothing much else to paint this far inland, and unless she moves to the coast, she'll soon run out of vistas.

Gabby Rackham is seriously weird. Her regular job, the one that earned her a living before she came here to paint, was as a psychotherapist apparently. Her hair is streaked pink and purple, and she has multiple silver studs piercing her ears, with a random one on the side of her nose. She dresses in baggy clothes, and unattractive footwear. Black boots seem to be a staple. She's got a pretty face, but it's hard to pick out her features through the bulky mane of multi-coloured hair. A couple of tattoos, one on her wrist, and one on a shoulder blade, up the threatening appearance.

I'm not sure why she wants to look so unattractive, but I've too much to think about without worrying what the tenant living in my apartment looks like. She doesn't seem to be short of money, and pays her rent on time. That's all I care about. She could be fleeing an abusive husband for all I know, but she's so not my problem.

When I put down the deposit on the apartment, I really believed I'd found my own corner of heaven. There was no way I'd ever rent it out. That was the plan, until the hidden costs came to light. They'd been buried under the slickness of the sales spiel, which I'm now having to recite to equally naïve customers. I did the maths, thinking I had enough to make the purchase while at the same time setting up shop as a sales agent in the vacant offices across the way.

I couldn't have been more wrong. The costs just kept spiralling after I'd signed my life away. Renting out my apartment was the only option to keep me afloat.

One of the things that wowed me the most was the Spanish Village itself. It's like the set of a commercial for *Selling Sunset*. The pristine plazas, lit by low-energy LED bulbs, are immaculate. Not a scrap of litter anywhere, not even the glimpse of a cigarette butt.

In the daytime, it is beyond amazing. I cycle around, and walk up and down, breathing in the perfection of it all. But at nighttime in the winter, the orange bulbs encased in smoky glass give the place a really creepy feel. Like an old black and white movie. Atmospheric, but beyond eerie.

And there's one thing missing which makes me really uncomfortable. CCTV cameras. I'd feel safer knowing someone was keeping an eye out. The resort admin has promised cameras will be installed later this year, but as there are so many unoccupied properties, it's likely a mañana-type promise.

If anyone attacks me, no one will be any the wiser.

9

I dig out my office keys, unlock the grille over the door, and somehow manage to yank it off. In the mornings, there's usually someone to help, forgoing the need to yank. A security guard, or Seamus, the guy who mans the drinks and tapas kiosk opposite.

Or if I'm really lucky, Marcus from the office suite next door: Hola Sol. He's my main competitor when it comes to flogging a place in the sun. Although he's far too cool to yank. He slides the grille off with seamless effort. A six-foot hunk of charm and charisma. Recently, I've had to remind myself he's the competition.

After the Marbella disaster, I've learnt my lesson. No more handsome cads. At least this time round no one could mistake me for a millionaire, as I don't have two cents to rub together. At this rate, I'll soon be sleeping rough.

That said, I'm learning plenty of slick sales patter from Marcus. He's been in the game a long time. When people browse in our adjacent windows for properties to rent, and if we're lucky, properties to buy, he's outside in a flash. All sparkling veneers, suntan, and designer stubble. It takes me longer to appear, my spiky heels losing it on the tiles.

If the potential customers are women, I don't even bother. No point when Mr *Love Island* appears. But when a single guy follows me back inside, it's beyond satisfying. I stick my nose in the air with a smug backward glance.

Marcus has an arrogant twinkle in his eye, and I find myself battling not to get sucked in by his charm. I watch him with clients, drawing them in with his smooth, easy manner. When he directs his attention my way, it's hard not to weaken.

He's always trying to inveigle information out of me. Where have I come from? My background? Family? Significant others?

I give nothing away, and don't intend to. I know his sort. Once bitten, never again. I'll have to contain my more lustful imaginings to bedtime.

Having yanked the metal grille off, I step inside and flick the light switch. The single bulb explodes, and I duck to avoid the glass splatters.

'Shit. Shit. Shit.'

This is all I need.

I turn on my phone torch, and creep around like a cat burglar, trying to avoid the spiky shards.

Across the plaza, I look up at my apartment. I want to howl all over again. There she is. The lovely, lonely Gabby Rackham, with her purple hair, resting her arms on the rail of *my* balcony. The red-tipped glow from a cigarette end is just visible, but she's too far off for me to see if she's looking my way.

I can't dwell on the squatter (that's what I call her, even though she pays the rent). For now, I'm the one who needs somewhere to stay tonight.

The villa owners' keys are secured inside a metal wall box, hidden behind the door of the kitchenette. Coats camouflage the box, and I squish them aside to input the combination code: 2904. Hard to forget the flight number of that fateful trip to Malaga as it's etched in my memory. Forever. It was the number of the plane I was on when I met Isaac Marston. I shiver every time I input the code.

My fingers graze over the keys. There are fifteen sets in total. Fourteen, once I've handed back Avery's spare set. How could I have been so stupid? Then again, what choice did I have? A place in the sun was to be a whole new beginning. *Selling Sunset*, in a little corner of paradise. Forget phoney millionaire status, this was to be about hard work. I was still set on making my fortune.

My fingers come to rest at Bernard and Pat Roper's keys. Number 3, Avenida del Mar. It's nowhere near the sea, but the swimming pool is the largest on the resort. I have no idea why I decamped to Avery's modest corner property when I could have stayed at the Ropers'. The Ropers don't pay me much more in maintenance fees, but for some weird reason I was more reticent to stay in a five-star property than in the modest villa in Las Colinas. Misguided logic told me that staying in a smaller property was somehow less of a crime than choosing somewhere more palatial.

One thing that bothers me about Avenida del Mar, though, is that it's so remote. It's on Phase 1 alongside other larger detached properties. No community feel. No friendly barbecues with neighbours. But tonight, it's my best option. I can't wait to get there and crawl into Pat and Bernard's king-size bed.

A sudden noise outside, and I fall back against the sink. It sounds like the wail of an animal caught in a trap. An enormous squeal of pain is followed by silence. I don't move for a minute. When I dare go and look through the window, I see the security guard and Rottweiler stroll past. The dog seems to be shaking something in its mouth. Something live.

Fear permeates my every pore. I'm back in Marbella. In Isaac's villa, unable to escape. Why do I now feel trapped again? I'm in the open air. There's no one out to get me. Okay, the Rottweiler isn't giving me the most welcoming vibes, but the solitude should be comforting.

Images of the 4X4 trying to run me off the road earlier pop into my mind, and I start to feel really panicky. I need to get to bed, have a good night's sleep and worry about everything in the morning.

Once I get the grille back into place, I don't linger. My last glance, before I head back to the car, is towards my beautiful apartment. And towards Gabby Rackham. It pains me that this single woman, with a pie-in-the-sky notion to be the next Van Gogh, is living the dream.

And at my expense.

10

HAYLEY

I can't believe this is really going to happen.

Since telling me everything he overheard on the plane, and all about Astrid Olsen's offer for him to move to Spain, Teddy and I have been making plans. While he's relishing his part in a whole new adventure with the potential for serious money, I'm secretly concocting a plan for the Pulitzer Prize. I'm pretending my excitement is all about the money he's going to make. But truth is, it's got nothing to do with the money. Teddy's move to Spain might provide me with the scoop of my career, the one that changes everything if I play my cards right.

He left this morning with a new suitcase, and an upgraded wardrobe. With his neat new haircut, and freshly shaven face, he's back to looking like a teenager.

His parting shot as he dragged his suitcase out the door was, 'Are you sure you don't mind? If you really don't want me to go, I'll stay.'

Over my dead body. This is the first time ever that I'm desperate for him to go.

My eyes moistened over (we do go back a long way), but I was eager for him to leave. It might be a whole new chapter for him, but this time I'll not be left out.

Ten minutes after he's gone, I boot up my laptop and start googling. I reckon three months tops should give me time to piece together a story. The plan is to message Teddy daily, nudging him for titbits of information without giving the game away. Teddy is a talker, and confides in me as if to a mother confessor. I'm after names. Dates. Details. Descriptions of the villa. And especially feedback on Astrid Olsen, his new employer.

Casa de Astrid sounds pretty plush, but I can't help wondering what she sees in Teddy. Well, Stephen to her. I look at the teddy bear tattoo on my wrist, a memento of when we first hooked up. Together forever.

My insides tighten when I wonder what Astrid might want from Teddy. If she's as loaded as she seems, she could throw money at any random male.

* * *

Three weeks pass pretty quickly. My phone is glued to my side for updates. It certainly hasn't taken Teddy long to fit in with the jet set, his excitement bubbling through the texts.

> Astrid is a hoot. I'm able to save 100 euros a day, can you believe it?

Really? Teddy saving 100 euros a day? There's got to be a catch. I dread to think what he's doing to earn that much.

> She's parading me around Marbella. Great fun! Went out on a yacht today.

There's no hint of concern that he's living with an assassin, and I'm starting to wonder if he made the whole thing up, or embellished details of what he overheard.

When I tell him I've a new flatmate moving in he doesn't seem at all fazed. I stressed that it's a temporary thing, but I needn't have worried; he said he has no plans to return anytime soon.

Damon is great. He's been here just over a week, and has paid two full months' rent upfront. He cooks for me every night, puts the toilet seat down without being asked, scrubs the bathroom, and likes a cocktail or two. And is incredibly hot. I don't share any of this with Teddy, as I don't want to piss him off, especially when I'm desperate for more information on what's happening at Casa de Astrid.

True to his word, Teddy messages regularly.

> And wait till you hear what she told me last night...
>
> You'll never believe this...
>
> Astrid is quite the character. She's hilarious...
>
> Oh, and she wants to know why I don't have a girlfriend. I've mentioned a sister, Hayley, but never a girlfriend...

I fill in each new piece of information on to a spreadsheet.

I'm excited, but uneasy. Keeping a girlfriend out of the equation was a smart move on Teddy's part. Astrid might open up more if she's not concerned about a jealous partner. If he ever lets slip, in an unguarded moment, that his 'sister' is a journalist, then the game's up. Both for him and me.

It's hard to forget that he's likely living with a murderer, but he seems happy enough. My job is to concentrate on building a story during my six-month sabbatical from the paper.

I've been googling extensively to find anything that might support what Teddy overheard. I'm starting to doubt everything, almost ready to throw in the towel, when I see it. Bingo!

There's an article in today's *Telegraph*. It's only small with a grainy photo attached, but it's enough. It's about a man who died on a roof terrace. Died. Not murdered. The story is pretty succinct, but gets my heart pounding.

British Conman Found Dead on Marbella Roof Terrace

British man, George Stubbs, aged 38, from Peckham, South London has been found dead on a roof terrace in Marbella.

Recently married to a Norwegian millionairess, Astrid Olsen, Stubbs got locked out of their villa, getting stranded on the roof terrace in 40-degree heat, and wasn't able to get back in. According to police, he would have died through dehydration within twenty-four hours of being trapped.

Ms Olsen and Mr Stubbs split up several months before his tragic demise, and while, at the time, it was believed that Ms Olsen may have committed suicide, it was later revealed that at the time of her estranged husband's death she was travelling around England.

Ms Olsen states that she walked out on Mr Stubbs, claiming he was a violent and abusive husband.

Ms Olsen made the grim discovery when she got back to Spain, some three weeks after her husband's death. His body was so badly burnt, an autopsy wasn't carried out.

It appears to have been a tragic accident, with no suspicious circumstances. Ms Olsen confirmed that the handle on the fire door leading from the terrace back into the villa had needed replacing for some time. Sources believe that the heavy fire door slammed shut, locking Mr Stubbs outside. Unfortunately, there was no mobile phone signal on the roof.

Since the report of his death, several women have come forward with claims that Mr Stubbs conned them out of their life savings. However, as the women seem to have handed the money across to Mr Stubbs willingly, no legal action can be taken, and the money is unlikely to be returned to the victims. Ms Olsen has so far refused to comment further on this matter.

I reread the article over and over, and then start scribbling a long list of questions. I'll not bombard Teddy all at once in case he gets suspicious. Or more worryingly, in case Astrid starts to smell a rat if Teddy can't keep his mouth shut. Whenever I think of this crazy woman, I shiver. Teddy and I could be playing with fire, but I can't stop now. Excitement is bubbling up, nudging the anxiety to one side.

I'm perched on the wobbly kitchen barstool in the kitchen, hunched over my laptop, when Damon sneaks up behind me.

'Shit. Don't creep up like that,' I yell.

I have to claw at the counter to stop from falling off, and when I turn round, Damon is standing there with only a hankie-sized towel round his waist. He's been in the shower, and his body is covered in a damp sheen. I don't know where to look.

He leans over to peer at the screen.

'What are you reading?'

I quickly close down the laptop.

'Nothing important. It's just work,' I snap.

I'm not sure I want to share what I was reading, although it would be good to tell someone. But I hardly know Damon, nor if I can trust him.

He might be good in the kitchen, and at scrubbing surfaces, but it feels too early to open up to someone I've only just met.

When I feel his hands on my shoulders, I realise he's totally disinterested in my work. No interest at all in murder, Marbella, or Teddy. As his towel slithers to the ground, I realise I might have bigger problems.

11

While I'm panicking about what my lodger might have on his mind, he scoops up the towel, holds it over his private parts, and scurries back to the bedroom. When he reappears a minute later, looking decidedly mortified and red-faced, it's hard not to laugh. Actually, he looks pretty cute. He's pulled on a T-shirt and jogging pants, thank goodness.

'I couldn't help seeing you were googling Marbella,' Damon says, his long shapely feet now dangling over the end of the sofa, while I sit on the hard chair, declining an invitation to join him.

'I'm working on a story.'

'Anything interesting?'

'Doing a bit of research on something that might have more to it than meets the eye.'

'Sounds intriguing. Want to share?'

Do I? Don't I?

When he tops up our wine glasses from a bottle he bought earlier, I think, *what the heck. It'll be good to share.* Now Teddy's gone, I've no one left to talk to. I've spent the last seven years trying to please Teddy, leaving little time for girlfriends.

I tell Damon that Teddy overheard a very interesting conversation on his recent flight back from Malaga, and his summations of the storyteller.

'He said she was so large that she barely squeezed into her seat.'

I instantly regret belittling Teddy to someone I hardly know, but I can't forget how his opinions of Astrid quickly changed after she made him an offer that was too good to be true. She seemed to suddenly slim down overnight from a size 18 to a size 0.

When Damon doesn't say anything, I carry on.

'Teddy has very good hearing. The sort of ears that can drill through concrete.'

Damon laughs. He's damn cute when he laughs, his eyes crinkling at the corners, and with obscenely cute dimples popping up on his cheeks. The wine is definitely emphasising the cuteness.

'So what did he hear?'

Maybe later I'll blame the wine for loosening my tongue, but Damon is rapt, willing me to carry on.

I take a large gulp of wine, and start to talk.

I tell him that Astrid is a millionaire, linked to the Norwegian royal family, and she confessed to the lady sitting next to her on the plane that she had masterminded the murder of her estranged husband. She got someone else to trap him on a roof terrace in 40-degree heat with no escape route.

'The guy didn't have a mobile phone?'

'No signal.'

'Teddy must have really good hearing to pick all that up across the aisle of the cabin. Was she shouting?'

The dimples are back. He's trying to suck information out of me by using cuteness as a tactic.

'I think Astrid might have talked a bit louder than she meant to. Or a bit louder than she thought she was.'

'Who was the person who actually trapped him up there? Aren't they the guilty party?'

'According to Teddy, Astrid persuaded some woman to lock her husband on the roof, assuring her she'd let him out soon. The plan was only meant to make him sweat.'

'Oh, so she never let him out.'

Damon swivels round and plonks his slim and perfectly shaped feet on the ground, and sits up straight.

'That's how it looks. But...' I go and pick up the copy of the newspaper, and set it on the floor in front of Damon, open at the article.

'The paper reported it as an accident. I only read about it today.'

Damon's eyes scan the article, concentrating on every word.

A wave of doubt rolls over me. Was I wise to tell all? I need to keep a lid on the story until I have the full facts. This Astrid could also be a dangerous number.

'Jeez. You could have a real scoop here,' he says, his eyes agog. He's genuinely excited.

'You think so?'

'Yep. I think so indeed.'

He puts the paper to one side, and doesn't say anything for ages. I've no idea if he's going to yawn, suggest he gets an early night, or offer to slip into something more comfortable. Like another handkerchief-sized towel.

My pulse picks up speed, the soporific effect of the wine losing its magic. This guy could be a madman. I remember his Flatshare application, when he was looking for a room to rent. He didn't share much, other than he lived locally, and was eager to move in straightaway. He didn't mention family or friends, but after interviewing a smarmy estate agent, a divorcee wreck, and a Margot Robbie lookalike, I was desperate for someone half approaching normal.

'You know what, Hayley. I've got a week's holiday coming up soon, and I've got a bit of money saved. What say we pop over to Marbella and do a bit of research on site? You and me.' He points a finger to me and back to him in case I've trouble digesting what *you and me* means.

'Why would you want to do that?'

'I've nothing better to do.'

Really?

It takes a moment to digest what he's suggesting, but the excitement soon kicks in. You know what? It might be a bloody good idea. Damon might actually help me get my scoop.

'Let me think about it, and decide when I'm sober.'

I knock back a full glass, just to confirm the reason for not agreeing immediately.

But I've already made up my mind.

What fun. Marbella here we come.

12

I'm not sure how to broach the subject with Teddy about coming out to Marbella. Not to mention telling him I'd like to bring my new flatmate. A flatmate that, so far, I haven't admitted is male. That said, Teddy hasn't been curious, too wrapped up in Marbella life.

It's only when I get a message late one night from my soon-to-be ex-boyfriend (I suspect he's drunk) that I think I might have solved the problem.

> Guess what? Astrid is having a Playboy Mansion type of pool party in a couple of weeks. All of the Marbella jet set will be there! And... I'm her plus one.

This is my chance to play jealous. Let down. Abandoned. Miserable. But hey, I'm anything but. This is my chance to up the ante.

> Oh. Sounds fun. Any chance I could gate crash? Tell her your sister is keen to catch up? Ha ha.

(I add in a couple... okay, a dozen sad emojis here, emphasising the lonely girlfriend role.)

When Teddy first arrived at the villa, he told Astrid he'd been living with his sister off and on between travels for the past seven years, also mentioning that he hoped she could come and visit sometime. Fortunately for me, Astrid agreed. 'Of course, Stephen,' she'd cooed. 'Any time.'

Damon stands behind me now as I type. He dares rest a hand on my shoulder again. This seems to be his modus operandi, but it sends a tingle down my spine.

We stare at the screen, transfixed as Teddy types.

> I'll ask Astrid. So many people coming, she probably won't notice an extra person. Till later xx

'Not sure how I'll explain to him who you are.' I grit my teeth, and look at Damon.

'We'll think of something together. It'll be fun.'

I hope so, but anxiety palpitations are suggesting otherwise. Going to the Playgirl mansion of a suspected assassin might not be the wisest move. Also, I must be crazy going with a random flatmate whom I've only just met. But I remind myself a journalistic award never got won through timid journalism. Time to take some risks.

An hour later, Teddy sends a new message.

> Yay. Astrid is a game old bird. Of course you can come, Scrivens. She didn't even ask who my guest was. I'll send you the details. Can't wait to see you. Oh, and btw... a brother of Astrid's dead husband has just turned up at the villa. He's fun too! XX

My heart beats a little faster. This is a juicy titbit.

Give Damon his due, he's less interested in hearing about the dead husband's relative, more concerned that Teddy has added kisses. He needs constant confirmation that Teddy and I are history.

And to top it all, Damon is now anxious about how Teddy will react when I ask about bringing a plus one.

'When are you going to ask him?'

Poor Damon. He's so keen to come that he's petrified of being left out.

I start typing.

> Can I bring my new flatmate Donna? If you're with Astrid, I'll need company!

'Perfect. You're a dark horse, Scrivens.'

'I'll blame the wrong name on predictive text.'

It feels weird to hear Damon calling me Scrivens. He's picked up from Teddy's messages that this is what he calls me.

When Damon swivels me round, and plants a soft kiss on my lips, I'm not sure what to do.

Maybe it's the excitement of what we're planning, the Marbella trip, or the fact that Damon is getting hunkier by the minute, but when he pulls me off the chair, I melt into his arms and the kissing continues all the way into the bedroom.

It's only later, when we're snuggled up under the duvet, that I start to worry. Dealing with Teddy's jealousy over a random male guest, and possible anger at me for misleading him on his name, shouldn't prove too difficult. I know how to deal with Teddy.

My main concerns are nothing to do with him. They're now all centred around Astrid, whoever she is. She's wealthy, connected, conniving, and... possibly a murderer. The pool party might sound like fun, but am I wise to put myself in the firing line?

Not to mention Damon.

13

JADE

Having been chucked out of Avery Knowles's villa, I've been left with no choice but to squat in another client's property until I sort myself out. I'm so desperate to get some sleep.

I drive round to Phase I, the first area of the resort to be developed on what was once a harsh desert environment. It's where the most luxurious properties are located.

As I head towards the Ropers' villa, I start worrying about Gato. My stray cat. I can't go back now to find him, as he's likely hovering by Avery's front door waiting to be let in for his bowl of milk and tuna chunks.

I'm distraught thinking about it, but I'll find him tomorrow, and then decide what to do. Perhaps I can house him in my office until I find somewhere more permanent to stay. But tonight, I can't let this cloud my mind.

The Ropers' villa is one of the most palatial on the resort. Not Marbella luxurious, but next best thing. B-list rustic rather than A-list ostentation. The views over the golf course are amazing, with the silhouette of rolling sierras in the distance. Not to mention the inside is kitted out like a *Place in the Sun* show home.

Only issue, it's beyond isolated. I park up outside on the street, and use my phone torch to light up the path towards the front door. I look left, right, and then do a full 360 before I slip the key into the lock. Lucky I have my phone to hand, because all the electricity is kept turned off when a property is vacant.

I find the box, trip the switches back on and the whole villa lights up like a West End stage. No. No. No. The neighbours could be watching. Well, neighbour singular. As far as I'm aware, there's currently only one other villa occupied at this end of the Avenida. Jolene Sanderstead, the widow with the frizzy orange perm. She's one of Marcus's clients, naturally (a single woman, after all). I'm hoping she won't tell anyone that she saw lights on in the Ropers' villa, even if she jumps to the conclusion that they've arrived on the resort early. But worrying about Jolene on top of Gato and everything else will have to wait. I'm near to collapse.

I wander round the villa, turning off all the lights, except for the one on the landing.

I suddenly stop in my tracks when I hear a noise. It's a whine, accompanied by a faint scratching noise. I'm now at the top of the stairs, and lean heavily against the banister. I hear it again. It can't be burglars, can it? I want to laugh, it's so ludicrous, but I'm more on the spectrum of madness than mirth.

I peek over the railing, and realise I've left the front door open. The noise is coming from outside, and is becoming more and more persistent. Images of the wildebeest-like creature from earlier flash through my mind. It could be an Iberian lynx, or a species of European wildcat. More useless general knowledge about indigenous Spanish predators.

'Can't you take up cooking? Study Spanish recipes rather than Trivial Pursuits?' my mum is always saying. She's horrified at my part-time hobby of trying to master pub quiz knowledge.

She'd prefer I got married, have a couple of kids, and become normal. Fat chance.

If it is an animal, then I've got the light on my phone to scare it off. The torch is blinding, and there's always the pepper spray in my bag.

I tiptoe downstairs, and breathe more easily when the noise dies down. Jeez, I must be beyond tired if I'm imagining things, and hearing noises in my head.

As I go to close the front door I see it.

It's Gato. My stray cat. The one who sits outside Avery's villa every night until I feed him tuna bites. How the heck did he get all the way here? Phase 2 is at least a mile round the resort. He couldn't possibly have known where I was. Unless someone dropped him off. Things couldn't get much freakier.

I bend down and give him a tickle behind an ear, before heading down the path into the road. There's no one around, and no signs of life anywhere. This part of the resort is so creepy, and even quieter than where I was staying before.

Luckily, when Avery chucked out my belongings, he also hurled out some provisions from the kitchen. Crystal kindly stuffed them into carrier bags, which should still be in the car.

I open the boot, and hey presto. The tins of tuna chunks are in there, along with a leaky carton of milk. Gato's trip won't have been in vain.

'Why do you call the cat Gato?' Marcus asked me once. He thought it was hilarious. 'You know Gato means cat in Spanish?'

'Duh. Of course.'

I wasn't going to explain my choice of name. Marcus is so superior with his supercilious smile and gorgeous set of teeth. He is bloody handsome, but beyond irritating as he seems to relish making fun of me.

I also like that Gato sounds like Gateau, which would be a cool name for an English cat. Rich, creamy and squishy.

My furry companion follows me inside, slinking low across the marble tiles with his bony ridged back. The sight breaks my heart. He comes up close, rubbing against my legs as I fiddle with the carrier bag. Two minutes in, and he's greedily devouring the gourmet treat.

The Ropers have a no-pet rule for renters. But you know what? I couldn't give a toss. I've had enough for today. Tonight especially.

Gato and I are going to crash out. He can sleep on the end of the bed, and keep an eye open for Iberian lynx or wildebeest.

14

There's no sign of Gato when I wake up. It's nearly eight o'clock and the sun has only just appeared.

I toss back the curtains of the Ropers' master bedroom, and instantly feel better. The sky is azure blue, not a cloud in sight. Heaven. It's easy to forget it's cold out. Despite the illusion of heat, I'm shivering. The chill won't abate for a couple of hours.

At least I remembered to switch on the hot water before crashing out, and a steaming shower gets me ready for action. I need to sort out where I'll stay for the next few weeks, and after the fiasco with Avery, there'll be no more squatting free of charge. Perhaps I can offer gratis or discounted maintenance in return for a bed at one of my clients'.

But first things first. I dig out a relatively uncrumpled dress from the pile of clothes Avery dumped outside his villa, and slip into my battle-ready heels. Not too high, but high enough to encourage male interest into my office rather than Marcus's. I need to keep my work hat in place while I try to sort out the mess.

It's only when I'm downstairs that I notice the back door is slightly ajar. Gato must have gone out that way, but how? I can't remember if I left it open, or if I opened it at all. I came in the front door, didn't I? I have a quick scout around but everything else seems to be as it was last night.

I drive up to the edge of the Spanish Village, leave the car, and set off for my morning trip to the clubhouse. I skirt round the Village rather than going through the middle as it's quicker, and I'm desperate for my morning coffee and tomato bread. My stomach is seriously rumbling. I tug my cardigan round me to pad out the chill, and walk as fast as I can.

Early-morning golfers have beaten me to the clubhouse. At least six sets of clubs are stacked by the front door, and the noise of laughter ricochets through the foyer.

Shit. Shit. Shit. Avery Knowles is holding court, laughing and joking in the midst of a group of sporty types. When I try to sidle past, he glowers at me. He's all I need this early.

I notice Padraic Mullen in amongst the group. I look after his villa which is four properties down from Avery's. I raise my hand in a rather feeble greeting, but he doesn't look my way. I suspect Avery has already told him he caught me squatting. That could be another contract I've lost.

When I enter the cavernous clubroom with its towering ceiling, I feel a thrill go up my spine. This space, along with the plush terrace through the glass doors, is what finally made up my mind to buy the apartment, and move permanently to Murcia.

This single imposing room sold it to me. It's always spotless, the black and white marbled floor tiles gleaming, with an enormous crystal chandelier accentuating the luxury. This resort is where I wanted to live, and work. With £120,000 left in my bank account, I snapped up a discounted apartment in the Spanish Village (well, Marcus told me it was discounted, now I'm not so sure), and also signed a contract to lease the property offices across the way. I had enough for a year's rental, and this is where I was to make my fortune.

Javier, the regular clubhouse barman, grins when I appear, and without me having to ask, serves up my usual cortado.

'Tomato bread, *señorita*?'

Okay, I have this every morning, but it tastes so good. The tomatoes are rich and sweet, unlike those in my Crouch End Asda. Olive oil, and a generous sprinkling of salt on top, and it could be a Michelin-starred recipe.

'*Gracias*, Javier.'

It only takes him a couple of minutes to prepare the tomato bread, and soon I'm heading out to the terrace with my food and coffee. I pause outside, take a deep breath, and inhale the view. The lush green of the fairways, and the sierras in the distance. It really is a tiny corner of paradise.

While I try to decide on which end of the terrace to sit, as far away from the clubroom as possible to avoid Avery's entourage, I spot a familiar face in the corner. Suddenly the shivering starts up again. It's Crystal. Crystal of the bizarrely long fingers and toes. I've got goosebumps up and down my arms, even under a woolly cardigan, while she's reclining with her eyes closed and looking up into the sun. Not sure if she's registered it's freezing, as she's only wearing a skimpy white top, with thin shoulder straps barely holding it in place. Even from this distance, I can see she's not wearing a bra.

It's impossible to pretend I haven't seen her, even if I tiptoe off in the opposite direction, because her eyes spring open.

'Hi.' Her face lights up as she sits forward and waves.

'Hi.'

Looks as if I've no other choice but to join her.

She's soon indicating an empty chair. 'Join me. Here, have a seat.'

I sit opposite, rather than beside her, and set my cortado and plate on the table.

'You're up early,' she says.

'And you. I'm off to work.'

'Oh,' she says with a curious tic of a very arched black eyebrow. Funny, her black eyebrows are at complete odds with her translucent skin, and silky blonde hair. If her hair was black, she could pass for Morticia Addams. The vampire look is weirdly unsettling.

'Avery probably told you, I manage properties round the resort. And also act as a sales agent.'

'He did tell me. He's such an unfeeling rotter though,' she says, leaning closer across the table. 'I'm sorry about last night.'

'Oh, it was my fault. I shouldn't have stayed at his villa without telling him.'

'Give him a few days and he'll calm down. He doesn't hold grudges.'

'I hope you're right. Anyway, I'll pay him what I owe for my stay.'

Do I own up to several months' worth of free accommodation, or do I pretend it was only for a few days? I needn't have worried, though, as Crystal splays her generous fingers on top of my hand.

'Tell him you were only there a couple of nights. He's a sucker for a white lie.' She winks.

Is she for real? Her high-pitched laugh is even more disconcerting than the vampire look, especially this early in the morning. She's definitely a bit cuckoo, but don't look a gift horse in the mouth, as my mother says.

Maybe if Crystal and I strike up a friendship, Avery will soften.

I knock back my cortado, and am about to crunch into the tomato bread, when the sight of Avery appearing through the terrace door makes me jump. He's certainly not as bright and breezy as Crystal, and gives me another death stare.

Thankfully he doesn't join us, but it's my cue not to linger. With minimal small talk, I guzzle the lush tomatoes despite the effort of swallowing. My insides are seriously in revolt, and for the first time ever, I leave food on my plate.

Five minutes later, and I'm saying goodbye to Crystal.

'Must dash,' I say, wiping my lips with a tissue. 'Work to do.'

'*Adios*,' she says, trilling her long fingers. '*Hasta luego*. See you later.'

I scurry down the back stairs, past the putting green, and head for the Spanish Village.

15

I'm puffing heavily by the time I reach my office. Marcus has already opened up, and waves from behind his desk. We both have an open-door policy, giving us equal chance to talk up punters browsing in the property windows.

'Need a hand?' he calls out.

'You're okay.' No idea why I say this, as it's a nightmare getting the grille off. He watches, and smirks.

'Here. Let me help.'

He's alongside me in a flash, arms outstretched. His light blue short-sleeved linen shirt showcases his rippling biceps. How he can have such a perfect tan beats me, because he never seems to leave his office, let alone sunbathe.

'Thanks.' I blush. My heart races a tad when he nudges me away, and slides the grille effortlessly to one side. 'Shall I lift it inside?'

'Please.'

I follow meekly behind, as he slips it up against the back wall.

'At your service, madam.'

A couple strolls past outside, and he's off like a bullet from a gun. 'Must go. Catch up later.'

Bastard. He's now got his smarmy sales hat in place, and appears to be browsing in his own window alongside the pair. It doesn't take long for him to launch into his pitch.

'Three hundred and twenty days of sunshine a year. A communal swimming pool on each phase of the development. Yes, there's even one due to be built in the Spanish Village.'

He spouts the same spiel ad nauseum. The young man takes his partner's hand, and tries to edge her away from the oil slick. With a promise of getting back to him, they wander off, past the kiosk, and on through to the central plaza.

I settle at my desk, turn on the computer, and wait for it to boot up. Outside, Seamus O'Halloran is opening up the kiosk. He's the patron of the bijou bar and coffee outlet. He depends on the sun for business, as there's barely room inside the kiosk for Seamus to squeeze between the coffee machine and the serving hatch. Customers have no choice but to sit outside.

He's setting out tables and chairs like he does every morning. Seating for at least fifty. It's definitely overkill, and each morning it takes him at least twenty minutes to unstack and arrange the furniture.

He wants it to look as if it might get busy. *The place to be seen* is the pitch. Seamus makes me smile with his leprechaun looks. His ginger beard, wonkily shaven sideburns, and generous belly remind me of one of Mum's garden gnomes.

As he raises the shutters, opening for business, I spot Gabby Rackham wandering over. She's the last person I want to see.

I know it's ridiculous, but I'm so jealous of Gabby Rackham. Not the fact that she's a femme fatale or because she's rolling in money. Simply because she's staying in my apartment, and can afford to stay there with no apparent responsibilities. Other than occasionally hosting quiz night and the odd shift behind the bar in The Three Bulls, she's living a life of leisure. I haven't seen her in painting overalls, or sitting in front of an easel, and am starting to suspect she might just enjoy lounging around.

I, on the other hand, am officially homeless with hardly anything left in my once very healthy bank account.

She looks so relaxed, sitting down outside the kiosk waiting for Seamus to bring over her morning pot of tea. Like Crystal, she does the turning-the-face-up-towards-the-sun thing, and stretches out her muscled legs. I'm being bitchy, but suspect that under her generous kaftans she might have thighs like a horse's haunches, and calf muscles like a shot-putter's. If she wasn't so well built, why the heck would she dress in such voluminous outfits?

Funny thing about Gabby, she speaks so quietly. She squeaks like a mouse, with a faint but distinct lisp. Her voice and scary appearance are a total mismatch.

I set to work, and try to call the Pedersens, the Danish couple I wined and dined last night. They were 90 per cent smitten with the swanky townhouse, and I'm praying they'll confirm a purchase today. When they don't pick up, I do a double-pronged attack with a courteous email telling them I'm here all day.

Next I compose an email for all my remaining management clients. I enquire about dates when they might be coming out, and dates they might have guests staying in their properties.

I'm about to chase up Jim and Julie Johnson, the couple who do private pool maintenance, as the Ropers' pool needs serious attention. I can't risk them turning up unannounced and discovering scum coating the water surface. But as I'm keying in their number, I freeze and put the phone down again. Gabby Rackham is heading my way. She looks so sunny, almost skipping towards me on her horses' haunches, that it's a real effort to get my own smile in place.

Ever since she moved into my apartment she's been trying to engage me in girly chats. She's far too nosy by half, and even half an hour in her company sharing coffee takes a Herculean effort. If she's not questioning me about the business, or Marcus, she's asking about my past. *Where am I from? How did I end up on this resort? Has selling properties always been my thing?* The questions are endless.

'Hi, Jade,' she whispers from the doorway.

'Gabby. Everything okay in the apartment?'

'Yes, it's amazing. Thank you so much. I wish I owned such a fabulous place. Maybe one day.'

Be careful what you wish for. It's Mum in my head again.

'Good. Glad you're enjoying it.' My teeth are seriously gritted.

'I was curious about security cameras. Are there no CCTV cameras on the resort? I can't see any in the Spanish Village? It's so dark at night, and so quiet. It can be quite scary.' She grimaces.

'There aren't any in yet, but they're going to be installed soon.'

'That would be great. I know private properties have their own cameras, especially on the more isolated parts of the resort.'

Where the heck is she going with this? She seriously needs to get a life, as I've work to get on with. I smile, managing to unclench the jaw lock, and aim for an end-of-conversation expression.

But she's going nowhere.

'I see Russell is installing cameras on Mr Roper's villa up on Phase 1. Maybe you should think of one for your flat?'

'Pardon? Mr Roper's villa? I don't think so.'

'I did my 5K walk this morning, and Russell was up a ladder. I was being nosy.'

My stomach lurches but I try to not let it show in my expression. 'Oh, yes. Sorry. It took me a minute to twig. That's right, the Ropers asked me to sort cameras out for them.'

'Maybe ask Russell about putting one in your apartment. I'd be happy to pay for it.'

Over my dead body.

Why is Russell installing security cameras at the Ropers' villa? It's the first I've heard of it. Mr Roper has never mentioned security cameras. Why now?

My chest tightens. I can't be found out again sleeping in another client's property. Has Avery really spread the word this quickly that I'm not to be trusted? But he only found out last night that I'd been staying in his villa. What the heck is going on?

Gabby reluctantly slopes off, no hurry to go anywhere, and as soon as she rounds the corner, I grab my bag, car keys, and lock up.

'Where are you off to?' Marcus yells through his doorway.

Bastard. He probably heard the conversation with Gabby. Sometimes I imagine he has hidden speakers inside my office.

But I ignore him, as I need to get to the Ropers' and find out what the hell is going on.

16

I drive like a lunatic round to Phase 1, catapulting the car in the air over the speed bumps. I'm so queasy that I'm scared my breakfast might come back up.

There's no sign of anyone in the circle of properties that houses the Ropers'. That is until I see Jolene Sanderstead.

'*Hola*,' she yells. She's English, from Brighton, but insists on speaking to me in Spanish. Well, holiday-maker Spanish, intermingling random words and phrases into lengthy sentences spoken mainly in English.

I offer a feeble wave as I lock up the car. She's the last person I want to talk to. I flop my back against the car, and stare up at the Ropers' front wall. There are two cameras facing out onto the street that weren't there when I left this morning. The one on the left is flashing, and is directed straight at my car.

I scrabble for the villa keys, scoot round the back of the building to gain entrance that way. And would you believe it? There are another two cameras round the back. The right one facing directly on to the swimming pool with its coating of scum.

I'm now seriously sweating, my forehead as damp as my

neck. The chill in the air is slowly abating, but I feel so hot it could be mid-August. The Ropers' villa is so isolated I get why they might want security cameras. But the fact they've installed them now has my pulse racing. And why didn't they go through me?

My hands are shaky, as well as damp, and my fingers slither over the villa keys. I need to get inside, away from Jolene Sanderstead, and clear out my stuff from last night. Thank goodness I left the bulk of my belongings in the boot.

There are a couple of security cameras inside as well, which is curious. There's nothing in the villa worth stealing. The TV isn't even a flat-screen. It's so old, with fuzzy reception, and a lumpy backend. There are no computers, laptops, or personal belongings of any value. Even the safe is empty.

As I hurry up the stairs to collect my clothes, I'm too late to duck under the flashing red light in the landing. No. No. No. I can't afford to lose maintenance on this property as well. It's one of my best earners.

I have such an uneasy feeling that Avery is in some way involved with this. What bothers me most is not that he's warned the Ropers that I'm not to be trusted, but that he must have told them well in advance of last night. The installation would need planning, and equipment bought specially. This is the only explanation.

I clear out all traces of my occupation, and am about to lock up when Jolene sneaks up the path behind me.

'*Hola*, Jade. *Cómo está*? How are you?'

Although it's broad daylight, it's like a boo in the dark. I nearly jump out of my skin.

Jolene looks deranged, her eyes wide and staring. Her frizzy orange hair sticks out at all angles, as if she's had an electric shock.

'All good, Jolene. Sorry, can't stop. Got a very busy day.'

'Why all the cameras? *Por qué?*'

I wince when she pronounces it 'porky'.

I get that she's bored, who wouldn't be up here? It's like being exiled to a very exclusive leper colony, everyone hiding under rocks.

'Oh, security. You know. It's so isolated.'

I throw my arms wide while trying to skirt round her, but she won't budge.

'Strange. Mr Roper was only saying last summer how safe he felt leaving his property unattended. Told me there was nothing worth stealing. Wonder why he's changed his mind?' She settles a thoughtful finger on a chin dimple.

'Sorry, I really can't stop for a chat. I'm really busy. Catch up later.'

This is a lie, as I'll be avoiding Jolene like the plague.

I zap open the car door, throw my gear on the back seat, and set to make my getaway. Jolene stands motionless on the pavement, arms folded, and stares after me as I drive off.

When I get back to the Spanish Village, Marcus is out of his office, and is leaning up against the kiosk, sipping from a plastic coffee cup that's covered in shamrocks.

'Fancy a coffee?' he yells.

I'm beyond anxious to get in touch with Mr Roper, and Russell (the installer of the cameras), but from Marcus's smirk, I'm starting to suspect he might somehow be involved in what's going on.

I throw my shoulders back and amble over. I'm aiming for nonchalant, so-not-worried, but my insides are rebelling. My hair is sticking in clumps to my head, and I have a ghastly thought that I might look a bit like Jolene. Wild and unkempt. But Marcus doesn't seem to notice.

'You're looking good today. Love the dress.'

His eyes flick up and down my red and white polka-dot dress, and my stomach lurches. He's not unlike Isaac. Smooth, handsome, and much too charming. Well, no way, José. I'll not fall into that trap again. I need to pick his brains, nothing else.

'What's your poison?' he asks.

It can't be heatstroke, as my arms are chicken-flesh chilly, but my heart is racing. It's the memories. Marcus's smile. His tanned, slim fingers. His perfect teeth. He's shorter than Isaac, with cute crater-sized dimples on either cheek when he smiles. But this time my heart's not beating through lust, but rather through fear.

I still have nightmares of Isaac's charred torso on the roof terrace.

'Cortado, please.'

I opt for a table nearest our offices. If a punter appears, I'll be first out of the blocks. Marcus comes over, sets our coffees down, and slips in alongside me. Couldn't he sit opposite, keep a professional distance? He seems to forget I'm the competition.

'You okay?'

'Yes. Why wouldn't I be?'

I narrow my eyes. Why is he asking? Do I look that bad?

'You hurried off shortly after you arrived this morning. I wondered if there was a problem.'

'No. I'd somewhere to be.'

He smiles. It's pretty innocent looking, and he's sunny-Spain relaxed. One thing I'm definitely getting better at is reading people. Isaac taught me to trust no one, but Marcus doesn't seem to be hiding anything. That said, he doesn't need to know about my life. All I want to know is whether he has anything to do with the Ropers' new security measures.

'Avery Knowles popped round when you were out. I know he

was one of your clients, but he told me what happened last night.'

'And?'

The coffee gurgles in my throat. Of course I know what he's going to say, but I feel sick to the core.

'He's asked me to take over the maintenance on his property. Is that okay with you?'

It's far from okay, but I've no choice. At least Marcus isn't gloating, and looks rather sheepish.

Although we haven't talked about it, he likely guessed I was staying at Avery's.

'No worries. Congratulations on your new client.'

I sniff, pout my lips, roll my eyes.

'Listen. If you need somewhere to stay while you're sorting yourself out, I have a spare room.'

No. No. No. I've fallen into that trap before.

17

I must have turned a whiter shade of pale because Marcus looks really concerned.

'Are you sure you're okay?'

'Why wouldn't I be?'

I knock back the coffee, toss the paper cup towards the bin, and miss. Could things get any worse?

'Here. I'll get it.' Marcus unwinds his legs, and retrieves my cup, and chucks it, along with his own, into the bin.

'Thanks. I need to get back to work.'

I don't know how many times I've said that this morning, but Marcus's proximity is freaking me out.

Mum told me not to jump into any new relationship until I knew the guy properly. No sleeping around. Something more cerebral is where she's coming from, not to mention a desire to get me married off.

I'm opening up my office for what seems like the umpteenth time, when Marcus taps me on the shoulder.

'Do you fancy doing the quiz tomorrow night? I'm organising

a table, and your reputation as a general knowledge genius is going round the resort.'

How can I not fall for this guy though?

I wrote myself a list of things I was never to do again. Things I'd learnt from sour experience.

Never trust a man
Follow your instincts

(This is confusing, as Marcus is so damn hot. I know I shouldn't trust him, but nevertheless...)

Do not go for looks over substance
Go for sense of humour, intelligence, and decency over bank balance

This is the tip of the iceberg, but the only points I can remember at this precise moment. Marcus's proximity is clouding my memory.

'Erm. I'm not sure I'm around tomorrow evening,' I say, aiming at mystery. Why am I bothering? There's nothing mysterious about me from where he's standing. I've been caught red-handed squatting in one of my owner's properties, and having less than Christian thoughts about nearly everyone I meet, Gabby Rackham being top of the list. With little effort she seems to have achieved everything in life I'm after. Including my flat.

'Going anywhere nice?'

The smug bastard. He's assuming I've nowhere to go, nowhere to stay, no friends to see. Well, let's see about that.

'You know what? I'll come to the quiz. I can change my other arrangements.'

'Marvellous. I'll meet you there at seven?'

'Fine.'

'And don't forget. If you need somewhere to stay a few nights, the offer's on the table.'

His dimples are back. His eyes are soft, squishy, and my heart does a little blip.

I smile, no idea why it's a coy effort, but what else can I say? Yes, I'd love to move in with you. Make use of your spare bed. But I'm more concerned that if I did, I'd never get out alive.

I barely managed it last time.

18

HAYLEY

Damon and I book a cheap Airbnb not far from Malaga airport.

We're already acting like a committed couple, unnerving after less than a fortnight together. One suitcase. One tube of toothpaste. One travel-size shampoo. One shower gel. The trip has the feel of an unplanned honeymoon.

'Well, Scrivens. Ready for the off?'

I flip off his baseball cap.

'Hayley. My name is Hayley.'

'Hey. Watch it.'

Another kiss, or three, on the lips, and the Uber horn beeps. Luton airport here we come.

Travelling with Damon is different from travelling with Teddy. Damon keeps a clear head, no alcohol on the flight, whereas Teddy is usually legless when he clambers on board. Teddy is asleep within two minutes of take-off, but Damon is wide-eyed, like a kid on speed.

I work on my iPad after take-off, and Damon reads. I'm beyond nervous, but excited about the trip. It's fun being with Damon, but the adrenaline about a potential scoop (I've already googled TV/film agents to get ahead of the game) has my heart pumping.

I've a list of questions that need answers. There are so many bits to the story, and too many gaps. George Stubbs's girlfriends. Relatives. But my top priority is to talk to Astrid. She's the key to unravelling the tale, although getting her on her own might not be easy. I doubt she'll be too keen to answer questions about her late husband, if there's any truth in what Teddy overheard.

The party is in two days' time. Luckily the weather is perfect, even though we're heading into winter. At least Astrid's infinity pool is heated (like a tepid bath according to Teddy), and with a cloudless sky, the forecast is looking good.

When we land at Malaga airport, we pick up a cab, giving the driver the address of our Airbnb. At first I think he's dropped us off at the wrong place. I look up at the drab six-storey concrete block and inhale deeply.

Opting for the exercise, we forgo the lift and trudge in silence to the top floor. The apartment inside is even worse than it looks from the outside. So much for the 'stunning views'. Through the lounge window, the sea is a speck in the distance, barely visible through a host of other concrete blocks.

The apartment is literally one room, with a piddly corner kitchenette (complete with kettle, a two-ringed electric hob, and a wobbly fridge).

Damon starts yanking at the fridge door, and when two empty ice-cube containers fly out, he tuts. He then searches frantically for something to balance the fridge on to keep it upright.

Despite the dingy accommodation, Damon is still smiling. He's determined to enjoy himself, reminding me why we're here.

'We'll not be spending much time in the room. We've work to do, remember?'

I simply nod.

'Any word from Teddy?'

'Not yet. I'll text him now.'

> Arrived safely. All good. See you this evening? We can get a taxi to the villa? XX

Two minutes later a message pings back.

> I'll send you an address in the port where we can meet. Astrid wants quiet tonight, no guests. Is Donna with you?

'Time to come clean.' Damon pulls me down on to the threadbare sofa-cum-bed. It seems to be a sofa for one and a half people, it's so damn small.

I grit my teeth, and text.

> Yes, Damon is coming too. What time?

I leave out the kisses this time. I can feel Teddy freaking through the handset.

> Who the hell is Damon?

> I told you. My new flatmate.

> Damon? A guy? You said Donna

His ears will now be crimson. He's like Spock when he's angry, and his ears are all you notice.

> I'll fill you in later. Message me time and venue, and we'll be there. Can't wait.

I turn the phone off. Teddy doesn't harbour anger for long, so I'm banking his will have abated by this evening.

Anyway, he's shacked up with Sugar Mummy. What did he expect?

19

Can the guy heading towards us really be Teddy? I do a double, more like quadruple take, as he strolls over.

Damon and I arrived early, and have been waiting in the very exclusive, dimly lit bistro in Puerto Banus that Teddy suggested. It faces out to sea, with stunning views of all the millionaire yachts. The panorama might be great, but I'm more worried about how much the meal is going to cost.

I'm not big on designer gear, but the lookalike Teddy is dressed head to toe in exclusive brands. His white Nike trainers are pristine, no hint of his trademark mud splatters. The Ralph Lauren polo shirt makes him look like a catalogue model. And... oh my God... he's wriggling a Rolex on his wrist. A gold Rolex, no less. Well, it looks like a Rolex, but it can't be real. Can it?

Damon looks even more shocked than I do. The guy in the designer gear can't surely be my ex-boyfriend. Okay, I painted a pretty shabby picture, despite trying to embellish Teddy's good points while sounding less than convincing.

'Scrivens. Come here,' Teddy says, throwing his arms wide.

The Girl on the Balcony

I get up, push my chair back, and let him zoom in for a hug. It doesn't last long when he spots Damon over my shoulder. He releases his arms, then rakes his manicured (yes, really) fingers through freshly gelled hair.

'Teddy? Is that really you?' I ask, seriously shocked by his appearance.

'Yep. It's me.'

At least his trademark blush reminds me he's a guy I once dated. Or else he has an uncanny resemblance to the guy I once lived with.

I turn to introduce my new flatmate-cum-lover.

'Teddy. This is Damon.'

I glance at Damon, who is still seated and looks decidedly uncomfortable. His clothes might be dowdy in comparison to New Teddy's, but he makes my heart beat faster. The way Teddy used to do.

'Hi. Pleased to meet you, Damon. Scrivens has told me all about you... *not*.' Teddy emphasises the last word really loudly, then tuts, rolls his eyes and stares me down.

'Damon's my new flatmate. That's all.'

Not sure Teddy believes me, but rather than shake hands with Damon, he slips his manicured fingers into the pocket of expensive trousers. They've got to be expensive because they fit him. His long skinny legs are fully covered with no sign of an ankle.

If this was the first time I'd met Teddy, I'd think it was my lucky day. I dread to think what he's doing for Astrid in return for the high-budget gear. But that's no longer my problem.

We form an unlikely trio round the table, with me piggy in the middle. Teddy starts things off by ordering an extortionately priced bottle of wine for 240 euros.

Damon is unusually quiet, so I grip his hand under the table when Teddy isn't looking, and feel a reciprocal squeeze.

'So tell me. How's it going?' I direct my glare at Teddy, slowly uncoiling my fingers from Damon's. 'With Astrid?'

'It's going great. Astrid is amazing,' Teddy says, knocking back the millionaire-price-tagged wine like shandy from our local.

'She's not the monster-murderer then?' I laugh, trying to make light of a very loaded question.

Teddy glowers at me, and Damon looks at the floor.

'What are you talking about?' Teddy shrugs. He knows exactly what I'm talking about. It looks as if New Teddy has had a memory transplant as well as a makeover.

'It's okay. I filled Damon in.'

'On what? Filled him in on what?' The glowering gets worse.

'What you overheard on the plane. Remember? He won't tell anyone.'

'I don't remember. Anyway, it's not important. Astrid is great.'

'So you got it all wrong?'

Likely she's paying millionaire wages to her staff in exchange for loyalty and tight lips.

'Probably.'

Teddy is now really uncomfortable, shifting awkwardly in his seat. He's not going to give anything away, and certainly not in front of a stranger.

'Does she ever mention her husband, the guy who died?'

'Not really. Top up?' Teddy lifts the wine bottle and tops up our glasses. He then begins to study the menu.

Damon and I open our menus too, but I'm not ready to choose my food.

'You texted that a relative of Astrid's dead husband had turned up at the villa.'

The Girl on the Balcony

'Did I?' Teddy continues to concentrate on the *Menu del Dia* as if it's an exam paper.

'Yes. An uncle, cousin, or brother? I can't remember which. Have you met them?'

Teddy knows me well enough, that when I want an answer I'm like a dog with a bone.

'His brother, I think.' His eyes don't leave the menu as he runs a finger down the list of options.

'Brother. Oh, that's interesting.'

I continue staring at him until he finally throws me a crumb.

'He's just staying at the villa for a few days.'

'You said he was fun.'

'To be honest, he's out most of the time. But he should be coming to the pool party.'

Teddy tries to cut the conversation by clicking his fingers at a waiter, indicating that we're ready to order.

My heart flutters with excitement. This might be an important lead.

'What's his name?'

'Er... I can't remember. Emery, I think. That's it. Or was it Oliver? Not really sure, to be honest.'

Teddy is desperate to quash the direction of the conversation. Likely Astrid has warned staff not to discuss villa matters with strangers.

'Is he older or younger than George was?'

Teddy exhales through frustration.

'No idea. Now can we order some food? I don't know about you guys, but I'm starving.'

Damon nods, and the waiter takes our order. When Teddy insists it's going to be his treat, Damon opts for a starter, a main course, and dessert. He winks at me, and I want to burst out laughing.

I'm suddenly feeling much hungrier, now I've got a possible lead for my story. Emery, Oliver... whoever he is.

Here's hoping he'll turn up at the pool party.

20

Although Teddy didn't ask us (or even me on my own) back to Astrid's villa for a nightcap, and to meet his mysterious benefactor, he was quick to assume I'd be at his beck and call for the next few days.

This morning, after a steamy night with Damon, I feel really bad going off to meet Teddy, who still thinks he's my boyfriend. I'm scared to tell him we're over, as he'd likely cut loose and I'd lose the vital link to my story. But I feel even worse leaving Damon.

'You don't mind if I go, do you?' I ask him for the umpteenth time.

I feel really shitty leaving him in the concrete block, but that's short-lived when he says he's off to do a boat trip round the coast.

'Without me?'

'Yep. Without you.'

He holds aloft a skimpy pair of swimming trunks, and wiggles them. He certainly knows how to play me.

'Maybe I'll tell Teddy I can't make it. A headache. Covid. Or perhaps I should tell him the truth, that he and I are history.'

'You can't do that. Not until after the pool party. Remember, you're here to work? Piece your story together?'

Is he trying to get rid of me? I wish he'd stop wiggling his swimming trunks. I can imagine him parading his fit body along the beach, or diving off the side of some yacht. Okay, it's November, but it's still pleasant, and the thought that he might catch the eye of a Spanish girl makes me panic. But he's right. I need to meet up with Teddy, at least once before the pool party, and do some digging. And also to get our brother/sister story straight before I meet Astrid. I'm desperate to talk to her, see what I can find out.

I look out the window of the dingy apartment, and on to the street below. There's a tall, well-dressed guy standing near the block entrance, fiddling on his mobile phone. It's only when a text pings on to my phone, I realise I'm staring at New Teddy.

> You ready, Scrivens? I'm here. Down below. T xx

I don't know why I jump back from the window, rather than wave down. It all feels a bit weird, and watching Damon pack his rucksack with the skimpy trunks, goggles, and water bottle makes me feel sad. I'm starting to really like Damon, and wish I was going with him rather than with my ex. But work needs to come first if I'm to break open the story.

I text Teddy back.

> On my way!

I leave out kisses, and instead lift my bag, and land a last lingering kiss on my new boyfriend's lips.

'Have fun.'

'You too.'

Although I'm sort of hoping he doesn't have fun without me.

* * *

Teddy is talking to a man in a suit when I appear. The man tells Teddy he'll wait for him and then walks back to a large black car parked across the road.

'Scrivens. Great to see you.'

When he approaches, I brace for one of his Labrador-type kisses, but instead get a peck on the cheek. Over his shoulder I notice the man in the black car watching us. I shiver. He could be the reason Teddy doesn't act too lovey-dovey, as the man has possibly been told Teddy's picking up his sister.

Anyway, a peck on the cheek is fine by me. Especially when I glance up to the sixth floor of the concrete block and see Damon with his nose pressed against the glass. I giggle when he wiggles his skimpy trunks down at me, and my heart somersaults.

'Teddy. Good to see you too. What's the plan?'

'You're coming back to meet Astrid.'

'What?' This wasn't part of the plan. I thought he and I were off sightseeing, and I'd get the chance to pick his brains in private.

'We've got a lift back. To be honest, I didn't want that Damon hanging around. Astrid wants to meet you, not your flatmate.'

New Teddy seems to have learnt new skills from Sugar Mummy. Telling lies top of the list, as I know it's more likely *he's* the one who doesn't want Damon tagging along.

'Oh. What fun.' So not fun, but this is it. Maybe today I can find out more about George Stubbs's death, and his ex-wife, Astrid Olsen. If I'm really going to write the story, I need my work hat in place, and to get snooping.

Soon we're in the sleek Mercedes with the blacked-out

windows. Teddy and I sit in the back seat with a huge gap between us, while the swarthy Spanish driver keeps one eye on the road, the other on us.

I'm relieved, but surprised, that Teddy doesn't reach for my hand. The feeling that the driver might be keeping tabs on us makes me nervous.

Teddy talks about the weather (yes, really), food (not a big surprise here, but his enthusiasm for spicy local dishes is certainly one up from Big Mac and chips), and the amazing villa.

'Wait till you see it,' he says, wide-eyed.

'Can't wait.' Actually, I'd like to turn round now, and head back to Damon for a bit of snorkelling. I have really uneasy vibes about Astrid, and my insides have started to somersault. It's not just because of what Teddy overheard on the plane, but the fact she's turned Teddy into a whole different person. He seems distant and edgy, where he's usually so laid back.

'Have you got your costume?' he asks me. 'The pool is heated.'

'No. You didn't tell me. I thought we'd be going out, just the two of us.'

'Sorry, Scrivens. Astrid needs me for work this afternoon...'

'Oh. No worries. Whatever.'

'But she's really keen to meet my sister.' He winks behind a hand. At least he's sticking with the sister story.

But is it my imagination, or is the driver now staring at us through his rear-view mirror?

By the time the Merc cruises up to a huge, white-walled property with a *Casa de Astrid* plaque on the gate, my anxiety is sky-high. Despite Teddy overhearing Astrid's tale of murder, he now seems to be part of her team.

Maybe she's fed Teddy a completely different story to what

he heard. He's so gullible, and I'm starting to think he might have sold his soul to the devil.

21

Teddy is right. The villa is amazing, and absolutely huge. I wander round behind him as he takes on the role of tour guide.

'Cool, isn't it?' New Teddy has certainly mastered the art of understatement.

'It's fantastic.' My eyes are agog. The place is out-of-this-world stunning.

However, my 5,000-star rating plummets when we go inside through a half-mile stretch of glass doors. What a mess!

'Wow.' Meaning I can't believe what I'm seeing. The inside is covered with all manner of things. Clothes. Dirty plates. Cardboard boxes. Even a generously cupped bra hangs over a chair back.

'It's a bit messy, but I haven't started to clean up yet,' Teddy says.

'You clean up?' A laugh pops out. Teddy cleaning? He usually chucks his shoes across the hall when he gets in, and Scrivens does the clearing away. If he's actually cleaning – and I'll believe it when I see it – Astrid must pay *really* well.

He lifts a couple of plates, a couple of mugs, a bowl of

satsuma peel, and a carrier bag filled with stuff, and disappears through a door at one end of the enormous living space.

The walls are covered with huge random paintings... so random I've no idea what they represent. The colours are vibrant, but that's about all I can say about them. Teddy told me Astrid likes to paint, so likely these are her efforts.

'Hayley. *Hola.*'

I jump out of my skin when a well-built woman (likely the owner of the generous bra judging by her voluptuous chest) appears at the top of a huge winding staircase running up from the centre of the room.

She inches slowly down the stairs, gripping the railing and puffing heavily from the effort. At the bottom she extends a very bejewelled hand. At least two rings per finger, and a set of gold bracelets jangles on her wrist.

'How lovely to meet you. I'm Astrid. Welcome to my home.'

I feel my cheeks redden as I take her hand. Ouch. She grips tightly, and a knuckle-duster ring grinds against my finger.

'Hi. Lovely to meet you. Teddy has told me so much about you.'

'Teddy?' She raises an eyebrow. 'Teddy?' she repeats.

'Sorry, Stephen. Teddy's a nickname.'

'Oh. Yes, of course. I almost forgot you're his sister.'

Instinctively I tug down the sleeve of my cotton jumper to cover the teddy tattoo on my wrist. Astrid's narrowed eyes watch me like a hawk. Could she suspect I'm not his sister? I simply smile and hover, no idea what to do next.

Suddenly she yells out, and breaks the impasse.

'Stephen. Stephen.' She stares towards the door Teddy's just gone through, and a second later he reappears.

'Astrid.' He pulls himself up like a guard on duty.

At first, I suspect he's just getting really well paid for being a very willing cleaner, and he's not keen for me to know that this is his role.

But I couldn't be more wrong. Astrid flounces towards him, generous ankles peeking out from under a maxi-length dress. She stretches out a hand, and entwines Teddy's neatly manicured fingers in her own.

'Let's go outside. The weather is lovely today, don't you think?'

I nod in sync with Teddy, who looks mortified by Astrid's hand-holding.

'But first,' she continues, freeing her hand from Teddy's, 'Stephen. Or should I say Teddy...' She laughs wildly, and hairs stand up on the back of my neck.

'Yes?' Teddy hangs on her every word.

'Bring us a nice cold bottle of something fizzy. Champagne, perhaps?'

She looks at me.

'That sounds lovely,' I say.

Teddy scuttles off. Jeez. I can't believe my free-spirited ex has sold his soul for money. It must be a *hell* of a lot of money.

We settle outside on an enormous terrace tiled in shiny marble. Teddy appears with an ice bucket holding two bottles of champagne, and goes back inside for a platter of olives, cheeses, nuts, and snacks. Astrid is soon dipping her bejewelled fingers in and out of the assortment, and licking the tips between dips.

The champagne tastes good, and along with the clear blue sky and warm sun, I could almost be envious of New Teddy's life choice. But Astrid makes me uncomfortable. Not sure if it's the murder story, or just a general vibe. I could be having drinks with Hannibal Lecter, that's how queasy she makes me feel.

Twenty minutes in, I decide to bite the bullet. The drink is helping me relax, and I start off gently. A question every few minutes is the plan.

'Teddy, oops, Stephen tells me you're widowed. I'm sorry.'

'Oh, don't be sorry. My husband was a *monster*.'

She emphasises the last word, as she pops another olive in her mouth.

'A monster?' I aim for casual, quizzical, and so-not-bothered if she rises to the bait or not.

'He was abusive, controlling. And I thought I was in love with him. Can you imagine?'

'That's awful. I'm sorry.'

'Do you know what it's like to be in love?' Her eyes narrow, and her lips pout. Why do I get the feeling she's trying to sum me up?

'Yes. I thought I did.'

Teddy reddens, and fiddles with a handful of nuts. Not sure which of them is the most ill at ease.

'What was his name?'

I'm supposed to ask the questions. But she's slippery.

'Reuben.' The made-up name pops out.

'Reuben? Tell me about him.'

Teddy's eyes widen, and as he swivels his glass too quickly, champagne dribbles over onto the terrace.

'Oh, it was a long time ago. I'd rather forget him.'

There's a few seconds' silence before I dare ask another question.

'I hear your husband died in the villa. On a roof terrace? Teddy mentioned it.'

Teddy gives me daggers, but I'm not here to help him build a lifestyle with a madwoman. I'm here for the Pulitzer Prize.

'Yes. He burnt to a frazzle.'

'That must have been dreadful.'

'Stephen, you've gone very quiet,' she purrs, and leans across and takes his hand for a second time. I can almost feel the thick gold rings bite into his bony knuckles.

'What?'

He has no idea what to say, so I carry on.

'Was it an accident?'

'An accident? What a funny question.'

Astrid stares at me. If looks could kill, I'd be dead.

22

I thought I'd be the one asking the questions – how wrong was I? I'm quizzed like a game-show contestant.

How long am I staying? This is the first question.

'Just a few days.' I drink the champagne faster, desperate to ask my own questions.

'I hope you'll be coming to my pool party,' Astrid purrs. She kicks off her sandals, and hoists her broad ankles onto a chair.

'I'd love to. It's the day after tomorrow?'

She nods.

'And do bring David with you. Is he Reuben's replacement? *The one*, perhaps?' She wiggles fingers like inverted commas, and laughs again.

'Thanks. He's only my flatmate. We're just good friends.'

Teddy's shoulders visibly relax.

'Really? Just good friends?' Astrid asks with a sceptical puff of air.

'Yes. Stephen was living with me in between travels, but I need a more permanent lodger to help with the bills.'

'Oh. I see.' Astrid watches me over the rim of her bubbly drink.

'And it's Damon. Not David.'

'Oops. Whatever. I'm looking forward to meeting him.'

As Teddy pushes his chair back, and goes to get up (he's looking really uncomfortable – and not just from his tight trousers), Astrid throws in the curveball question. The million-pound jackpot, that if I get it wrong I'm back to zero.

'And Hayley, what do you do for a living?'

Teddy leans his head behind Astrid's, shakes it rather violently from side to side. I'm not to say I'm a journalist, I know that. Although I've prepared plenty of lines and questions I need to ask, I'm thrown by this particular question. It takes me a couple of seconds to come up with an occupation that is as far removed from journalism as possible.

'I'm a hairdresser.'

No idea where that came from. I've been going over and over possible questions and scenarios, preparing for such an interrogation, but why the heck didn't I anticipate being asked what I do for a living?

'Oh, are you really? I should have guessed from your gorgeous auburn hair. It's so silky, and beautifully cut and styled.'

She starts fiddling with her own wispy hair, curling the ends round her podgy fingers. Teddy, now standing directly behind Astrid's chair, rolls his eyes. He can't believe I came up with such a stupid occupation.

'Perhaps you can do my hair? I could do with a cut and colour.'

Her eyes bore into me, and I have to look away. Does she suspect I'm not a hairdresser, or has Teddy told her a different story? Whatever, she's trying to suss me out.

I take a sip of champagne, my fingers shaky, conjuring up a reply.

'I'd love to, another time perhaps. I haven't brought my gear with me.'

'That's no trouble at all. I have everything you need. Scissors. Hair dyes. Shampoos. Mousse. Sprays. You name it. I've got a mini-salon upstairs.'

This feels like a test. Could she already know I'm a journalist? Teddy said he hasn't told her, but who knows? I get the feeling there's no pulling the wool over this madwoman's eyes. Although she lives in a mess, and looks a mess, I get the impression she's as sharp as a tack.

'Astrid.' Teddy's voice saves me from dealing with the hairdressing issue.

'Yes, Stephen. Or should I call you Teddy? It's soooo cute.'

She tugs at his hand, using a firm grip to help her out of the chair.

'Is it okay if I show Hayley round the grounds before I tidy up?'

'Of course, Teddy darling. Then afterwards, I'd like you and I to go into Marbella for lunch. What do you say?'

'Yes, of course. Shall I book somewhere?'

'That would be lovely. A nice surprise.'

Astrid strolls off, and doesn't look back. She doesn't say goodbye, and hopefully I'll be long gone before she reappears. It'll certainly be a quick look round the grounds, as I'm desperate to get away.

The whole set-up makes my skin crawl. Teddy has turned into a complete stranger, someone I don't recognise at all. Money seems to be his new god, as there's no way he could fancy Astrid.

As Teddy marches ahead of me across the terrace, and down a path towards an olive grove, I look back towards the villa.

I shiver when I see Astrid by an upstairs window staring down. She stabs two fingers in the direction of her eyes, then points them my way. She's letting me know she's watching me.

23

Teddy leads me past an olive grove, and then down a few steps.

'Well, Scrivens? What do you think?'

In front of us is the most amazing infinity pool. It's so huge, it swallows up its surroundings.

'Wow. It's even better than the photos.'

'Photos? Maybe best you delete them.'

'What? Why?'

'All our messages.' Teddy stuffs fidgety hands in his pockets. He's so unrelaxed, jittering from foot to foot. 'Astrid doesn't let staff take pictures, and we're told we'll be sacked for forwarding so much as a single snap.'

'Bit late for that.'

'I didn't realise when I sent you those pictures. Can you delete them, please?' He pleads with his eyes.

'Okay. I'll delete them, but seriously, Teddy. Are you staying here much longer? Astrid seems more than a bit crazy.' I swivel a finger near my brain. 'Totally loco.'

'She's not that bad, and the pay is amazing. I've now got a few thousand pounds saved.'

'Already? You've only been here a month. I dread to think what you're doing to earn that.'

His cheeks redden, and he looks across the pool. Anywhere but at me.

'It's not what you think. She's just lonely.'

'Really? Thousands of pounds lonely?'

'Listen. Give me three months tops, and I'll be back. Then we can get a deposit down on somewhere more permanent.'

He lowers his voice to a murmur. Even if Astrid hurried outside, there's no way she could be within earshot so quickly. Teddy might be obeying orders, but I'm picking up something else. He's scared of her.

'Whatever. One day at a time. Have you found out any more about her husband's death?'

'She doesn't talk about it. Shuts down any mention.'

'Have you tried to talk about it?'

'Not really, to be honest.'

Although disappointed, I feel relieved that he hasn't snooped. Who knows what Astrid would do if she knew why I was here.

'At least you haven't let slip that your sister is a journalist.'

We laugh together.

'A hairdresser though? Really?'

Teddy leans in, winds a strand of my auburn hair behind my ear, and lets his fingers linger.

'I've missed you, Scrivens.'

He's about to lean in closer when I stretch out an arm against his chest. Lucky I do, because at the same moment, there's a rustle in the bushes behind us. Astrid appears, wearing a wide-brimmed straw hat, and is talking to someone who looks like a gardener. But at the same time, she's got one eye on us.

* * *

By the time I get back to the concrete Airbnb, I'm strung up and exhausted. I haven't got much fodder for my story, and Teddy fed me nothing new. The only things I learnt today are details about Astrid's character.

'She's crazy,' I say, tossing my bag onto the bed. 'More than a little.'

'That bad, eh?'

Damon looks so relaxed, and genuinely pleased to see me. It makes me realise that Teddy and I are definitely over. For good. Teddy is now almost as creepy as Astrid, and I need normal. A partner, a home, and a family. As well as the scoop of my career.

'What did you do while I was gone?' I ask. 'Did you go snorkelling?'

'Actually, I just went for a walk. It wouldn't have been much fun without you. I've been twiddling my thumbs since you left.'

Although I'm chuffed that he's missed me, I'm a tad surprised. He's been going on about how much he's wanted to snorkel, and this was his chance.

He stretches out his arms, pulls me down on to the sofa-cum-bed, and starts smothering me in kisses.

For half an hour at least (okay, more like an hour) I forget everything except my hot new flatmate. Even the potential career-changing exclusive sinks to the back of my mind.

When Damon pops into the bathroom for a shower, I wander over to the smeary window and look down on to the street below.

The same black car is there, or a very similar one to that which picked me up this morning. And the same driver is leaning up against the bonnet with his phone out. He seems to be taking pictures.

They're certainly not selfies, as he's holding the screen up in the air, and pointing it directly towards the sixth floor of the concrete block.

24

JADE

Once I've fired off emails to Harry Roper, and all my other existing clients (those that haven't yet asked for their keys back), I scribble a note and stick in the office window.

Working round the resort. On mobile if urgent. Back at 1.

First stop will be Las Colinas community. I urgently need to find Russell. Firstly, I've a growing list of maintenance jobs that need attention in the properties adjacent to Avery's, which are handily on the opposite side of the road from where Russell lives. More importantly, I'm desperate to find out who asked him to install the cameras on the Ropers' property.

I feel so edgy, verging on paranoid, that I park the car round the corner from Las Colinas. I'm not sure why I feel the need to sneak about, as doing so won't bolster my CV. But I have an uneasy feeling about everything that's going on. Something doesn't sit right.

I'm in luck, because straightaway I spot Russell working on

The Girl on the Balcony

the house neighbouring his own, pruning an olive tree whose branches stretch across the whole expanse of the front garden.

But before I reach him, he scoots round the back.

'Yoo hoo. Russell?' I yell, shielding my eyes from the glare of sunlight. Where the heck has he gone? 'Russell?'

I push open the gate, trip over the lopped-off olive branches, and sidle round the back. It's then I hear an engine. Through the back hedge, I see his van (*Russell's Sunny Services* painted in bright red letters along the side) take off. He's left shears, ladders, and expensive branch cutters on the ground.

I wave after him, but that only seems to make him speed up, and soon the van has disappeared from view.

My mind is swirling. Why is Russell now ignoring me? It's not the end of the world that he installed cameras without my knowledge.

'Jade?'

I jump round, stubbing my toe against an ornamental rock.

'Crystal.'

All I need.

Somehow I manage my PR sunshine smile.

'I thought it was you.' She wanders over, her enormous feet in open-toed strappy sandals, covering the distance in a couple of steps.

It looks like I'll have to say 'must get back to work' for the umpteenth time today. Also I'm not sure I want her watching me as I do my checks on the adjacent properties. She doesn't strike me as a snoop, but who knows? My judgement is seriously skewed, and everyone is making me feel uneasy. Marcus. Russell. Avery. Gabby Rackham. Even Seamus at the kiosk.

'Fancy a coffee?' she asks. 'I'm sitting round our pool and could do with the company.'

Her shoulders are starting to acquire a faint pink tinge, but under a floaty sarong, her legs are still alabaster white.

I take a moment. 'Go on then. Why not?'

Maybe I can use her to get back in Avery's good books. She may have some sway with him. Also, maybe she might have intel on Russell and the Ropers. The more I think about it, I'm convinced Avery is at the root of everything. It looks like he's more than a little pissed off by me staying at his villa. He's likely trash-talking me to everyone, but it doesn't explain Russell's over-the-top reaction. Russell is solid, and we go way back. Maybe Avery threatened him, but I can't believe he'd be set on such an extreme course of revenge.

I push the gate shut to the property Russell has abandoned, and follow Crystal across the road.

'Maybe you'd prefer something stronger? I've opened a bottle of cava,' she whispers behind her fingers with a giggle. 'But don't tell Avery.'

I don't remind her that Avery and I are no longer on speaking terms. But you know what? A glass of cava might be the way to go. I'm slowly running out of things to tackle on my agenda, as my clients are ignoring me – both in person, and also my digital attempts at communication. Despite the fact that the only person I've wronged has been Avery. He's certainly been quick at filling everyone in on my untrustworthiness.

'Cava? I guess one glass won't hurt.'

The way I feel at the moment, a whole bottle might be better.

25

'Oh, Marcus is quite dishy,' Crystal swoons, pipe-cleaner limbs draped across the sun lounger. She keeps fiddling with the sarong, pulling it over her bony legs, but letting it dip off her increasingly pink shoulders. She also toys with her hair, twirling the ends round her fingers. When she tugs out a couple of strands, I wince.

I noticed her yanking out hair once before, and thought it was a one-off. Now I think she's got a serious issue.

'Marcus? You think so?'

I gulp the cava, the pre-planned sips having gone by the wayside.

While Crystal lounges, I sit perched on the edge of a second sun lounger which wobbles like unset jelly. If I lift my feet off the ground it tips like a rocker.

'Yes-I-do.' She says each word slowly, like a robot. Hard not to think Stepford Wife. 'Is he single?'

I'm not sure if it's a rhetorical question aimed to see if I'm interested, or if she genuinely wants to know. He's certainly dishier than Avery with his not-to-be-trusted pebble eyes. Thinking about him makes my skin crawl.

'I think so. Not sure though. We're working neighbours, but that's as far as it goes.'

'He's the competition, right?'

She closes her eyes and lies back as if we're in 30-degree heat, despite the fact the sun has dipped behind a rapidly developing band of sinister-looking clouds.

'I suppose so,' I say. 'He's now looking after Avery, I hear.'

'I'm sorry about that.' She twists her neck round. 'It was unlucky he caught you out. We weren't due out for a couple more weeks.'

'Avery emailed that he wasn't coming out until May.'

'It was pretty last minute. He loves his golfing trips, and couldn't resist the invitation.'

'You haven't been out here before, have you?' I ask.

'I came with him when he first looked round. I met you briefly, don't you remember?'

'Vaguely,' I say. I remember someone being with him, but didn't take much notice as I was much too keen to pull off a sale.

'Avery stayed on and sealed the deal while I headed back.'

'Oh.' I'm not sure what else to say, as I now feel mortified that I ended up comatose in her boyfriend's bed after drinking too much celebratory sangria. Although the more I get the measure of Avery, the more I'm convinced that he must have spiked my drinks.

'He's been out a couple of times since on his own. This is my first time staying at the villa with him.' She giggles.

How can she be attracted to Avery? I can see why he's drawn to her, she's attractive in a willowy fragile sort of way, but how did she fall for him? He's such a creep, and certainly no looker. Perhaps it's a father fetish – he's got to be a lot older than her. Or maybe he's got money, though his villa is pretty average in the grand scheme of things.

I don't ask where they met. London. Spain. Timbuktu for all I care. I'm more concerned about getting up without tipping over the sun lounger, and in the process not smashing my skull on the tiles. My head is already squiffy from the cava, which doesn't help.

I empty my glass, and manage to sidle off the contraption.

'I must get back.' Here we go again. 'Work to do.'

When I roll my eyes, she looks at me strangely.

'No worries. Thanks for the company. And, by the way, I hear you're doing the quiz tomorrow night. See you there.'

'Are you doing it too?' Oh, no, that means facing Avery in front of other people.

'Marcus invited us to join his table.'

Why didn't Marcus tell me this himself? I'm not sure who I thought would be on his table, but certainly not Avery and Crystal. Marcus knows what happened with Avery, so why is he throwing us together? Perhaps he wants us to make up, or else he's rubbing my nose in it, but I can't believe Marcus would be so mean.

As I slouch back to the car, I've already started panicking as to who the other two people will be. Knowing my luck, one of them will be Gabby Rackham.

As I approach the car, I notice a white piece of paper tucked under the wiper. At least it won't be a parking ticket. I rip it off, and as I do so a wooden crate alongside the passenger door catches my eye. What the heck? It's a load of mouldy satsumas.

I lift out a couple, and rancid mould from the rind coats my fingers as juice dribbles to the ground. I'm tempted to rip up the note without reading it, as I'm seriously freaking. But, of course, I don't.

Enjoy.
PS I'm watching you

I do a full 360, and although there's no one around, I nearly jump out of my skin when a large black 4X4 drives past. My insides turn to liquid when the driver opens his window and waves. It's one of the guys who drove me off the road the other night.

And the registration number confirms it's the same car.

26

I crawl into my car after dumping the crate of orange gunge on to the back seat. My head is spinning, and nausea is battling with the panic. What the hell is going on? Who are the guys in the black car, and what do they want? If they left the mouldy oranges as a joke, it was so not funny. My skin prickles with the sense I've got a stalker. Dealing with Avery is one thing, but this is something else entirely.

On the way back to the office, I tip the mouldy oranges into a large rubbish bin at the back of the hotel.

My mind is all over the place, but the most immediate concern has to be where I'm going to stay tonight. The Ropers' is out of the question, with their new state-of-the-art security system. Crashing out on the office settee is a last resort as I'm so hot and sweaty, screaming out for a shower.

I park up, slump my head against the steering wheel, and bang it up and down a few times. This was meant to be a whole new phase of my life. I genuinely believed hard work and energy would reap its own rewards. My bottom lip is seriously quivering, and as I'm about to explode into tears, I see Marcus talking to Gabby outside his office.

Did he touch her shoulder? I'm soon sitting bolt upright, tears having been swallowed back as I stare at the pair. She's doing her coy act, teasing pink strands of brittle hair behind an ear. I'm surprised the hair doesn't get snagged in the array of ear piercings.

When Marcus sees me get out of the car, he takes a couple of steps back from her. I know they've spoken before, but today they look like old-school besties.

'Hi. You're back.' He moves over to meet me, as Gabby scurries off in the opposite direction.

'Yep. I'm back. Anything happen since I was away?'

I try to keep my voice steady, but it's hard to talk calmly.

'The Pedersens came by.'

My heart skips a beat, and I manage a smile. Thank goodness. This could be the bit of good news I need.

'Any message?'

I zap the car door, and walk as casually as I can alongside my nemesis. I don't want to show too much excitement that the Pedersens have been, but Marcus has gone unusually quiet. He's biting his lip with perfect white incisors.

'I'm really sorry, but they asked if I'd sort out the purchase for them.'

'What? Why? Because I wasn't in the office?' I give him daggers.

This can't be happening. They are my clients. Oh my God. Has Avery somehow got to the Pedersens as well?

'To be honest, Jade, I don't know why they came to me as you've done all the hard work.' He takes a deep breath. 'What say I take it from here, and we split the commission?'

He turns his head, his expression sheepish like a kid caught with their fingers in the sweetie jar.

'Bloody hell, Marcus. You've got to be kidding me,' I snap, scared to look at him as I'm about to lose it completely. I march ahead, desperate not to make a scene in public.

He grabs my arm, hauls me back.

'Whoa. Hang on,' he commands.

'I'm not a bloody horse.'

We're now level with the kiosk, and Seamus yells out. '*Hola*, Jade. Marcus. Coffee?'

Marcus and I are Seamus's best customers, but my head is already spinning from everything that's going on. Not to mention from the cava.

I simply shake my head, and scrabble for my office keys. They fall on the ground, and Marcus bends to pick them up. As I go to snatch them back, our fingers graze, and a jolt of electricity shoots through me. Tears sting in the corners of my eyes, and Marcus holds my hand for a few seconds. Despite what's going on, his warmth feels good, although I know it shouldn't.

'Want to talk about it?' he asks.

When I don't say anything, he propels me towards his office with a firm palm against my lower back.

Seamus whistles behind us. Not sure if he's whistling at us, or whether it's just his sunny disposition, but something tells me it's the former.

When Marcus opens up, then turns the door sign to *Cerrado* (closed), the floodgates open.

27

'Why don't you tell me about it,' he says, handing me a wad of tissues.

I wonder what he wants to know. That I'm losing clients by the hour, I have some mad stalker after me, or that I was nearly run off the road last night by a maniac driver? Instinct tells me everything is connected, with Avery somehow involved. At least with the losing-clients part.

Marcus doesn't sit down, rather wanders into the kitchen at the back of his office, and clatters around. A couple of minutes later he's back with a bottle of cava, and two what look like half-pint glasses.

'Sorry. They're all I've got.' He gives a sheepish grin.

'I'll stick to water if you don't mind. I've already had a drink.'

'Have you? Already?' He checks his watch with an irritating smirk.

He's about to put the bottle to one side, when I weaken.

'I suppose one more glass can't hurt,' I say with a watery smile.

'A small one then,' he says, popping the cork and filling up the half-pint glasses.

'That's not a small one.'

'Leave what you can't manage.'

He's guessing I'll finish it all.

What's worrying me about Marcus is not the fact that he's taking all my business, but that he's so magnetic. I can't help but find him attractive. He looks nothing like Isaac did, but I'm starting to feel about him the way I did my previous boyfriend in the beginning.

Marcus isn't as perfectly handsome, but he's really cute, and caring. While Isaac never had a hair out of place, Marcus's hair flops all over the place. He's got the casual dishy look down to a T.

As the cava slips down more easily than I feared, I have to remind myself that psychopaths can be pretty dishy.

'Shit,' Marcus says, as foam from his glass dribbles on to his marble floor tiles. I breathe more easily when he doesn't make a dash for a mop and bucket, the way Isaac did when so much as a drop of water landed anywhere.

I hold my glass up. 'Thanks.'

'My pleasure. Cheers,' he says, clinking his tumbler against mine. 'Go on. Tell me everything. I'm a good listener.'

'What do you want to know?'

'Well, what's going on? Why are you so upset, and why have the Pedersens come to speak to me?'

'I've no idea.' It's true where the Pedersens are concerned, as I've no idea why they've suddenly homed in on my competition. I don't want to sound churlish by bad-mouthing Avery and suggesting he might be involved. Last thing I want is to come across as a hypocrite.

As for other reasons for my meltdown, I doubt he'll want to

hear about my past and the nightmares that keep me awake at night. What happened in Marbella stays in Marbella.

'Why are you so upset? You can trust me.' Haven't I heard this before?

But Marcus isn't going to give up.

He's so bloody relaxed, lounging back with his legs spread out, his feet inches from mine. I have to reel my toes back in to avoid contact.

'No reason really,' I lie, gulping on the cava.

As the bubbles hit, again, everything doesn't seem quite so dramatic.

Marcus watches me with his chocolate-brown eyes, and my stomach flips. He's waiting for me to carry on.

'I'm desperate for a few sales so that I can move back into my apartment. The one Gabby Rackham is in.' I roll my eyes, as if she's the villain. Pretty mean, considering she's not to blame.

'I was surprised you had to rent it out. I didn't have you down as short of money.'

Really? Maybe I perfected too well *how to live like a millionaire*. I've still got the book I bought on the subject squirrelled away. The one that taught me how to pretend like I was loaded. From the way Marcus's eyebrow is quizzically raised, I wonder what rumours he's heard. Perhaps bloody Gabby has repeated what I told her (in confidence of course). That I spent all my hard-earned savings on the apartment and in setting up shop, and I don't have a spare euro in the bank. I don't want Marcus feeling sorry for me.

But he looks concerned, so I spill the beans.

'While I was trying to set up the business, the expenses of keeping up payments on my apartment became too much. All the hidden extras.' He'll know this is true. He's the master sales agent who avoids mention of extra costs when offering up his

The Girl on the Balcony

sales patter. Who can blame him though, as it's often the only way to make a sale?

'Oh, I see. So where are you going to stay now?'

He knows I've got nowhere to stay, and he's not going to give up. At least, unlike Isaac, I know he's not after my fictitious millions. Perhaps he really is interested in me. Well, if not me, at least in my wellbeing.

'Want the truth?' Bloody cava is wringing the truth out of me.

'Yes. I do.' His chocolate-brown eyes are now tinged with a fleck of gold.

'Absolutely no idea. Probably I'll sleep in the office. I can't risk losing another client by squatting.'

Hearing the words out loud brings back the panic. I really have nowhere to stay. No money to rent somewhere. And no one to turn to.

He gets up, goes to his plush, slick designer desk (the sort I promised to buy myself when sales picked up) and unlocks the top drawer. A weird thought kicks in. This is where handguns are kept. Too many crime dramas, but it's always the top drawer of well-appointed desks.

I uncross my legs, plonk my half-pint glass on the coffee table, and am about to get up, make a speedy exit, when he chucks a set of keys my way.

I slide to the right, fling out a hand, and they land in my palm.

'Well held! The address is attached to the tag. My finca is about two kilometres outside the resort. The spare room is yours.'

Holy shit. He's got to be joking me. I need to say *no. No. No.* But...

'Are you sure?' No idea who asked this. It can't be me, surely not.

'Providing you share the Pedersens' sale with me.'

He's laughing at me, the bastard. I'm not sure if it's the cava, lack of sleep, lack of food, panic, anxiety, but I'm drained of fight.

Looks like I'm back in some guy's house. This time not because he's a hot-shot millionaire, but because I've no other choice.

This time I'm desperate for a place to sleep. And a hot shower.

28

I manage to get some work done after I leave Marcus's office, despite the squiffy head. Seamus doesn't look surprised when I present at the kiosk for a double-shot cortado.

While all the cava might have mellowed my mood, I'm soon sobering up. This back-up plan could have serious flaws. The thought of moving in with a strange man, albeit the guy who has been working in the office next to me for the past few months, is crazy. I don't know him at all, the same way I didn't know Isaac, and look what happened there. He ended up dead.

The big plus is that I won't have to sleep rough, and the chance to shower followed by an early night is hard to resist. Marcus assured me there's plenty of hot water.

I'll stay tonight at least. Two or three nights tops, until I get myself sorted. I've about enough money in my bank account to rent one of my owners' apartments for a month or two. I've already fired off several emails, and a bite should come back soon.

I'm still worried about Gato, as there's been no sighting of him since he disappeared from the Ropers' villa. Hopefully when I do find him, Marcus won't mind letting him stay.

Marcus disappeared mid-afternoon, sticking his suntanned, wrinkle-free face round the door to tell me that he'll be back really late tonight, and not to wait up. Otherwise I'm to make myself at home.

I didn't like to ask where he was going, as it's none of my business. Although I am more than curious. Maybe he has a girlfriend, but asking about significant others doesn't feel right.

I lock up around five and wave goodbye to Seamus who is stroking his beard. Maybe I'm paranoid because again he's looking at me oddly. It's not a lustful look, more a wary one, as if I'm deranged. The way I look at Jolene Sanderstead.

A last glance up at my apartment, and there she is. Madam bloody Rackham, sitting on my bijou balcony with a book in one hand and a glass of something pink in the other. I try to blot out the image, as I need to get to Marcus's finca while it's still light.

Although it's only a couple of kilometres away, I pop the address (Finca Encanto, El Escobar) into Google Maps. Another piece of trivia. Notorious drug baron, Emilio Escobar, once known as the King of Cocaine. I wonder whether Marcus knows this. It'll be fun finding out how good his general knowledge is at tomorrow night's quiz.

The car hiccups into action, and I set off down the long drive-through, past The Three Bulls, the resort's very own British pub, the nine-hole practice golf course, and the tennis and padel academy.

I slow down on approaching the security kiosk, and the safety barrier immediately goes up when Santiago spots me. He waves with one hand, the other gripping a comfort handful of tortillas. He's so laid back that I suspect he'd let anyone suspicious in or out. Even men in balaclavas, or gold-medallion-toting drug barons. Anything rather than engage.

A sudden image of the hairy men in the 4X4 pops into my head, and I shiver. How did they get past Santiago unless they're staying on the resort? Or know one of the owners? It's likely Santiago didn't bother to check or was asleep at the time.

Although it's still daylight, the country roads radiating away from the resort are deserted. They're not as freaky as they were in the darkness, but they all look as if they're leading to dead ends or the Sahara Desert. By seven, it'll be pitch black again.

When Google Maps announces I've reached my destination, I start to panic. There's nothing. No houses. Only dry deserted landscape as far as the eye can see. Other than what looks like a disused cow shed. It can't be, can it?

My tyres rumble over another pitted surface towards the ramshackle shell. It's not even a track, it's just caked mud, strewn with random mini-boulders. I park up outside and tiptoe towards the wreck.

When I get round the back, I breathe more easily. There's an add-on, of sorts. A very basic extension, but at least it's got glass in the windows, and a front door with a lock on it. Yep. *Finca Encanto.* The rustic name plaque isn't much of a welcome as it hangs askew with the help of two very rusty nails. But at least I've got the right place.

I open up, and voila. It's like Doctor Who's Tardis, much bigger inside than the shell would suggest. There's a huge living space with a stone tiled floor, and I count four huge sofas. The room is simply whitewashed, with a strange array of carved wooden masks on the walls. A couple of crossed spears over an open hearth suggest Marcus might have been to Africa.

It could be the headquarters for an isolated cult. Again I do the tiptoeing thing, glancing back over my shoulder every couple of seconds. It's bizarrely quiet. Bizarrely decorated. Just bizarre. At least there's no danger of comparing Marcus's lifestyle with that of Isaac's. This is not a £5 million villa, that's for sure. If Marcus isn't after my money, at least he'll not suspect I'm after his.

He told me there are two bedrooms, and mine is the smaller of the two. I poke my head through an opening in the wall a couple of yards from an open hearth, and a single bed is slotted snugly up against an unrendered stone wall. Rather than a normal window, there's a small glass skylight. It's unlikely an intruder will break in overhead, fortunately, as the skylight slants at a perilous angle. The only thing that makes me uncomfortable is the lack of a door.

Perhaps Marcus hasn't got round to renovating properly yet, but how will I be able to sleep without a door on the bedroom? For all I know, my host could be a creepy voyeur.

I slump on the bed and finger the blanket. The room has the feel of a prison cell, but it'll do. I'm ready to lie down and pass out.

I take my phone from my pocket, and text Marcus.

> Arrived at Finca Encanto safely. All good thanks.
> Jade

I press send, but it doesn't go through. I move the phone round and round, holding it up towards the skylight, in a vain attempt to get a signal.

Just my luck. Some kind of connection would be too much to hope for.

29

It takes a few seconds to get my bearings. Where the heck am I?

I'm not sure if it's the sunlight streaming through the skylight that has woken me up, but when I check the time it's already 8.30. Holy shit.

My heart pumps like a piston, and I sit bolt upright in the bed. The place is eerily quiet, until I hear it. A very soft whimpering noise. A mewing, and it's coming from outside the back door.

I start creeping around again, even less idea why this morning, as there's definitely no one about. There's no sign of Marcus, and no one has been here since I crashed out last night after a scalding shower.

I carefully inch open the door, and that's when I see him. It's Gato. How the hell did he get here? He looks up at me with the most soulful eyes you've ever seen.

'Gato. How did you get here, little man?'

He's in a snug cardboard box, and looks so malnourished that I can't hold back the tears. I lift him out and hug him close. His purr is so faint, as if he's barely alive. I've been worried I mightn't find him. Relief at seeing him is overriding curiosity as to how he got here.

I bring him inside, and I'm in luck. In the fridge is a carton of milk. Not much else, other than a plastic packet of Serrano ham, some mouldy unrecognisable type of cheese with the most horrendous smell, and a half-drunk bottle of white wine. I find a bowl, and pour in the milk. Gato struggles to bend over, but a pink sliver of tongue is soon lapping.

I gather up my things, check my phone (still no signal), and get ready to lock up. I go outside and look around. There's still nothing. No one. Marcus might have brought Gato round this morning, and didn't like to disturb me.

But I remember, when sobbing into his tissues, telling him all about Gato on top of everything else, that he said he was allergic to cats. So it's unlikely Marcus was the one to bring him here. Also, I can't imagine him creeping round outside Avery's villa hunting for strays.

Once Gato has finished lapping, he stares at me, as if to say, 'What now?'

I need to get to the office, open up, and find Gato something more substantial to eat. I also need to find out, if it wasn't Marcus, who the heck brought the cat to the finca. There's no way he could have got here by himself. Even if he had the energy, and certainly not in a cardboard box.

It takes me only ten minutes to get to the resort, another five to reach the office. I carry Gato in the box, leaving my overnight kit in the car.

Still no sign of Marcus. Where the hell is he?

While I'm struggling with the grille, my phone pings. At least I've got a signal again.

> Hope you slept well. Sorry didn't make it back.
> See you mid-morning. Marcus.

I manage to get inside, heaving the grille up against the wall, and settle Gato in the cool corner by the kitchenette.

'Listen, kitty, I'll be back soon. I'll get you some fishy bites.'

When I look up, I see Seamus's enormous green eyes pushed up against the glass. He's watching me intently with a hand shielding his eyes. I hope he's seen Gato, or he'll think I'm nuts, talking to myself.

'Coffee?' he mouths, jiggling a hand up and down as if holding a mug.

'Please.' I nod and mime at the same time. I certainly need a coffee, or three, to get my mind in gear.

'Coming up.'

I kiss Gato on his little bony head, and it breaks my heart when I notice the bald patches. But at least he's asleep.

Once Seamus delivers the coffee, I knock it back while standing up. I've so much to do. First stop the Mercadona for cat food, and paracetamol. My head is thumping, and I'm having trouble focusing. Then I want to find out who the heck brought Gato to the finca. A part of me wonders if it's just some seriously weird person worrying about stray cats and has me down as the resort sucker.

Yet a cold sweat makes me think it might be more than that. It feels stalkerish, as if someone has an agenda. If they mean to freak me out, it's definitely working.

30

When I get back from the supermarket, I realise I need to eat before settling down to work. My insides are gurgling from anxiety and lack of sustenance. Deciding Gato should be okay for another half an hour, I head through the plaza towards the clubhouse.

The place is buzzing with a large group of foreign-speaking golfers with very white faces. Possible clients. A few weeks ago, I'd be manoeuvring to get close, do a bit of schmoozing. But I need to sort out my own living mess before I start googling witty phrases in whatever language they're speaking. I've mastered how to say: *how are you, would you like a coffee, where are you from, 320 days sunshine a year* in an array of languages. Recently I've added Icelandic to the list, as their national football team is due to visit in the early spring.

I carry my tomato bread and cortado out to the veranda, and before I've a chance to backpedal, Crystal is waving me over. It's then I see she's got company. Shit. Bloody Gabby Rackham. She's everywhere. Either sitting on my balcony, drinking out of my cut-price wine glasses, or my designer cat mugs, or lounging somewhere on the resort. She's living the dream all right, albeit my dream.

'Hi, Jade. Come and join us,' Crystal whoops. She's dressed in a canary-yellow floaty top, see-through again, with matching yellow earrings. Her earlobes are nearly as elongated as her fingers and toes.

'Hi,' Gabby echoes with a feeble wave. She has seriously gorgeous eyes, with to-die-for lashes, but it's hard to see past the hair and grunge. She's dolloped a rosy blob in the centre of each cheek, and resembles a circus clown.

'*Hola*,' I say, aiming at levity. I feel anything but light-hearted, and would much prefer to slink off into a quiet corner with my tomato bread. No such luck.

Crystal is up, pulling a spare chair over to their table, and pats the cushion.

'How are things?' she asks, her voice dropping in pitch. She's aiming for sombre concern, as she knows I'm struggling. Where do I start?

Mum tells me never ask anyone how they are in case they tell you. That's where I am now. I'd love to tell Crystal how I really am, the shit having started with her boyfriend, Avery, but I don't. There doesn't seem much point.

'Fine, thanks. At least the sun is breaking through.'

I sit down, and cut my tomato bread into miniscule pieces. My throat is so dry, I'm scared of choking.

'How's business?' Gabby jumps in.

'Booming.' They'll both know this is a lie because the resort is deserted, but I'm not going to tell them I've nowhere to live, no money in the bank, no one to turn to, and a half-dead cat in my office.

Crystal fiddles with the ends of her hair, and suddenly pulls out a couple of strands.

'Ouch,' she yelps.

Gabby and I look at each other, finding it hard not to gawp. When Crystal continues to fiddle with the ends, I now suspect she might have TTM (another ridiculous piece of quiz trivia. Trichotillomania. An urge to pull out one's hair, strand by strand). It's a condition usually linked to mental health issues.

Crystal yelps a second time. 'Ouch. I need to stop this.'

I need to get away. As I knock back my cortado, Gabby breaks the silence.

'I've seen your little cat, Gato, around your office,' she says.

'Gateau?' Crystal giggles. 'A piece of cake. Great name.'

'It's Gato, as in Spanish for cat,' I clarify. 'Not as in Black Forest.'

Did Gabby just chuckle?

'Are you keeping him in your office now?' she asks, not seeming to have picked up that I'm trying to get away.

'For now. When I get settled somewhere I'll have him move in.'

I'm so wound up that I can't take any more questions or inane chat. I get up, push my chair harshly under the table, and swing my bag over my shoulder.

At least Crystal doesn't ask where I might be settling. She'll have guessed I've found nowhere permanent yet, and as she reinstates her sympathetic look, she pulls out another strand of hair.

'At least it'll keep Marcus away from your office,' Gabby pipes up.

'Sorry?'

'Marcus. He's dreadfully allergic to animals. Cats especially.'

'Really?'

I don't own up that Marcus might have already shared this fact with me. All I do know is that I need to escape from these crazies.

'He gets such bad asthma when they're around him. Apparently he nearly died once.'

That's all I need. Being accused of killing off the competition by suffocating them with cat hair.

As I wander back through the plaza, it crosses my mind that keeping Gato in Marcus's finca won't be an option. I need to sort out a place to live, and fast. I can't leave Gato alone every night in my office. Also, something in the pit of my stomach tells me it mightn't be a wise move to stay with Marcus anyway. For one, he's the competition, and secondly, I'm starting to have disturbingly lustful thoughts about him.

Also, why is Gabby Rackham so concerned about my cat? A rogue thought hits that she might somehow be involved in Gato's mysterious appearances in the middle of the night. Could she be that crazy? Why not tell me if she's worried about him?

I seriously need to get to work, and away from these madwomen. I speed up, now desperate to check which of my clients is willing to rent out their property to me. At least for a couple of months until I'm back on my feet. Then I'll be moving back into my apartment, and the aspiring artist will have to find somewhere else to live.

Bloody Gabby Rackham. I'm starting to really resent her, despite the fact she's done nothing wrong.

As I head through the Spanish Village car park, a large black people carrier passes on its way out. It looks familiar. When I catch the number plate, I know why. It's the car that seems to be following me round the resort. The one that nearly smashed my car to pulp.

As I stare after it, the passenger window rolls down, and a hairy hand gives me an obscene middle finger gesture.

31

My legs are like jelly, but somehow I make it to the office. My mind is in overdrive. Who the heck are the men in the black car? I keep getting flashbacks to Marbella, the terror, and trying to escape. It's illogical that the hairy men might be connected to what happened, as how can anyone know I'm here?

Gato has his nose pressed up against the glass when I get there, and looks even worse than I feel. But at least he's managed to extricate himself from the box.

He sticks to me like a limpet as I open his tuna chunks. When a weak purr starts up, I hunker down and stroke his mangy coat.

A knock at the door, and I smack my head on the top of the desk.

'Shit.'

I struggle up, tug down my dress and flick hair off my face. I rub my eyes, as tears are pooling in the corners. I couldn't feel any worse.

'Jade. I've been looking for you.' It's Marcus. He stands in the door frame, and blasts out a sneeze. Gato freezes, and his spartan fur stands on end.

'You okay?' I ask. Marcus's eyes are swollen, and he hasn't even been that close to Gato. It's like a competition between the three of us to see who looks the worst.

'It's my cat allergy,' he wheezes, turning his head away and sneezes again, before pulling out a very starched white hankie.

'Don't get any closer. Gabby told me how bad your allergy is. I didn't realise it was this serious.'

A pain shoots through my head, and I rub a finger across a burgeoning bump.

'Did she? Funny, I don't remember telling her.'

He looks bemused, rather than concerned about my possible concussion.

'Anyway, enough of cats. A couple of things,' he continues, after a last almighty honk into the hankie.

Looking at Marcus, I manage to forget my woes for a minute. His eyes are seriously puffy, and doleful. Even more so than Gato's if that's possible. He pushes back his luscious fringe, and I pray he's not going to start pulling out strands.

He takes a deep breath, as if deciding whether to tell me what's on his mind or not.

'Hit me. What's up?'

My heart beats a little faster. I'm praying it isn't more bad news which seems to be following me round like a stalker.

'The Pedersens are definitely going for the townhouse. I told them we're working together, and despite a moment's hesitation, they've agreed to go ahead.'

'Seriously?' I know I should thank him, but I'm anxious about being in his debt. He'll likely expect something in return.

'You did most of the work. Seems only fair.'

I'm so desperate for money that I'd be crazy not to accept. Yet memories of Isaac are never far away. I can't forget the dangled wealth, his *Love Island* looks and honed physique, and his attempts at ensnaring me with caring concern.

Marcus is just as attractive, and I know the need for caution. But I've run out of options.

'Thanks.' I keep it simple.

I sit down, turn on the computer and wait for it to boot up. Work hat in place seems the way to go, as I need Marcus to leave.

'The other thing,' he says, scratching a finger across rare morning stubble.

'Yep?' I open my eyes wide, willing him to get on with it.

'I'm afraid the cat can't stay at my finca. You get why?'

'No worries. I'll find somewhere else. No problem.'

I set to open my emails, thinking he's going to move off, when he throws the curveball.

'Gabby says you can stay at hers. As you know, she's got a spare room, and I think she's quite the animal lover.'

You've got to be kidding me. It's my bloody apartment, and she's acting like it's hers, making magnanimous gestures most likely to impress Marcus.

I'm even more irritable now (if it's possible), thinking that I've been discussed round the resort. Gabby is in *my* flat, and she's happy for me to stay there?

'Thanks for letting me know.'

I can't look at him, deciding to keep my eyes latched on to the computer screen instead.

'Okay. See you later.'

When I don't respond, he reminds me, 'And don't forget the quiz – 7 p.m. prompt.'

I give him a single thumbs-up.

32

An hour later, I finally get a rare piece of positive news.

One of my clients, Marlon Langford, has confirmed that I can rent his villa for two months tops in lieu of free management charges. Problem is, he's only two doors down from Avery and Crystal. I have no idea how long they're staying for, but that will be top of my list of questions tonight. The thought of facing Avery at the quiz makes my insides curdle, but needs must.

By the time I lock up, I'm feeling slightly more upbeat. Except when I look at Gato. He's mastered the art of pressing his nose against the glass. He does a better miserable face than an undertaker. It breaks my heart, and I can't look at him.

I promise that as soon as I have somewhere permanent to stay, he'll be my roommate.

'Promise, little guy.' I wave over my shoulder.

Once I'm in the car, heading to Marcus's finca to get changed, I turn on Spotify, more optimistic now I've got a plan. Tomorrow, I'll do a full loop of all my properties and make sure everything is shipshape, and then start attacking online sales enquiries.

George Ezra. 'Green, Green Grass'. I screech out the lyrics as I bump along. Maybe, just maybe, things will work out. Once I can start saving, get back in credit, then I'll set to moving Gabby Rackham out. If I've got two months at Marlon's villa, then Madam has two months tops in my apartment.

When I get back to the finca, the spartan landscape quashes the exuberance. It's like a desert, minus the cacti, and there's absolutely no sign of life as far as the eye can see. Marcus left his office a couple of hours ago, so hopefully he'll be home soon.

The finca has got a split personality. From the front, it looks like an abandoned outbuilding, but round the back, new brickwork, a small, landscaped terrace with barbecue, and table and chairs (for two), bring it to life. It's still pretty basic, but a start. I must remember to ask Marcus who owns the rest of the surrounding moonscape.

The front door (round the back) is ajar, and my voice echoes as I step inside.

'*Hola? Hola?*' I repeat.

There's no sign of Marcus. Or anyone. It's really creepy wandering around, poking my head into the eerily quiet rooms. My heart speeds up as panic kicks in. I'm definitely suffering from PTSD after my escape from Marbella. My nightmares tell me I should have been the one who died, not Isaac. Being alone in a seriously isolated stone shack is bringing it all back.

Hopefully I'll feel better after a hot shower. But first I lay out my red *go-get-'em* dress on the prison cell bed. I need to power dress if I'm to face everyone at the quiz. I need confidence, especially where Avery is concerned. Confronting him won't be easy, but I'm past caring what he thinks, especially as he seems hellbent on destroying me.

Once I'm washed and dressed, I've got half an hour to spare, so I dig out Volume 10 of E. W. Egghead's pub quiz book series from my bag. I brought it with me to help get in the mood for tonight. But first I lift out the half bottle of white wine from the fridge, and sniff. It'll do. I'm in desperate need of Dutch courage.

I sip the wine. Heaven. Well, the first sip tasted like heaven, now I'm not so sure. It tastes more like vinegar, possibly cooking wine, and the label is half torn off. It's all I've got, though, so I stick with it. A couple of glasses and I should be ready for action.

For some reason, I'm relying on the quiz book to get me in the mood for tonight, but my confidence spikes when I know the answers to all the general knowledge questions.

> Who is the longest-reigning English monarch? Which chess piece can move the most spaces in any direction? In 1903, the first woman ever won the Nobel Prize. What was her name?

If the wine is going straight to my head, knowing the answers fills me with resolve. I'll show them.

It's the first time in ages that I've been looking forward to doing something. Something other than drinking alone, or trying to flog apartments. I whisk a white pashmina round my shoulders, and prepare for action. I even start humming 'Budapest' as I lock up. If things pick up, I'll maybe have a bash at the karaoke evening.

When I pull into the car park of The Three Bulls, I struggle to find a space. It's so packed. I don't immediately spot Marcus's VW Polo, until I notice it in an unlit corner. I manage to squeeze my car into a slot in an opposite corner.

I never ask Marcus where he goes after leaving his office, in case he gets the wrong idea, but I freeze when I see him and Gabby Rackham strolling together towards the bar. He opens the door, and with a theatrical gesture, ushers her ahead.

Seeing them together sets my teeth on edge. Maybe he's been

staying over at Gabby's apartment (*my* apartment to be more precise). He can't be sleeping with her, can he?

The wine from Marcus's fridge is now curdling my insides, and acid reflux hits the back of my throat. I get out of the car, zap it closed, and straighten up. Goodness knows how I'll cope, but Mum's voice is breaking through the angst.

Face things head on. The best way out is always through.

Here goes.

33

When you watch *A Place in the Sun*, all the Brits talk about is *living the dream*. Which has a pretty standard wish list: paella, Rioja, sun, sea, and sand. But The Three Bulls, the resort's drinking hub, couldn't be any less Spanish.

Inside has the feel of an East End pub, with the smell of fish and chips, six flat-screen TVs playing football on a loop, and filled with noisy beer-swilling punters. At least I don't feel overdressed, as one table seems to have come in party gear. Either that or they always venture out in February in tuxedos and ball gowns.

The mix of wine and nerves is playing havoc with my insides, and the place is so dimly lit that it takes me a minute or two to spot Marcus. He's at the table farthest away in an even darker corner. Gabby is sitting next to him, their shoulders very close. It looks as if she might be his plus one. They couldn't really be an item, could they?

'Hi, guys,' I say, making my way over.

'Hi. Good to see you. You're looking good,' Marcus says, eyeing my dress. My blush tones in with the colour, but I doubt anyone will notice. It's so dark that it's hard enough to see who you're talking to, let alone the colour of their cheeks.

'Jade.' Gabby nods.

'The others not here yet?'

'Avery is at the bar, and Crystal is on her way.'

'And Russell. The maintenance guy is making up the numbers. You use him, I think?' Gabby raises a questioning eyebrow.

Of course I bloody know him. You've got to be kidding me. He's the last thing I need.

'Oh. A full house then.' I aim for my happy face, but my jaw has sort of locked. I unravel my pashmina, slide it over a chair back, and let Marcus pour me a glass of wine from an already-opened bottle.

I sit on the edge of my seat, jiggling my legs up and down. I'm desperate to go home, well, at least back to the finca in the desert. Then I spot Crystal making her way towards Avery who is leaning on the bar. He kisses her on the cheek, and hands her a glass of something in a tumbler with a piece of lime stuck to the rim.

I didn't realise quite how tall Crystal is compared to Avery. She's almost a whole head taller. Her white floaty dress is demurely feminine, all silk and lace, and it seems to do the trick with Avery. He kisses her again, this time on the lips, pouting for all to see. He looks quite relaxed, but I'm picking up a more rigid vibe from Crystal.

I'm relieved when the music starts up, and random sixties tunes blast out on a deafening loop. Although the quiz doesn't start for another twenty minutes, the noise kills any prospect of stilted conversation which suits me fine.

When Russell arrives, he does a double take when he sees me. He's been avoiding me with the stealth of a covert operative since installing the Ropers' security cameras. Being in the same room as both Avery and Russell isn't going to be easy, as I feel really anxious and on edge.

Russell mumbles an embarrassed greeting, appearing even more shocked than I am at being on the same table. As he sits down, I glance over at the bar and see Avery scowling in my direction. The thought that he's harbouring a vendetta against me makes my hair stand on end. He's definitely got a misogynistic streak, and it looks as if he's intent on punishing me thoroughly for staying at his place. I get why he'd warn friends on the resort not to use my services, but he seems to be going to extreme lengths, especially if he's contacting clients he doesn't even know. Then there's the 4X4. Could the guys really have something to do with Avery, or am I being overly paranoid?

Marcus looks at me and mouths, 'Okay?' He's picking up on my struggle.

I simply nod, desperate to get back in the mood for the quiz.

Marcus acts as team captain, and hands round scribble sheets with biros. His fingers brush mine, and I feel a tingle. Also, his thigh is dangerously close to mine under the table as the seating is very snug. He's now sitting closer to me than to Gabby, which bizarrely lifts my spirits.

The quiz master appears dressed as a cowboy, and tap-tap-taps on the microphone, with an endless rendition of, 'One two, one two. Testing. Testing. One two three.'

Marcus grins, and winks at me, and I freeze when I feel a warm hand on my thigh. I'd love to put mine on top, forget all the shit, but I'm much too scared. Especially as Avery and Crystal are approaching the table, and Gabby is staring at me. She's tapping her pen up and down on the table. If looks could kill, I'd be dead meat. I gently remove Marcus's hand and move my chair over a bit, but it doesn't stop him winking again, and making my heart flutter. If it wasn't for Gabby's miserable pout, and Avery's dagger looks, things might be looking up.

Avery greets the others, totally ignoring me as he smacks his beer glass down on the table. His eyes turn to slits when he glances my way.

Crystal is the only one, apart from Marcus, who appears to be on my side. She reaches across and pats my hand, asking how I am. Again I simply nod, willing the ground to swallow me up.

John Wayne, the cowboy host, soon has everyone's attention. The music has been turned off and the TV screens muted. You could hear a pin drop.

'Here we go. Round One. General knowledge.'

Marcus is tasked with filling in the answers for our table. Table number eight. My lucky number. And, ten minutes in, I'm wondering if it's working. I know *all* the answers, but so do the others. The longest-reigning English monarch didn't give the others too much trouble. Elizabeth II. Which chess piece moves the most spaces in any direction? The Queen. Russell plays chess so he leant across and made sure we all knew this. Then everyone but Gabby knew that Marie Curie was the first woman to win the Nobel Prize.

We all lean back at the end of Round One, smug that we might have got full marks on this round at least. I certainly won't be owning up to the fact that the quiz, so far, has come directly from E. W. Egghead's tenth quiz book. The general knowledge questions were from quiz number five, the one I've just genned up on. I mightn't be the smartest, but I have the memory of an elephant.

When no one but me knows the answers to the entertainment section, I'm soon queen of the evening. Gabby gets glummer by the second. When I offer up confident answers to the history and sport questions, Marcus beams.

'You're good. I knew you liked quizzes, but I had no idea.'

He claps his hands together, making me more embarrassed. I'm now red all over.

Little does he know. Anyway, I'm certainly not going to own up to knowing where all the questions are coming from. I feel like a cheat, but it feels great.

When we get equal marks with the resort's resident boffins, who seem to be a mix of accountants and bank clerks, it goes to a tiebreak question to decide the winner. Gabby looks completely pissed off, and Avery even more so. He laughs, and whispers loudly behind a hand in Crystal's ear, loud enough to hear him bad-mouthing the table's egghead.

Give Crystal her due, she gently moves the hand covering his mouth, and gives me a consolatory smile. But instantly, with a quick glance at Avery, she puts a protective hand up to her throat. The gesture happens in sync with a death stare from her partner. Small comfort that my problems with Avery mightn't be as bad as those Crystal might have.

John Wayne taps his microphone, and screeches out the tiebreak question. All eyes are on us and table number two. They're all dressed in suits, even the women. They're the resort champions apparently.

'How many of the world's countries are landlocked?' our host yells.

Of course I know the answer, I remember it from earlier this evening. Crystal also seems to know, and scribbles the number forty-three on her scrap of paper.

I'm warming to Crystal, but it's not the right answer. Although I'm surprised that she's so close. Looks can be deceiving, that's for sure.

'Are you certain?' All eyes look her way. At least Gabby has brightened up now that someone else other than me is in the limelight.

'I think it's forty-four,' I scribble and whisper at the same time.

'Are you sure?' Marcus is going to have to choose who to believe.

'Ninety-nine per cent.' I can't say 100 per cent without appearing a know-it-all.

'Crystal?'

'I'm pretty certain, but if Jade is confident, go with her.'

She starts tugging at a strand of hair, and takes one almighty tug. Avery scowls but she ignores him.

Marcus takes up my answer and hands it across to the guy with the microphone.

My heart is thrashing against my chest. What if I've got it wrong? Maybe I should have let Crystal have the limelight.

'Well done to table number eight. Forty-four is the right answer. Table number two was very close, with forty-three. Bad luck.'

There's a gentle round of applause. It gets a bit louder when the host announces that table number eight have won this week's pot of money. And a bottle of champagne.

34

HAYLEY

Since meeting Astrid, I can't relax, and have started looking over my shoulder at every turn. That's how uneasy she makes me feel.

Even when Damon and I go sightseeing, or are making love and eating nachos in bed, her face keeps popping up. She was even in my nightmares last night, and at one point she was wielding a machete. Damon is in seventh heaven, saying it's his first real break in years, and doesn't get why I'm so paranoid.

'Teddy's the one living there, not you,' he snaps, not at all concerned that my ex might be living with a psychopath. He gets irritable when I mention Teddy, his laid-back nature becoming intense. I'm flattered he might be jealous, but it feels over the top for such early days.

The morning of the pool party, I'm so on edge that I'm tempted to forgo it, and instead get the first plane back to England, but not so Damon. He can't contain his excitement.

'What do you think?'

He catwalks through the lounge, wiggling his snake hips. He's wearing slim-fit Levi jeans, and his *Climbed Everest* T-shirt. I was impressed when he first wore it before he owned up to a fear of heights. Apparently even steep staircases make him dizzy.

The T-shirt helps kick-start conversations though, and he's perfected tales of snow blindness and altitude sickness. Not to mention how to build a bivouac.

He looks so good, I'd happily spend the day in bed, and not leave the dingy apartment.

Since I got up, I've been battling a full-blown panic attack. But Damon's sunny mood helps keep me sane.

'You look great,' I tell him. 'Have you remembered your swimming gear?'

'It's all packed.' He grins, rapping his rucksack, and clipping the clasps together. 'And you look good enough to eat,' he says, wandering over and squeezing my bottom with strong fingers.

I've opted for understated. An A-line navy linen dress, functional over glamour, although Damon seems to like it.

I nudge his hands away, fighting the urge to pull them back. Even this high up in the concrete block, it's hard to relax.

I freeze when a horn blasts, and I conjure up an image of the driver peering through the window, having scaled newly erected scaffolding.

'The car's here.'

Of course it's not an Uber. Teddy arranged with one of Astrid's drivers to come and pick us up. Pick up his sister and her nosy flatmate. That's what he told Astrid. I think he smells a rat where Damon is concerned, but he's going to let it go for now. Apparently the pool party is going to be like a Playboy Mansion bash. Celebrities. Bunny Girls. Hunky *Baywatch* guys. And lots of food and drink. Damon can't wait.

I can. I don't want to go.

We walk down the concrete stairs, no longer talking, and I nearly jump out of my skin when a uniformed driver accosts us by the entrance to the building. He's wearing a chauffeur cap, and tips it with a subservient finger.

'*Hola.*' The guy is bulky, and looks like a *Miami Vice* extra. There's a bulge under his jacket, possibly a handgun, which makes me feel even more nauseous.

Damon is not worried in the slightest, beaming in anticipation.

'I could get used to this,' he says as we slip into the back seat of the Merc.

What can I say? I'd much prefer to be back in London, in my cosy flat eating fish and chips out of yesterday's newspaper. Sod the story.

I have the most awful feeling of doom.

35

It's exactly midday when the Merc purrs through the gates to the villa. Red, white, and yellow helium balloons float high above the sky-high perimeter walls.

'Cool. Spanish colours.' Damon points.

I untangle my fingers from his grip when I spot a security camera directed through the car windscreen. Now could be the time to turn back.

The driver opens the car door with a flourish, and we step out on to a red carpet of all things. A sudden drop of rain, and I shiver. Overhead, there is a smattering of grey clouds but Teddy says the pool is heated and Astrid will still insist everyone goes in.

'She's had a huge awning erected at one end of the pool,' Teddy told me last night when he called. He also told me what was on the menu. What cocktails he had to prepare. And about the live band performing on the roof terrace.

'The roof terrace? Isn't that where her husband died?' I nearly choked on my question.

New Teddy has also mastered the art of silence. Even his

customary groan when he doesn't want to engage has been replaced by a tight-lipped silence. He quickly changed the subject.

Damon tells me it's best if I don't tell Teddy, ever, about my idea for a story. Certainly not while it's in the making.

'He might let slip to Astrid.'

He has a point. The last thing I want is Astrid to suspect I'm a reporter who thinks she's an assassin. Who knows? I might be the next person locked on the roof terrace.

I spot Teddy instantly, no idea how, as he's even more unrecognisable as my ex-boyfriend than he was the other day. He's dressed again in designer wear, a jumper thrown casually round his shoulders as if he's Brad Pitt. If I wasn't with Damon, and if I didn't know Teddy's default mode was *slob*, I'd be intrigued. But today, I've no time for Teddy. I need to mingle, schmooze, talk, ask questions of anyone and everyone. This might be my last chance to break open my case. And then get the hell out of here.

'Morning, Hayley. And...?' Teddy asks, nodding towards Damon. As if he's forgotten.

'Hi. Damon. I'm the flatmate, remember?' Damon's tone oozes sarcasm.

Teddy ignores Damon, and leans in to kiss me on the cheek. When I see Astrid watching from a few yards away, I'm relieved he remembered that I'm supposed to be his sister.

She's standing by the open patio doors, guzzling a bright green cocktail through a pink straw. I move away from Teddy and Damon and head her way.

'Helena. How lovely to see you again,' Astrid gushes, while continuing to guzzle. She clicks the fingers of her spare hand, and a waiter dressed in a starched white jacket is instantly alongside, appearing out of nowhere.

I don't correct her for getting my name wrong, guessing it was deliberate.

'Astrid. Thanks for having us.' I turn and nod in Damon's direction, getting even more freaked when I notice him talking to Teddy. It's hard to tell from their twin expressions which one is the more pissed off.

'Will you have one of my special cocktails?' Astrid asks me, holding up her almost empty V-shaped glass, and scooping out an olive from the bottom.

'Thanks.'

'Make that two then, Leonardo. And start handing round the canapes, please.'

She clicks her fingers again, and Leonardo scuttles off.

People are piling into the grounds, the front gates thrown wide, as vehicles drop guests off in their droves.

'Helena. You must start mingling. Teddy will introduce you and David to the other guests. He knows quite a few of them.'

'Thanks. Will do.'

Astrid waves her arm, in the manner of shooing away a rabid dog. My cue to mingle.

Why do I feel like a kid at a first birthday party? Nervous, anxious, and desperate to hide in the toilet.

I head back across the terrace, threading my way through the milling throng. At least the rain is holding off, and a glimpse of sun is peeking through. Even though it's quite mild, I'm shivering head to toe.

Teddy has disappeared, no doubt to double up as waiter, lifeguard, plus one, and then I spot him in the distance talking to a guy in a tuxedo. Four other guys, dressed in the same penguin outfits, are holding all manner of instrument cases. Likely the band.

'We're supposed to mingle,' I whisper to Damon.

'Can't we just mingle between ourselves?' Damon smiles, and I'm so glad he's here. Teddy must suspect he's more than a flatmate, but Astrid's keeping him so busy I doubt he's much time to worry. Astrid is definitely suspicious though. She's now standing up close to Leonardo, the waiter, and whispering behind a hand.

Paranoia flags up she's talking about me.

36

After a few drinks, I calm down and stay close to Damon. He seems to have mastered the art of mingling, and is soon regurgitating his phoney ascent-of-Everest story. The more at ease he becomes, the more I'm smitten. Although I have started wondering about ex-girlfriends, as there's been no mention. Surely I can't be his first?

When Astrid heads our way, and squeezes between us, I decide to leave them to it. I head in the direction of the music blasting down from the roof terrace. A painted sign (painted in the same manner as the paintings on the walls... huge thick strokes in child-like blobs) leads me to a steep staircase.

These must be the stairs that Astrid's husband, George Stubbs (alias Isaac Marston) went up before getting locked outside in the 40-plus-degree heat.

The stairs are steep, and I cling to the railing as they're also slightly slippery. By the time I reach the top, I feel woozy and disorientated. The music is so loud that at least I won't be expected to make small talk.

I notice the door has been clipped back by a huge metal hook that looks as if it's been newly installed. I get out my phone, take a few pictures of the stairs, the door, and the hook, before I step outside.

Amazing. Wow. Wow. Wow. The roof terrace is huge, but the noise is horrendous. The harsh rasping jazz is torture. It might be worse being trapped out here with this noise than in the heat.

I wander round the perimeter of the terrace, which is festooned with more balloons and banners. Paintings are hung on the walls every couple of metres. I wonder if they're meant to represent foliage, but it's hard to be sure. They're just very green, with no definition. Likely more of Astrid's masterpieces.

In the far corner, standing on his own, is a middle-aged guy wearing a bird-patterned shirt and navy shorts. He's also wearing dark glasses and a Panama hat, dressed more for the tropics than Spain in the off-season. He's not looking at the view, because there isn't one. The whole terrace is encased by enormous white walls, and there aren't any views of the Med. Or anywhere for that matter. It's like a very exclusive open prison.

I take out my phone, and surreptitiously take a few more pictures. Although I capture the man in one of them, I'm careful not to be noticed. It's only as I put my phone in my pocket that I spot another security camera. What's with all the cameras? Who would want to break out on to the roof terrace?

'Hi. You'll not get a signal up here.'

I swivel round to face the guy in the Panama hat. I'm amazed I heard his words, as my ears are ringing. But at least the band seems to have taken a break.

'Oh. I did wonder.' I take my phone back out from my pocket. 'Yes, I couldn't get a signal at all.'

'Did you know that the guy who died up here had his phone with him?'

My stomach knots. Keep talking.

'Really? Astrid mentioned her husband got trapped up here, but I didn't realise there was no signal.' This is a lie, as the newspaper article pointed this out.

'All a bit suspicious if you ask me.'

The guy takes off the Panama hat, pops his sunglasses on top of thinning hair, and extends a hand.

'Avery. Avery Knowles. The dead guy's brother.'

37

It takes only a millisecond to twig. Teddy said a brother of Astrid's dead husband had turned up at the villa. He said his name was something like Emery. Or Oliver. I wonder if he really forgot, or has been told not to discuss guests. My heart races with a sudden adrenaline shot. This guy could provide a huge piece of the story.

'Hi. I'm Hayley. Hayley Scrivens.'

Avery and I shake hands, before he proceeds to drag over a couple of chairs and indicates for me to sit. Sitting down seems like a plan, as I feel disorientated and lightheaded. Also the roof terrace is giving me really bad vibes. I keep checking the door is still open, despite the fact there is a five-piece band, and at least twenty people milling around admiring the green splatters. That would be a lot of people to murder in one go.

'My boyfriend, sorry, my brother...' I blush, on the careless side of drunk, 'Stephen is working for Astrid.'

'Is he now? Interesting. I thought his surname was McDonald?'

It takes a moment to concoct a response.

'It is. I was married briefly, hence the Scrivens.'

Avery motions a waiter hovering by the door. It's Leonardo, the guy Astrid was ordering about earlier. I wonder why he's come up here. He can't be following me, can he? Or perhaps he's following this Avery chap. My mind is all over the place.

Leonardo presents us with a chilled bottle of Sauvignon in an ice bucket, along with two glasses. Avery and I sit facing one another. This is my cue to get my interviewer hat in place, while giving no hint of why I'm really in Marbella.

'You're Astrid's brother-in-law? But I thought her husband's name was Stubbs?' I need to tone down the excitement, but I'm now intrigued as to why they've also got different surnames.

He watches me over the rim of his glass.

'I changed my name by deed poll after George's death.'

'Oh?' My eyes are wide.

'He was reported as being a conman, so I thought it best not to be linked by name. You know how it is.'

I do indeed. The story's getting more interesting by the minute.

'I'm really sorry what happened to your brother. I hear he got trapped up here in the scorching heat.'

'Trapped? Or locked out deliberately? Now that's the question.'

38

Avery single-handedly knocks back the whole bottle of wine while I stick to water. I need a clear head to digest what he's saying.

'Did you know George had a girlfriend at the time he died?' he asks.

Lucky for me, Avery likes the sound of his own voice, as he's soon on a roll.

'No.'

Go on. Who? Where was Astrid? A girlfriend? I remember hearing Astrid and George were estranged, but where was Astrid when he died? The questions are swirling.

'Some gold-digger called Jade. I've forgotten her surname, but I do remember the last payment out of George's and my joint bank account was to her. Bit of a coincidence he died shortly after, don't you think?'

'Really? Who was she?'

'Good question. I intend to find out lots about her, as I'll be getting that money back with interest. I'm not convinced she didn't kill him.'

I don't ask why he and his brother had a joint bank account, as I need him to keep talking. They may have been close, with Avery looking out for his younger brother.

Avery drags his chair closer, until his thigh brushes against mine. I must look horrified because he pats me on the leg and apologises.

'There's such a lack of pretty girls around.' His double chin wobbles when he laughs.

Where the heck is Damon when you need him?

The brass band torturers are starting up again. They're cleaning down trumpets, saxophones, and other brass attachments. I don't have long to ask more questions.

'Do you really think she had something to do with his death?' I lean closer, sensing this might be the way to make him continue. Then I'm out of here.

'Yes, I do. Astrid says that Jade was the last person in the villa with him before he got locked on the roof terrace. She'd been staying here. My guess is she locked him up there deliberately before she fled.'

'How do you know this? Who said she was the last person to see him alive?'

I suspect Astrid spread the word, so as to keep herself in the clear. From what Teddy overheard on the plane, I presume it must have been this Jade that Astrid was talking to. Teddy overheard Astrid warning the woman in seat 2A that there was footage of her on the villa's indoor security cameras. This was no doubt to keep Jade quiet.

I mean, who would want to cross paths with Astrid? She's getting more menacing by the minute.

When Avery settles a more determined hand on my knee, I know it's time to go. Not to mention the fact that the torture music is about to start up again.

'Do you know where Jade is living?' I ask. 'Is she English? Back in the UK? Or still in Spain?'

'Oh, she's back in Spain. Murcia region, I think. Astrid thinks it's a great game that I want to track her down. She's even offered to help.'

'You're kidding me.' No, he's not kidding. The Norwegian assassin looks as if she's in cahoots with Avery. As he licks his bulbous lips, I feel panicky. I certainly wouldn't want to get locked up here with this creep. Or be in this Jade woman's shoes if he's after her.

'Nope. Not kidding you. I'm off to find her. She's working a bit further round the coast, I hear.'

I check my watch, and although we haven't been talking that long, it seems like forever. When the first note screeches out from a trumpet, I cover my ears. It's my cue to go.

But when I get up and turn round, guess who is coming through the door that's held open by the new strong brass hook? Damon. And alongside him is a very tall, willowy lady who is almost opalescent.

Avery staggers to his feet, pushes both our chairs back against the wall, and waits for the couple to approach.

'Crystal, darling. Where have you been?'

'I've been talking to this gorgeous young man. Damon.'

Give Damon his due, he looks suitably sheepish. He comes straight up to me, takes my hand, and suggests we stay and listen to the music.

I'm not sure which is worse, the thought of listening to more music, or staying in this chilling place a moment longer.

But I can't help the tingle of excitement. What a bombshell! Avery is the dead man's brother, out to get someone called Jade who conned his brother out of money. Maybe even killed him. I certainly wouldn't like to be in her shoes.

This could be huge.

39

JADE

I wasn't going to drink any more, but when Marcus pops the champagne cork, it's too tempting not to celebrate.

Avery is watching me, shaking his head, and giving me death stares. I'm determined not to let him spoil the moment, but it's tough as he's in my face. He's standing so close I can smell his rancid sweat.

But Marcus is so upbeat that I'm determined Avery won't quash the moment.

'Cheers.' Marcus shares out the drink, and as we smack our glasses together fizz spurts everywhere. The only other person, apart from Avery, who refuses a drink is Russell. He excuses himself and heads for the gents'.

Suddenly the lights come on, and blind everyone with a less than subtle hint it's time to go. The barman quickly upturns vacated chairs on to tables, and flings open the doors.

Marcus empties the last of the champagne into my glass, and winks.

'I'll drive you home,' he says, as we prepare to leave.

'I'm fine,' I say, knowing that I'm absolutely not fine to drive.

'You are not. Leave your car here, and you can pick it up in the morning.'

'Okay, boss.' I roll my eyes, but Marcus is definitely scoring brownie points for the masterful approach. He hasn't drunk any champagne, so should be fine behind the wheel, whereas I'm decidedly squiffy.

We all hover by the exit, waiting for Russell. The euphoria of winning soon drains away when I notice him scooting out through a side door. I've been building up to having a stern word with him, ask him why he's been avoiding me as well as who instructed him to install the Ropers' cameras. Now he's racing off through the car park.

'He's in a hurry. Not very polite.' It's Avery. He dares tap my shoulder and points. 'Wonder why.' He scratches his head thoughtfully. 'Hmm. I wonder.'

I don't think I've ever hated anyone more than I do Avery at this moment.

'Was it you who got Russell to install the Ropers' cameras?' I hiss in his face, shaking with anger, scared I might lose it completely.

'Now why would I do that?' He laughs so loudly, my fists ball in fury.

'Avery. Come on, let's go.' Crystal steps between us.

'Gladly,' Avery says before strutting ahead.

'Well done, Jade. You nailed the last question,' Crystal says in a calming tone.

'She's a bloody cheat, that's what,' Avery yells over his shoulder. 'But I'm watching her. She'll not cheat again. You can be sure of that.' He offers up a threatening two fingers for all to see.

I'm now beyond furious, ready to punch his lights out.

'Oh, ignore him,' Crystal says. 'You were great.'

It's hard to ignore Avery. He's determined not to let things rest, as if I'm the target of a personal vendetta.

But at least Crystal seems to have my back.

'Thanks. A bit lucky at the end.'

'No. You know your stuff. I wonder what country I missed out?'

I'm not sure whether she's patronising me, or genuinely trying to douse the flames of Avery's vitriol.

'The Vatican City perhaps. People forget it's classed as a country.'

'Oh. I'll remember that. Anyway, well done.'

I notice over my shoulder Gabby is tugging at Marcus's arm. She's sweating like a pig, likely due to the amount of clothes she's wearing. She's bulked up like a Sherpa. Her face and neck are so damp that sodden purple and pink strands of hair are sticking to her forehead.

We wander outside, and say goodbye to Crystal as she hurries after Avery. I'm shivering with only my skimpy pashmina for warmth, but at least it's more than Crystal is wearing. She must be freezing to death in her floaty silk dress, and flimsy diamante sandals. The goosebumps on her arms are hard to miss, and it crosses my mind that Avery might order her what to wear. Nothing would surprise me.

'Do you mind dropping me off?' Gabby is still tugging at Marcus's arm.

Give Marcus his due, he very gently prises her fingers, one by one, off his muscled arms. He looks so handsome, and when he winks at me, my heart melts. He's the one good thing about this whole sorry mess.

'Of course, Gabby.'

'You can both come back for a nightcap if you'd like?'

She directs her question at Marcus, totally ignoring me. I pray he's going to refuse.

'Maybe another time. It's been a long day.'

Marcus looks at me, and I simply nod agreement. The last thing I need is to go back to my apartment and be entertained by my bloody tenant.

Gabby starts walking off towards the car on her own, and I sense her disappointment. She really seems to have a thing about Marcus, but I doubt he'd be able to get past her grim appearance. The way I feel right now, I'm not sure I can deal with any more negative thoughts.

When Marcus zaps open his car, Gabby automatically gets in the front, leaving me to sit in the back. None of us talk on the short drive back to the Spanish Village. When Marcus parks up, Gabby reluctantly opens the door.

'Thanks. See you tomorrow.'

She gives me a rare smile, before leaning over and kissing Marcus briefly on the cheek.

When she gets out and slams the door, sloping off without a backward glance, Marcus lets out an enormous sigh of relief. When I do likewise, we both laugh.

'Right, young lady. Let's get you home,' he says, directing the car back the way we came. 'You want to sit in the front?'

'No. I'm fine here. Just ready for bed.' An enormous yawn escapes, and Marcus grins at me through the mirror.

He's bloody gorgeous, and for a mere second, his features morph into Isaac's. I pull myself up, and grip the overhead strap. My head is spinning, and by the time we're out on the bumpy dirt track I start to feel really queasy.

He speeds up, tossing us in the air like pancakes as he tries to negotiate the potholes. Neither of us speaks, but the silence feels loaded. I start to freak that I might be going back to another psychopath's lair. No phone signal, no way out, and no one for miles around.

What am I doing?

I can hear my mum's voice in my head.

I hope you've learnt your lesson.

40

I peel open an eyelid, and it takes a moment to work out where I am. As I come round, I start to panic. My eyes are so dry that I've trouble seeing, and my mouth is parched.

The last thing I remember was giggling as I collapsed on to the bed and Marcus slipping off my shoes. At least I'm alone, and still lying on the finca's single-cell bed.

My red dress is ruched up round my thighs, crumpled as hell, but thank goodness everything else is in place. Pants, bra, and even the pashmina is still hanging off one shoulder. I spot my shoes neatly placed by the door. It could be a rewind of Marbella. Of the first night I ended up in Isaac's villa, with no memory of the night before. Holy shit.

I freeze when I hear a clattering coming from the kitchen, with what sounds like the drone of a TV in the background. As I try to get up, hindered by a pounding headache, the events of last night trickle back. I dip my feet onto the cold tiles, but even as the chill hits, I can't help grinning. The champagne. The victory. Okay, it wouldn't be up there with winning Wimbledon, but it felt good being the resort boffin. Even the whole shitty saga with Avery can't take away my moment of glory.

It's only as I wander into the living room that I notice my E. W. Egghead quiz book open on the coffee table. And it's open at quiz number five, the one that provided the entire content of last night's questions.

I'm pretty quick at getting to it, and snapping it closed before Marcus appears with two steaming mugs of coffee.

'Sleep okay?' He's grinning like a Cheshire cat, likely guessing how I knew all last night's answers. At least he's got the decency not to mention it.

'Grand, thanks.' My voice has the rasp of a file. I cough a couple of times to clear the phlegm.

'You were out for the count and I didn't like to wake you.'

'I think it was all the champagne.'

'Listen, I need to get to the office. The Pedersens are coming in to finalise their purchase.'

'Oh.' The last thing I need reminding of now is the Pedersens.

'And I'll transfer your half of the commission once the contract is signed.'

'Whatever.' I grip the mug tightly in both hands, and dare take a sip. 'And thanks.'

He comes and sits beside me. Very close, and turns to face me.

'And about staying here, I love having you, but...'

He's going to throw me out on the street.

'I know about Gato. And how you want to take him in, but as you know I'm really allergic to cats. Not as in a minor allergy, but life threatening. I've ended up in hospital before now.'

'That must have been dreadful. Of course I'll not bring Gato with me. He can stay in the office for now.'

I don't want to confine Gato to the office, as he needs serious looking after. Going to the local vet is on my ever-growing to-do list. Gato won't be going back on the streets, but we can't both stay here, that's obvious.

'I've arranged with Gabby that you can stay there until you get back on your feet. I know you're struggling, but things will pick up when the season kicks in.'

While I'm trying to tone down the anxiety about my whole situation, his concern is making things worse. And why is he so desperate for me to move in with Gabby? It's as if they're plotting behind my back.

I don't mention the Langfords' offer to stay at their villa free of charge in lieu of management fees. My plan is to reply to them today and accept. I don't have much choice, as there are currently no other options on the table.

Problem is, it's only a couple of doors down from Avery (far from ideal), and staying there would mean losing more income. I can't really afford to lose the income.

But Gabby. He's got to be kidding me.

'Gabby?' My features squish up as they do when I'm anxious. He laughs.

'Why so horrified? She's okay. And it is your apartment. You can keep an eye on it while you're there, and treat Gabby as the tenant.'

He has a point, and the way he phrases it makes it sound not a totally bad idea. I'd have to stay in the smaller bedroom, but perhaps I could stomach it in the short term. Not to mention the satisfaction of helping her pack her things when she has to go. And rather than forking out rent, I'd get away with just discounting her rental payments. Financially it makes better sense than the Langfords' offer.

Yet there's something about Gabby that makes me edgy. She's far too nosy for one thing, and too close to Marcus for another.

'You two seem very close,' I say, steering the conversation away from my homelessness, and a feeling of being railroaded.

'I think she has a soft spot for me.' He blushes. 'She's nice, but not my type.'

I don't voice that I'm not sure who would be her type, but his words are music to my ears.

He pats my knee, and I have the most dreadful urge to take his hand and pull him closer.

'Anyway, Gabby also loves cats. She'd be more than happy to give Gato a home too.'

'Okay. I get the picture.'

Yep, the two of them are determined that I move into my apartment. I get a sinking feeling in my stomach, wondering if it's all Marcus's idea so that I won't have to stay at his finca any longer.

He gets up, lifts a jumper off a chair back, and knots it round his white linen shirt. I sense there's more to come.

'To be honest, I'm not sure it'd be a good idea having us both under the same roof.'

'Why not?'

Looks as if I'm right, and he's trying to get rid of me. So much for the celebratory glow.

He takes a deep breath, and I fear the worst.

'You're pretty gorgeous, and I am an unattached hot-blooded male.' He laughs, his cheeks now crimson. 'I couldn't be responsible for my actions if we were living together.'

He looks so uncomfortable that I guess he's telling the truth. Despite the disappointment, I know he's made a wise decision.

However, when he picks up his car keys, I panic that he might be leaving me here. Stranded or locked up in the desert.

'If you want to take a shower, I'll be back in twenty minutes. Popping to the shop for a newspaper, and milk. Do you need some for Gato?'

My eyes moisten round the edges. Marcus is a good guy, and I'm only tarnishing him because of the rotten guys from my past.

'Don't worry about milk for Gato. Apparently, according to Gabby, I should only give him water. Not full-fat milk.'

'No worries.'

And with that he's gone.

41

An hour later Marcus and I are back on the resort, opening up our respective offices. When I appear, Gato starts meowing, and hobbles round my ankles until I pick him up.

He snuggles in so close, his sharp little claws latching on to my T-shirt, and I can't prise him off.

'Come on, wee guy. Let's get something to eat.'

He reluctantly disengages, switching off his purr.

Once he's fed, I log in to work, and start going through my emails. The first one to catch my eye as I scroll down is from Marlon Langford, the guy who offered me his villa for a couple of months. The property two doors along from Avery's.

> Jade
>
> My villa is now not free for the period you requested. Also, it's with regret that we've decided to no longer use your management services.
>
> Regards, Marlon and Betty

I flop my head in my hands. Gato stares up at me, and starts up the meowing noise again. It's not only that I've lost the offer to stay at their villa, as well as another management contract, but it's the tone of the email. He must know that I squatted at Avery's without paying. How could I have been so stupid?

The lack of Hi or Dear at the start of the email, and Kind or Best at the end, lets me know he's not impressed. It looks like Avery isn't going to let it drop. My one stupid mistake could ruin my life if he keeps up the vitriol.

Looks like I no longer have a choice. With pros and cons on both options – Madam Rackham or the Langfords – I hadn't decided either way. But it doesn't matter any more.

When there's a rap on the door (even though it's open) I nearly jump out of my skin. It's Gabby, jiggling a takeaway coffee container from the kiosk.

'Morning.'

'Hi. You nearly scared me to death.'

I quickly put my computer into screensaver mode, forgetting that it's a picture of the view from my balcony. The balcony that Gabby Rackham enjoys every morning with her toes poking through the railings, as she reclines on my lovingly chosen bistro patio set for two.

'This is for you. Marcus called round and filled me in.'

Filled her in on what? That he suspects I'm a quiz cheat, a homeless loser, or a bit of a drunken tart?

'Oh.' I act nonchalant, glancing down at the pile of bills on my desk, and move them around. If I look busy, maybe she'll go away.

'Listen. I'm happy for you to come and stay until you get yourself sorted. Marcus explained.'

'Did he?' Am I really going to do this? I take a deep breath before I carry on. 'Well, only if you're sure?'

Any doubts I had about lodging with Gabby Rackham are no

longer relevant. After Marlon and Betty's email, I really have nowhere else to go. Sleeping in my car might be possible for a night or two, but when Gato's purr starts up again I know I've no other choice.

'As long as you're happy with the small room,' she says, plonking the coffee on my desk. It feels like a plonk, which makes me wonder how relaxed she really is about the whole idea, or if she's only offering to please Marcus. 'And I wouldn't expect to pay as much rent.'

'Of course not. Are you happy for Gato to come with?'

'Definitely. I love cats. Wait till you see your apartment.' She laughs loudly.

'Sorry?' I dread to think what she means by that.

'I'm a real cat fan. Listen, I'm in and out all day, but here's a key.'

She hands it over, assuming that I don't have a spare. When she glances outside, she starts fiddling with her pink and purple straggly hair. Toying with it, and coyly teasing it behind an ear.

I needn't have looked out the window. Of course it was going to be Marcus. Looks as if she's got it bad, so bad, that she's offering the only other single, available girl on the resort a spare room, just to keep in his good books. When he pokes his head round, I get such an uneasy feeling about the whole arrangement. It's as if everyone around me is conspiring to sort out my future. Or destroy it.

'Hi, ladies. All okay?'

I'm not sure if he's smiling broadly for mine or Gabby's benefit. But whoever, whatever, he's now in control. That's what it feels like, and is making me doubly unsettled. As if I'm being manipulated.

But why? And by which of them?

42

A couple of hours later, as I'm about to put Gato into the cardboard box and take him to the vet in Fuente for a health check, Russell appears. He has his hands shoved in the pockets of paint-splattered jeans, wearing a navy top covered likewise in paint splodges. He looks decidedly sheepish.

'Hi. Well done last night,' he says. 'You were amazing. No idea how you knew all the answers. I'm hopeless at quizzes.'

His smile dissipates when he picks up on my mood. What did he expect? That I'd have time to stop for pleasantries when he's been avoiding me like the plague?

'You rushed off quickly, last night,' I snap. 'And why have you been ignoring me?'

'Listen. Can I come in? I can explain.'

He steps into the office, pulling the door closed behind him.

'Go on then. Hit me.'

He sits down opposite, and fidgets in the chair.

'Avery Knowles asked me to put in the Ropers' new cameras.'

Why am I not surprised?

'And you didn't think to tell me first?'

'Avery said you were no longer acting for the Ropers.'

'How was he in touch with them? How did he get their details?' I glower at Russell.

'I'm really sorry. It's just...'

I keep glowering, too furious to speak.

'Avery said he'd give me some money if I didn't tell you.'

'What? You're kidding me. So you gave him the Ropers' details which were private and confidential?'

Nope. He's not kidding.

'I had Mr Roper's phone number, and gave that to Avery.'

'Bloody hell, Russell. How much money?'

I don't know why this is my first question, but it seems important. My heart is hammering in my ribcage, while Russell considers his answer.

'If you lie to me,' I say sternly, 'that's the end of us.'

'I'm really sorry. It was 500 euros.'

'And was that just to keep your mouth shut?'

'Avery sorted out the details with the Ropers, and I got paid my usual hourly rate.'

'I bet you did.'

Russell now hangs his head. Okay, so he's made 500 euros, sneaking around behind my back, but unless Avery can get him more work, he's up the creek.

The silence hangs like death in a morgue, and Gato picks up on the grim atmosphere. His sad meowing starts up, and his watery eyes look as if he's crying. I need to get to the vet's.

I start fiddling with documents again, willing Russell to disappear.

'I'm really sorry. I'm so desperate for money. Are we okay? It'll not happen again, I promise,' he says.

He's 100 per cent right. Over my dead body, it'll not happen again.

'I'll think about it. That's all I'm promising.'

This is a lie. I don't need to think about it. I need Russell more than he needs me, with maintenance jobs building up on the properties I still manage. But I'm so furious that I need time to calm down, and hold on to some pride.

'Thanks, Jade. I knew you'd understand.'

He doesn't know me at all. I wonder what he'd say if I told him Avery is out to destroy me, that I'm homeless, and have some guys stalking me on the resort, and possibly trying to kill me.

When Russell gets up, and hovers a moment longer, I start panicking there's worse to come. When I hear what he says next, I laugh so hard I think my sides might burst.

'I wonder if you'd fancy going for a drink sometime?'

'Really?' I try to swallow back the laugh, feeling ridiculously hysterical.

'Jeneva and I have split up.'

He's pretty quick at dipping his toe back in the water. I only spotted him with his fiancée last week.

'What say we stick to maintenance jobs?'

Talk about thick-skinned.

'Okay, boss.' He salutes, before slinking out of the office.

At least I now know I'm right about Avery. I'm furious with Russell, but he's not in Avery's league. The bastard is operating a one-man campaign to destroy me, but I can't work out why. Surely he could have sued me for lost rent, or demanded money with hefty interest. Even with mild menaces.

But this feels like something else entirely, and I've no idea what.

43

Once Russell leaves, I bundle Gato into the car, and head for the vet's. His little body gets so tortured by needles that he's out for the count when it's all over. I have to push the 200-euro vet bill to the back of my mind, as I'd no other choice. At least he's alive.

While he sleeps in the office, I start the almighty task of carting all my possessions over to my apartment. I dump everything on the pavement outside the apartment block, and keep adding to the pile. It's like the contents of a very drab car boot sale.

Thankfully there's no sign of Gabby, which is good news. She could be anywhere, hopefully back in England. But I mustn't be mean, as none of this is her fault, and she's a lifesaver for giving me and Gato a roof over our heads.

As I'm filling up a carton with a stash of quiz books, Marcus appears. With a female client in tow. Red hair. Red face. Red arms, and covered in freckles. Okay for some, as he's no doubt been prowling the resort for customers while I'm saving stray cats, not to mention saving myself from sleeping rough.

'Need a hand? Let me help with those boxes. They look heavy.'

'I'm fine, thanks. I can manage.' I can so not manage, but don't want to feather his PR opportunity in front of the cranberry redhead, whose pink toenails clash with red flip-flops.

'I'll just be a moment,' he says, turning to the woman and placing a hand on her arm. Could he get any more smarmy? When she nods, he hoists up the box of quiz books, but not before thumbing through the contents.

I pick up a large suitcase and start wheeling. Too much to hope that he'll not bring up the subject of quizzes.

'I can see why you're a quiz champion. You've got some serious knowledge in here.'

He bends in pretend effort at the weight, puffs loudly, and I have to laugh.

He holds open the door to the apartment block, and orders me in a very commanding voice to leave the suitcase and he'll bring it up after he's dumped the books.

I take the stairs two at a time, and have to take a deep breath when I'm outside my front door. I put the key in the lock, but it won't turn. I try again and again.

'Here. Let me.' Marcus takes the key, and suddenly the door springs open. He falls forward and nearly smashes into Gabby.

'Marcus,' she squeals, but her smile fades when she sees me loitering in the background.

'Gabby. Just helping carry some stuff up for Jade. Where should I leave this?'

She directs him to the cubicle. I'd forgotten how small the second bedroom is. *No room to swing a cat*, as Mum would say. Pretty apt considering Gato will be my roommate.

Ten minutes later, all my stuff has been deposited in the cell. You can't even see the bed any more, as it's covered with the overflow from the floor. Maybe I'll have to sleep in my car after all, as I'm having serious trouble negotiating the piles.

Gabby screeches through from the kitchen.

'Tea, coffee, anyone?'

Marcus taps my arm (what's with all the arm tapping?) and whispers, 'I'll make a move. Tell Gabby I've got a client waiting.'

'Will do,' I whisper even more quietly.

Gabby reappears, but her smile slips when she sees that Marcus has gone. We both listen to his retreating tread on the stairwell.

44

Oh my God. Gabby wasn't joking about liking cats.

Every visible surface in the apartment is covered in ornaments of them. China ornaments. Brass ornaments. Wooden ornaments. All shapes and sizes. The walls of the lounge, the kitchen, and the bathroom are adorned with pictures of cats. And a huge cast-iron doorstopper in the shape of a cat takes pride of place by the front door.

'You really are a cat fan,' I say, goggle-eyed. Understatement of the century, but at least Gato should be safer here than on the street. He'll think he's landed in feline heaven.

'Yep. Can't wait to meet Gato properly. Will he sleep in with you?'

'Maybe, or perhaps in the lounge or on the balcony? He's not used to being kept inside, but it's safest for now.'

'I'd prefer it if you kept him in your bedroom. There's so little room, and real cats do leave hairs everywhere.'

This is my apartment. My home. But I decide not to press the matter.

'Okay. Maybe I'll eventually put in a cat flap so he can come and go.'

'I'd prefer it if you didn't,' she says.

Is she serious?

'I don't mean now. In the future.'

The way I feel right now, it'll be later tonight when she's asleep.

I don't linger, and turn down the offer of tea, coffee, wine, sangria, and even a cool beer. While the latter is very tempting, another five minutes with Gabby feels like a challenge.

She seems really desperate for company, as it takes me a full fifteen minutes to get out the front door. I've had to promise to have a drink with her tomorrow, or the day after, so we can get properly acquainted. Problem is, the last person I want to confide in is my new flatmate.

'See you later,' I yell over my shoulder as I make my getaway.

The silent response tells me she's either really disappointed not to have the company, or else she'll be on the balcony nibbling crisps and nuts. And right enough, when I'm back outside, I look up. There she is, toes merrily poking through the railings, with a cold can of beer at her lips. She's definitely looking a little smug, as if she's won some sort of battle.

I've no idea how I'll cope living in the same apartment with her, as she's really getting under my skin. It's one more incentive to get my act together; the sooner the better.

* * *

By mid-afternoon I'm ready for a break. The weather is so glorious, sun high in a cloudless blue sky with temperatures nudging 20, that I decide to go for a jog.

The resort is circled by deserted roads, no potholes, gleaming white markings, and even better: no cars. If a vehicle does pass, it feels like rush hour. The place is still very quiet, but hopefully this will change with spring not far away. Tomorrow is 1 March, and I'll be counting down the days until summer.

Once through the Spanish Village, I pick up speed until I reach the edge of the last phase of buildings. There are so many vacant, unsold properties, which could house a boatload of migrants, it seems such a waste. Even Marcus can't shift the townhouses on the last phase of the resort, despite the pristine interiors and gardens. It's the lack of activity. His slick sales patter evaporates when he ventures this far up. I've heard his flattened monotone.

The road opens out after a steady incline, and soon I'm on the four-mile stretch which circles the resort and comes out by The Three Bulls and the tennis courts. Satsuma trees, lemon trees, olive trees, and fig trees line my route. Barren now, but not for long. Come May, hand-picked figs will be bulging in my rucksack.

I pound faster and faster, spurred on by Taylor Swift bellowing through my EarPods. When a car suddenly appears alongside me, I scream from the shock. I know I'm on a road but the last thing I'm expecting is a vehicle. When I see what sort of car it is, and worse still who is inside, I try to speed up. Not that upping my pace will be much use, because even though the Land Cruiser is crawling, it's still going faster than my top gear.

A glance at the number plate and the terror comes flooding back.

It's the bloody car that nearly bumped me off the road, the night of the stolen satsumas, the one I keep spotting round the resort. What do they want?

Isaac's face flashes up in my mind but I quickly suppress it.

My heart is seriously racing, and a stitch glues itself to my side. I need to slow down, and breathe.

As on the night of the stolen satsumas, there's a field off to the right. But with sturdy fencing protecting the resort perimeter, there's no obvious way through.

The same two bearded guys are now leering through their open windows, and catcalling. I've turned the music off, as I need to stay alert. When I can't push on any harder, I give up and slow to a walk.

'Jade. It is Jade, isn't it?' The driver speaks in a husky voice, with a leathery Glasgow brogue. I assumed these guys were Spanish, Portuguese, or maybe North African. Any nationality other than British.

'Who's asking?' I face them, hands on hips, aiming for brave. Who am I kidding? I'm shaking like a leaf.

'Wouldn't you like to know? Are you trying to avoid us?'

The passenger with the slithery tongue starts to laugh. As he slowly peels open his door I think I'm going to throw up.

I have the most dreadful feeling they're going to blindfold and gag me before tossing me in the boot.

But I'll never know because it's my lucky day. In the distance a car is heading our way. Before the bearded beast reaches me, an overhanging paunch handicapping his speed, I dash into the road, and crisscross my arms frantically in the air.

The oncoming car slows down, not having any other option as I move side to side. The 4X4 doesn't hang around, and as soon as the guy climbs back inside, it speeds off in a billowing shower of dust. A hairy arm waving out the window is the last thing I see before it disappears round the bend.

'Jade. Are you okay? You look dreadful.'

Thank God. It's Crystal. She's wearing a canary-coloured

sunhat, and dark glasses. I had no idea she had her own car, assuming Avery drove her everywhere.

'Crystal. Holy shit. Am I glad to see you.'

'Hop in. Who were the men in the car?'

I manage to manoeuvre my unset-jelly legs into the tight space, and my head falls between my knees. I feel so dizzy, and the nausea becomes too much. No sooner have I closed the door than I throw up all over the footwell.

'I'm so sorry,' I wail. Things couldn't get any worse.

'Listen. Don't worry. Let's get you back and cleaned up. Then you can tell me what's going on. First let's open all the windows wide.'

All four windows simultaneously roll down. At least she's being positive, but I can't stop shaking. She's so calm, and I'm a nervous wreck. Thank God she arrived when she did.

Otherwise I dread to think what might have happened.

I might even be dead.

45

HAYLEY

Damon and I manage another four hours of the pool party before we head off. Whereas he relished floating on waterbeds, drinking and eating far too much, I'm desperate to get away. Damon swats away my concerns when I tell him Astrid has been watching our every move.

'It wasn't my imagination. Everywhere I turned she was there. Lurking. She's a class-A lurker.'

He's not worried.

'Hm. Well, I've had fun.' He's dozing off in the car, his head lolling against my shoulder. He smells of chlorine and alcohol.

I'm sitting rigid, staring straight ahead. Leonardo, the waiter in the starched white garb, has doubled up as our driver and seems to be looking more in his mirror than at the road ahead.

As I'm also about to close my eyes, Damon murmurs. He's got a really sexy murmur.

'You know that Jade you talked about,' he slurs. 'Jade Willshire or something?'

'Yes?' I'm soon back in rigid pose.

'She's gone to Murcia to sell properties.'

'How do you know that? How did you get her name?'

'I was doing some digging on your behalf.' He goes to tap a finger against his nose but misses. 'Oops. She's selling sunset. Heaven.'

'Who told you?'

I jiggle his arm to keep him awake.

'Cryssal,' he mumbles, missing off the T sound. 'Jade Willshire. Something like that.'

'Avery's girlfriend Crystal? Avery couldn't remember Jade's surname, or perhaps he didn't want to share.'

'Cryssal told me that the mysterious Jade is flogging properties on some golf resort. I think that's what she said.'

'Which golf resort?' Come on, Damon, give me one more thing.

'Campo de... something. Campo de...'

Next thing he could be dead. His head has slumped across my thighs, and he's whistling gently.

Good old Damon. I run my fingers through his still-wet hair, and kiss him on his crown. Not only is he hot, but he's turning out to be a pretty canny snoop.

46

I take back my misgivings about Leonardo. Without him, I'd have never got Damon out of the car and into the lift of the concrete block.

Damon slumps on to the stone floor, and Leonardo manages to hoist him up until he's leaning against the steel walls. I opt to walk, as the sardine can only holds two people. Even at a leisurely walk, I'm outside our apartment before there's any sign of the rattling cage.

Leonardo somehow manages to keep Damon upright as they walk down the corridor. My flatmate is like a dead man walking. Once inside the apartment, Leonardo throws him down onto the sofa bed, before having a quick look round. I feel anxious that he's likely clocked there's only one sofa bed and no bedroom, and that it might get back to Teddy, via Astrid, that Damon and I have shacked up.

Not that it's Teddy's business, but for some reason I'd prefer he didn't find out.

With Leonardo gone, I put my EarPods in to block out the

snoring, and make myself a coffee before booting up the laptop. I input 'Campo de' into the search bar, adding Murcia on the end.

Damon mumbled the word *golf* before he crashed out, and I manage to pull up several resorts called Campo de Golf dotted around Spain. There's only one in Murcia, on the outskirts of a small town called Fuente Alamo.

Could this really be where Jade has gone? To sell properties on a golf resort? It's a long shot, but maybe. Just maybe I can track her down.

I spend the next couple of hours googling. I check out the Murcia Campo de Golf, scrolling through tons of photos showcasing a pristine resort. I then check properties for sale, the prices and availability. There are hundreds on the market, the prices a snip against Marbella prices.

When I input the name Jade Willshire into Google, nothing comes up. But there is a Jade Wiltshire who seems to be selling properties in Marbella. *Marbella Inmobiliaria.*

I bite the bullet and ring the number. It's already eight o'clock, but the offices should still be open. I hold my breath, and then a guy named Carlos picks up. When I ask to speak to Jade, he laughs. Not sure what's so funny, but I hang on.

'She no working here any more. She's in Murcia. I got her the job myself.'

'Where exactly, Carlos?'

'Who's calling?'

'A friend of hers from England.'

'Another pretty *chica*?' He laughs again. I can visualise him from his laugh. Pretty seedy from what I'm picking up.

'Can you let me have the address, please? I'm in Spain and thought I'd look her up.'

I was right. She's at Campo de Golf in Fuente Alamo.

'Four or five hours by car from Marbella,' he tells me, before hanging up.

I then google hire cars. The cheapest and smallest possible, and check Google Maps. It's possible, but I could be there in the morning.

It's a reporter's hunch. But I've a feeling this Jade will provide a major piece of the puzzle. What really happened to George Stubbs? I can see the newspaper headline now.

More excitedly, I can see the real-crime docuseries on Netflix. If I work hard enough, I might even get enough information to put Astrid in the frame for first-degree murder.

My phone suddenly pings with a new message. It's from Teddy.

> Did you get back okay? We need to talk. It's urgent!!!

47

When there's movement from the sofa I close down the message.

'Hayley? Hayley? Are you there?'

It's then I hear Damon make a dash for the bathroom, and throw his guts up. Teddy will have to wait. For now, it looks as if I've got some serious nursing to do before I tell Damon I won't be flying home with him tomorrow. I've got new plans to pursue my story.

Damon is so cute when he's ill, but I can tell from looking at him that he's really struggling. At least he hasn't got the energy to argue when I tell him my plans.

'Oh. You won't be coming back with me?'

He's now lying prostrate on the threadbare sofa. I suspect an infestation of fleas, as Damon is frantically scratching his head.

'It's a hunch. I'm getting closer to what happened. I'm going to email the paper to tell them I might be on to something.'

'Will they pay for a stay in Murcia?'

'Nope. I'm freelance now, remember? It's on my own time, and I've got savings. But I'm sure they'll pay big time if I crack open the story.'

'I'll miss you.' Not sure if his miserable face is down to the thought of me leaving, or down to how ill he feels. Either way, he looks so vulnerable. But when he says he'll mind the cat for me, my heart soars. Damon might really be a keeper.

'I'll be back for Christmas. Promise.'

'I'll keep you to that,' he groans, his cheeks now white with a definite hint of green. He throws a hand across his mouth and shoots off to the bathroom again.

While Damon throws his guts up, I suddenly remember Teddy's weird text, saying he needed to talk to me urgently. With Damon locked in the bathroom, I try Teddy's number. It goes straight to voicemail which is a first. Teddy usually hugs his phone close like a comfort blanket.

When I hear the toilet flush, I opt to send a message rather than leave a voicemail. No point in upsetting Damon even more by talking to my ex on the phone.

> Back safely. Tried to call. Let me know all okay.

The message doesn't seem to go through, but at least I've tried. No doubt I'll hear back tomorrow. Meanwhile I've got more pressing matters.

While Damon lounges on the flea-ridden sofa the rest of the evening, vacantly staring at the shoebox-sized TV screen, I sort a hire car and book a really cheap Airbnb in Fuente Alamo. On Google, the place looks like a ghost town from a Western, but only a mile from Campo de Golf. I must be crazy, but an adrenaline rush is backing up my hunch.

Once everything is booked and Damon has fallen asleep, I take a last peek out the window. That's when I see Leonardo down below. He's got his back to the concrete block, and is staring out to sea. Why the hell is he out there? I shiver, both from cold and the random sighting.

I tug the moth-eaten net curtain across, ripping it more in the process, and switch off the single dangling light bulb. It's only 10 p.m., but I need to get to sleep and block out the morbid images. As I'm about to get undressed, and crawl in alongside Damon, a sudden epiphany comes to me of something else I need to do.

I reboot my laptop, and open up all my social media. I then delete all traces of Hayley Scrivens, reporter and journalist. All photos, and related content. Thank goodness I'm now freelance, as the paper where I worked has already deleted my profile.

Tomorrow, I'll come up with a new profile, a new name, and work on a new appearance. I don't want anyone linking Hayley Scrivens, reporter, with the girl who turns up at Campo de Golf. Working undercover feels like the safest route.

As Damon snores contentedly, my mind buzzes with all sorts of questions. Leonardo being outside the apartment feels stalkerish. Could he really be keeping an eye on us? If so, why? Perhaps Teddy has let slip to Astrid the real reason I'm here.

Also it's hard not to link the timing of Teddy's text to the sighting.

I'm now exhausted from both the day's activities, and the macabre thoughts running through my head.

I spoon up with Damon, finally giving in to warmth and sleep. It's our last night together for who knows how long, as I've work to do in Murcia.

48

Thank goodness Damon is much better after a good night's sleep. He's not so green around the gills, but is really slow at getting his act together. As if he's dawdling deliberately.

When his taxi arrives, he takes forever to get out the door. For a moment I panic that he might refuse to go without me. With a long drive ahead, I need to get moving, and can only breathe more easily when Damon picks up his rucksack.

'You won't forget me, will you?' he asks for the hundredth time.

He's so unsure, so unlike Teddy who was cocky, and confident that I'd be around forever. Damon looks so miserable, as if he's been dumped.

'Of course I won't forget you, and I'll see you soon. Don't forget to feed Mitzy. Lots of cuddles. Now go...'

I give him a last big hug, before he reluctantly drags his rucksack out the door and down the stairs. He's avoiding the tin can of a lift, with a vague recollection of having thrown up against the walls. Without looking back, he yells, 'Bye. See you soon.'

And with that he's gone.

When a text pings through a few seconds later, I stiffen. I'd forgotten Teddy in all the drama.

> Missing you already. D XXXX

I grin from ear to ear, relieved, although surprised it's not from Teddy again. I send a couple of love hearts, and mute my phone. I'll try Teddy later, but for now I've got so much to do. If he really needs to talk, no doubt he'll chase me.

My first trip is into Marbella before picking up the hire car and heading for Murcia. It's a five-hour drive, but at least it's motorway, and I'm keen to arrive before dark.

I pack up my stuff, lock up and chuck the key back through the letter box. I'll certainly be glad to see the back of this concrete hell hole.

After my Uber drops me off, I head for the hairdressing salon I googled earlier. Once I'm done there, I've got an appointment at The Piercing Lab a few metres further down the road. I'm hoping no more than three hours should sort out a whole new appearance, and then I'll be on my way.

Four hours later, and I head to collect my Nissan Note from Marbella Rent-A-Car.

The guy on the desk gives me a weird look, and asks to check my passport. He finally gives up when I explain in pidgin Spanish that I've only just had my hair coloured. At least the visible tattoos aren't permanent. I had no idea you could buy stencilled tattoos that peel off, so I bought a whole stack from The Piercing Lab.

I set off, and with only a couple of comfort breaks, I manage the drive in five hours. The motorways are a dream compared to the M25, and I don't have to slow once the whole way, reaching my destination before dark.

My Airbnb in Fuente Alamo is in a little back street, with an Irish bar to the right of the entrance. Murphy's. Once I'm unpacked, I know where I'll be going. I'm so thirsty, it's a no-brainer.

I pick up the key from a neighbour, and am soon inside the miniscule studio flat. I'm excited, but my stomach is in knots. Up until now Teddy has been the adventurous one. Am I really going to do this?

When I catch sight of myself in the bathroom mirror, I have to laugh. Have I gone mad?

I dress in huge baggy clothes (an enormous jumper, along with jogging pants, borrowed from Damon) and sturdy walking boots. It's going to be tough adopting a whole new disguise, but to ensure anonymity, it's vital not to be recognised. If I bump into Avery again, the last thing I want is for him to recognise me and work out I'm a reporter called Hayley Scrivens. Even though Avery has already met me, I'm confident he'll have little interest in Gabby Rackham... my new alias. I look a complete mess, and aim to keep it that way. Huge cheap sunglasses, as well as tortoiseshell reading glasses, should keep my eyes well hidden.

It suddenly dawns that I haven't turned my phone back on since I left Marbella. When I check for messages, I'm surprised there's been nothing more from Damon. But a new message from Teddy sends my pulse racing. It was sent three hours ago.

> I'm in deep shit. I need your help 👻

I try to call him, but again it goes through to voicemail. I'm not sure what else I can do. He hasn't replied to my message from last night either, which is so unlike him.

I suspect Astrid might have stopped paying him, maybe even thrown him out on the street. But after seven years together, I know Teddy's a survivor. This time I can't suddenly pick up the pieces, as I've moved on, and perhaps now is as good a time as any to make a stand. If he's that desperate he'll call me back.

I don't text him, sending Damon a message instead, asking if he got back safely. I smile at his quick response of a thumbs-up emoji and a simple couple of love hearts.

I now turn my phone back off, relishing the peace and excitement of being on my own. I might look a complete mess, but nothing is going to stop me popping next door for a pint.

And tomorrow, first thing, I'll head up to the resort.

49

Campo de Golf is a huge, sprawling resort, according to the blurb.

I motor slowly through a raised entrance barrier, and past a very sleepy-looking guard in a kiosk. According to the website, there should be a palatial clubhouse about half a mile up on the left.

I drive past pristine apartment blocks, with the occasional set of furniture displayed on random balconies. Although it's November, and I wouldn't expect it to be heaving with sun worshippers, the place is deserted. The size and grandeur of what I can see all around takes my breath away.

I turn into the entrance for the clubhouse, and park up. I kill the engine, and dare check my appearance in the mirror. I'm now scared they'll not let me in. My hair no longer has a subtle pink tinge, but it's streaked through with a hundred different shades of pink, white and purple. The tortoiseshell-rimmed glasses make me look even worse. Actually, I look slightly crazy.

Anyway, it's too late to worry. My new look is to avoid recognition, and should hopefully stop people striking up random conversations.

I've managed to set up new social media profiles showcasing Gabby Rackham as a hippy, wannabe, aspiring artist. Painting is to be my new fictitious hobby, a notch up from hairdressing, which certainly doesn't fit in with the new appearance. I also add on to my profiles that I'm a trained psychotherapist. It's a job as far removed from what I really do that I could think of. But in case anyone wonders how I can afford a painting sabbatical, I need to be prepared.

Outside the clubhouse are half a dozen sets of golf clubs. It's comforting to know there must be someone inside, as I'm starting to suspect the resort hasn't opened for business yet. Or that it's a phoney stage set for a *James Bond* or *Mission Impossible* movie.

I take a tentative step through the entrance and notice off to the right, before what appears to be the huge bar/clubroom, a sign for the ladies'.

I make a dash for the cloakroom, and am soon freaking even more over my appearance. No. No. No. My hair looks even worse under the bright lights. And my clothes might be a bit over the top. The baggy jogging pants and voluminous sweatshirt of Damon's were meant to add the illusion of weight, but I look more like a sumo wrestler. To top it all, the tortoiseshell glasses are steamed up, and I have to wipe them with a paper towel to clear the plastic lenses.

Tempting as it is to go back to the car, I take a few deep breaths, stride out towards the clubroom and head for the bar. Apart from a barman, and a smartly dressed guy ordering a drink, the place is empty.

'*Hola*,' I manage, praying the lone guy might speak English.

'Hi,' he says. At least he doesn't baulk at my appearance, which is something.

'It's quiet,' I say. Understatement of the century, but it's the best opener I can think of.

'Always is this time of year. You just arrived?'

The guy turns to give me his full attention. At least he's not rushing off to join the lack of people.

'Yes. I got here yesterday. Couldn't wait to have a look round. The place is amazing.'

I make goggle eyes but doubt he'll pick up the expression through the chunky glasses.

'It is, isn't it? Have you walked right round the resort yet? It's spectacular.'

Perhaps he thinks I need the exercise, but he seems genuine.

His next suggestion throws me completely.

'If you like, I could show you round?'

Is this guy for real? Could he be Astrid's lookout? Because there's no way he could be chatting me up. It takes a couple of seconds to work out his angle.

He's an estate agent, of course. I should have guessed from his smooth appearance. He's certainly not a tourist. He flicks a business card out of his shirt pocket, and thrusts it my way.

'Oh, you sell properties.' Again, I don't know why I aim for a really interested expression, as he's now looking at my feet. The black sturdy boots would be more suited to a hike in the mountains than for having a beer in a very plush, albeit deserted, clubhouse.

'Yes. Marcus Ingram.' He extends a hand, all smooth and suntanned. My heart flutters, no idea why, as he'll not be feeling any spark talking to me dressed like this.

'Hi, Marcus.' I finger his business card. *Hola Sol*.

'At your service. Let me get you a drink, and maybe you'd keep me company on the terrace?'

'Thanks. That would be nice.'

'Beer? Wine? Coffee? What's your poison?'

'A small beer would be good. *Una cerveza*, I think it is.' I laugh nervously.

'Don't worry. All the staff speak English. They ignore our attempts at Spanish,' he whispers behind a hand.

I blush at the intimacy, amazed how quickly I've stirred up interest. Business must be really quiet this time of year is all I can imagine.

Yet when he hands me my beer, I get a flutter of excitement. This guy could feed me valuable information. Especially if he knows Jade Wiltshire.

If he does, I could be in business. A chance to build my story.

50

After we've finished our drinks, Marcus takes me on a tour of the resort. He's slick with his sales patter, and also very fit.

'You okay?'

No. I'm not okay. I'm sweating in Damon's huge sweatpants and baggy sweatshirt.

'I'm grand,' I lie. Truth is I'm near to collapse.

'Another half a mile, and we'll be at the tennis and padel centre. We can have a drink there?'

'Sounds perfect.'

Half a mile? Blisters are building under my army boots, and my feet are throbbing in pain.

We trudge on, conversation dwindling when he picks up on my discomfort.

'You mentioned there's only one other property company on the resort. I assume they're the competition?' I ask.

I don't look at him as we trudge on, in case he picks up on my intensity. At least it's downhill from here.

'Yes, that's right. Jade Wiltshire is the competition, and works next door to me. She's only been here a couple of weeks, setting up shop shortly after the last property team moved out. Too quiet apparently.'

'I can imagine.' Yep, I can imagine, we still haven't passed a soul on the four-mile hike.

'Apparently, some agent she worked with previously recommended her to this resort.'

'Oh. She'll have her work cut out to find clients.'

'Yep. Especially with yours truly as the competition.'

I sense he's smiling, a big Cheshire-cat sort of smile.

'There's a main sales office that deals with unsold and new properties, but I'm inclined to pick up longer-established owners, and resales. I do management as well,' he says.

'For the owners? Will Jade be doing that too?'

'Yep, I expect so. At least having her as competition should keep me on my toes.'

We finally reach the tennis centre. There's no one on the courts, surprise, surprise, but on an adjacent pristine bowls lawn is an elderly group of players dressed head to toe in white.

It couldn't be a more English scene.

Marcus points to the seating area by the tennis courts. I collapse into a very welcome chair, as he heads off to a kiosk by the bowls green to get refreshments.

I then sit up very straight, and come over doubly hot as my insides somersault.

Lounging at the bar of the bowls kiosk is none other than Avery Knowles. Holy shit. And keeping him company is his girlfriend. The one we met at Astrid's villa. What was her name? It started with C. My mind has gone to mush. Avery said at the pool party that he was going to track Jade down, and it looks as if he hasn't wasted any time. Although I'm shocked at how quickly he's got here. Thank goodness for my disguise.

Marcus returns with two bottles of water, and asks if I've got my breath back.

'All good.' It's so not good. Breathing is getting harder, rather than easier. I swivel my chair round so as not to be facing Avery.

It looks as if he and I are both after Jade.

For completely different reasons.

51

JADE

Crystal pulls the car up outside Avery's villa. She's so calm, whereas I'm a complete wreck. Thank God she arrived when she did, otherwise I dread to think what the guys in the black car would have done to me.

Thankfully Avery's car isn't parked outside, although at this point, fronting up Avery would feel like a minor irritation.

I crawl out of the car and follow Crystal inside. It seems a lifetime ago since I scrabbled together my possessions from the front garden, but it's been less than a week. Yet my life has been turned upside down since. Nowhere to live. A dearth of clients, and two dangerous members of the Scottish mafia after me. It couldn't get any worse.

Crystal puts the kettle on, and assumes I'd prefer herbal tea to coffee.

'Settle those insides,' she adds, jiggling a couple of camomile tea bags.

'Thanks. Do you mind if I use the bathroom, freshen up?'

'Of course. There's mouthwash under the sink.' She gives me

a mothering smile. 'While you do that, I'll do a quick clean of the car. Get the worst of the sick off.'

She could have saved my life, and is really trying to make me feel better, casually cleaning up the car where I threw up. I'm almost sorry that I beat her on the landlocked-countries question, as she might be my only friend on the resort. Apart from Marcus, of course.

There's something even odder about her appearance today though, and it suddenly dawns that she's wearing a floaty silken scarf wrapped several times round her neck. Also, she hasn't removed her enormous sunglasses, even though we're inside.

In the villa there are two small bathrooms. One has a bath, and the other a shower. I go into the larger one, and the first thing I notice is that the sink surfaces are bare, other than for a disposable soap dispenser. No toothbrushes, no toiletries. *Nada*. By the door is a small holdall, bulging, and zipped up. As if someone is moving out. Perhaps they're heading back to the UK.

I splash water over my face and neck, and scrub my hands until I feel mildly presentable. Before going back into the lounge, I peek into bathroom number two. It's chock-a-block with men's toiletries. Shaving foam. A pack of opened disposable razors. Aftershave. And two bars of disintegrating soap, most of which is caked on the sink surround. Avery doesn't look as if he's going anywhere. Just my luck that Crystal might be the one bailing out, and he's the one hanging around.

When Crystal reappears, she suggests we sit outside in the small garden again. In the summer months the noise from the communal pool beyond the hedge is deafening, but for now the silence hangs heavy in the air.

'Do you want to talk about it?' she asks.

She watches me like the therapist Mum made me see after the

Isaac saga. I don't know where to start, or how much to tell her. The past seems to be coming back to haunt me. The guys in the black car have reignited the whole nightmare. It's as if they're somehow connected to the past. To Astrid, or in some way to Isaac.

'Not really.' I sigh. 'It's too long a story.'

'Try me.' She's not going to give up.

It's then I notice, when she uncoils her scarf, vivid red markings round her neck. Without staring too intently, I'm certain they're finger marks. It looks as if she might have had a set-to with Avery. When she takes off her sunglasses, there's no mistaking the bruise on her cheekbone.

I'm about to comment when she plops her glasses back on, the huge rim covering the black mark. I sense she doesn't want to talk about it, and something warns me not to get involved. Avery could be dangerous, and the last thing I need is to wind him up any more.

I decide to give her a potted version of my woes. Especially as she could have just saved my life.

'I shouldn't have stayed here without telling Avery, and now I'm losing clients all round.'

'Avery's very unforgiving. I should know.'

A slight blush tints her porcelain cheeks. She's like a bisque porcelain doll, 1800–1920s. The red blobs on her cheeks match the shade of red markings round her neck.

As I'm looking at her neck, she turns the inside of both arms out, lifts up a floaty sleeve and displays two further areas of angry red.

'Oh my God. Did Avery do that?'

For a second, I forget my own woes.

She nods, and tugs the flowing sleeve back down.

'I'm leaving him,' she says.

'Oh. I'm really sorry. I had no idea.'

I don't know why I'm so shocked, as Avery is a pig, but this looks serious. Crystal might be in real danger.

'Don't be. But listen, you might be able to help me.'

'Me? How?'

If she's looking for room and board, she's come to the wrong place. I suspect the idea of her moving out is pretty recent, judging from the packed toiletries in number one bathroom.

'I actually love it here. On the resort. It's so peaceful after my hectic London life. I'm thinking of buying. Maybe you can help?'

Buying? Can she be serious? If it was me, I'd want to flee the country.

But if she is thinking of buying, who am I to suggest otherwise?

'You want to buy on the resort?' I pull myself up from slouch position, suddenly keen to look professional.

'Why not? There seem to be some real bargains, and I don't see why Avery should stop me living my dream. No man will tell me what to do.'

She's really going to make a stand. Looks like she's made of sterner stuff than her hair-pulling habit might suggest.

'Well, I can show you plenty. What sort of thing are you looking for?'

'Las Ramblas. As you come in? I had a look round there with Avery when we first got here. I love the views, the location, and the interiors are amazing.'

'Las Ramblas? Good choice. The two communal swimming pools are huge.'

I don't let on that I squatted in a ground-floor property there when I first set up shop. Only four months ago. Las Ramblas is expensive, out of my budget, but Crystal might be loaded. Who knows?

'Can you show me what's for sale? Oh, and don't tell Avery.

Please.' She taps a biro-length forefinger against her lips. 'Shhh,' she whispers.

I'll definitely not be telling that prick anything. Go Crystal. This could be the break I need.

'I've got quite a few on my books. You'll get a better price on resales than on a new one.'

'Sounds good. Do you have one of the penthouses going?'

Suddenly a wave of nausea washes over me again. The penthouses are the few properties that I avoid like the plague. I don't do lifts, and after Isaac burned to death on a roof terrace, I can't face high-up sun traps.

'Are you okay?' She puts two hands over mine. 'You don't look so good.'

'Sorry. I think I ran too fast. My insides are all over the place.'

I cover my mouth and make another dash for the bathroom.

52

As soon as I feel a bit better, I leave Crystal and walk back to the office. I'm still lightheaded, but hearing that Crystal might want to buy a property has certainly lifted my spirits.

I've arranged to meet her tomorrow by the back entrance to Las Ramblas, and show her what's available. She giggled, and said she'd come wearing dark glasses, and a baseball cap.

'I won't be telling Avery where I'm going.'

If he's as much of a control freak as I suspect, I doubt she'll be able to give him the slip. But that's none of my business, as all I'm interested in is a sale.

There is one penthouse, recently reduced in price. Also, it's the original marketing show home, and beyond luxurious. I'll have to brace myself to trek up there. At least phone reception is strong on the roof. My gut tells me that if I can flog this apartment to Crystal, it might be the sale I need to get back on my feet.

I collect Gato from the office, snuggling him in his tatty blanket before shutting up shop. A cosy cat basket is on my mountainous shopping list. I like having him at work, but need to start leaving him in the flat so he can acclimatise to his new home. A cat flap is still on my to-do list, despite Gabby's protestations.

Seamus gives me a weird look as I saunter past, as does Russell who is already outside the kiosk for happy hour. Happy hour lasts the whole evening, starting at 4 p.m., as Seamus is desperate for business. It only gets cut to one hour in the busy season.

I climb the two flights of stairs to my apartment. The door is ajar, and I can hear Gabby on the phone. It sounds as if I'm the topic of conversation.

'She's okay. Only for a week or two. Stray cat. Drinks too much. Pretty? So-so.'

'Yoo hoo. Gabby?'

When I yell, Gato's eyes fly open. His little body shakes like a leaf.

The phone cuts off pretty quick, and a second later Gabby's standing in front of me. She's dressed in another voluminous kaftan which could double up as a tent. I dread to think what's underneath.

'Jade. Come in.'

She flings the door wide and ushers me into my own flat.

It's so crammed with knick-knacks, it looks half the size I remember.

'I'm cooking risotto if you fancy?'

'Thanks. I am pretty peckish.'

Where do I sit? I feel like a student lodger turning up to share with the landlord. There's a very bijou sofa facing a miniature TV, and nowhere else. It's perfectly designed for solo living.

'Make yourself at home, and I'll get cooking. It'll be good to have company.'

When my phone pings, she halts in the kitchen doorway.

> Fancy a drink tonight? Going into Cartagena, and thought we could celebrate the Pedersen sale. Paella perhaps? M 🙂

Gabby watches to see if I'm going to respond.

'All okay?'

Why wouldn't it be okay? She's like my mother, and much too nosy by half.

'All good. But listen, don't worry about the risotto. Sorry, I'm heading out. But thanks.'

'Oh.' Her face droops, and she looks as if she might cry. She can't be that lonely, can she? I have a fleeting pang of guilt.

Gabby is even weirder than Crystal. She's got such a pretty face, huge soulful eyes and full lips, but I don't get the frizzy pink and purple hair, and metal piercings. Not to mention the tattoos.

'But thanks.'

'Going anywhere nice?' she asks, before sloping off towards the kitchen.

'To Cartagena.' I speak more loudly, as she's started rattling pots and pans.

'With Marcus?'

You could hear a pin drop. The rattling stops, and Gato starts clawing at my top.

'Ouch.' It's as if his claws are stapled to my sleeves.

'With Marcus?' She repeats this in a very loud voice for someone who has suddenly reappeared and is less than a metre away.

'No. A client.'

'That's okay then.'

I head into my cubicle bedroom, and set Gato down. He slinks cautiously round his new territory, before heading back into the lounge.

Once I'm ready to leave, I try to find him. A moment of panic, until I spot the duplicitous furball. He's on the sofa, snuggled up against Gabby's generous hips. He's also licking his lips, while she chomps through a bag of crisps.

I can almost hear them both purr.

53

I meet Marcus at the entrance to the clubhouse. I thought it best he didn't pick me up from the apartment. Gabby's mournful expression was too much.

I haven't overly dolled up, as Gabby was watching me like a hawk. Cut-off leggings and a T-shirt, and I could be popping to the supermarket. She might hear later that I've been out with Marcus, but I don't want her mind going into overdrive.

'Hi, gorgeous,' Marcus says, as he strolls towards me.

I'm sitting by the cascading water feature, which squirts water on each rotation and spits in my face. But I love it. It was the finishing touch to the sumptuous clubhouse.

'Hi.' Jeez, I wish I'd made more of an effort, as Marcus is dressed for the opera. He's in black slacks, and a blinding white shirt. He's so goddamn handsome.

'Are you ready? Cartagena, here we come.'

He puts a hand on the small of my back, and propels me towards his car. It's not yet seven, but the light is fading fast. As we reach the car park, I freeze. The black 4X4 that ran me off the road is parked only a few spots away from Marcus's car. I involuntarily start to shake, and my legs feel as if they're going to buckle.

'What's up?'

Marcus retracts the hand that was doing the propelling, and faces me.

'Nothing.'

'Liar. What is it?'

'Can we get going, and I'll tell you in the car.'

I manage to move quickly, and Marcus has to jog to catch me.

'Is it a race?'

He un-zaps the car, and as we close the doors after us, I see one of the bearded guys through my side window. He's walking our way.

I need Marcus to hurry up, but he's in chill mode, pairing his phone with the car, and getting a playlist off Spotify.

He doesn't comment when I bend down to tie imaginary laces. He must think I'm crazy, considering I'm wearing casual sandals.

Only when we're on the road leading to the security gates do I lift my head again.

Marcus swivels round and grins. He's actually laughing at me, and if I wasn't so wound up, I'd probably be laughing at myself as well.

As we drive off the resort, and take a left towards Cartagena, I begin to calm down. Marcus is oblivious to everything, tapping his hand on the steering wheel in time to Status Quo. He's out for a good evening, and some serious celebrating.

This doesn't stop me checking the mirror every few minutes. Not until we're on the motorway do I relax.

Well, sort of relax. The memories of being forced into the ditch by the crazy men are never far away, nor is the memory of my lucky escape earlier when Crystal came to my rescue. Maybe

Marcus knows who the guys are, but for now, I don't want to know. It's heaven to be away from the resort, and back in the real world.

What was supposed to be a little piece of paradise has turned into an open prison. I can wander around the resort, but it's bloody difficult to escape. I feel almost as trapped as I did in Isaac's villa.

I check my pocket. At least I've got my phone, and it's fully charged.

54

We park in an underground car park, not far from the old town.

It's a dark, grim low-ceilinged concrete bunker, and I'm glad when we make it back into the open. Claustrophobic underground garages are near the top of my list of places to avoid.

We come out right by the sea, and I can't miss the chance to air a bit of general knowledge trivia. Okay, I read up on it before I came out, but who wouldn't want to impress this guy?

'Hannibal spent the winter of 219–218 BC in Cartagena. Did you know that?'

Marcus walks quickly, but slows when I start spouting facts.

'Did he indeed?' He's got that laughing thing going on again, but you know what? I couldn't care less. Tonight I'm going to try to have some fun.

'You're pretty good at quizzes,' he says, once we're walking in line.

'Want the truth? I'm a bit of a quiz nerd.'

'I gathered that from all the quiz books.'

'What quiz books?'

It's all a game, but the flirting is slowly unravelling the knots.

The Girl on the Balcony

A couple of glasses of wine, something to eat, and who knows...? Maybe things will turn out okay after all. My heart is already beating a bit faster, and the excitement butterflies are fluttering.

I haven't dated anyone since the disaster with Isaac. Although I mustn't think of this as a proper date, more a professional outing. Albeit with the competition.

There seem to be more back streets in Cartagena than in Malaga or Marbella. History oozes from every pore, every darkened crevice, but it couldn't be more enthralling. If I was on my own, the dank, black cobbled streets wouldn't be so welcoming, of course, but with Marcus everything has a brighter sheen.

'Do you like Rabo de Toro?' he asks, stopping outside a small bar called Sabores Españoles. Flavours of Spain.

'Yes, one of my favourite dishes.' I sniff, tilting my nose in the air. He's assuming I don't know what he's talking about, and that I've likely never heard of Rabo de Toro. Well, two can play at that game. I'm even more of a nerd with food trivia than I am with Spanish history.

'Really? Well, it's a special of the day here. Fancy giving it a go?'

We wander in, and Marcus smiles at the waiter who scurries over, and points us to a small table (a very high up round table, with two very tall stools). My sandal slides off my foot as I try to scramble up, and Marcus bends to retrieve it.

'Cinderella, I think this could be yours.'

I blush, mortified when he slips it back on to my frozen bare foot.

He orders a carafe of white wine. Heaven. And before he orders the food, I ask him where the dish Rabo de Toro originated.

'In Spain. Ha. You can't catch me out.' He sips his wine, clinks his glass against mine, and smirks.

'Whereabouts? Go on, Mr Smart Arse.'

'No idea. It's oxtail stew. I know that much, and it's delicious. Especially with chunky chips.'

'It was made for after bullfights. Originally an Andalusian creation.'

'Another fact from E. W. Egghead's quiz books?'

'Pig.' I laugh.

You know what? I haven't been this happy in ages. With all the problems, I've almost forgotten how to have fun. The only blip in the contentment is when I think back to my first date with Isaac, when he told me the hake stew we had in Marbella was one of his favourite dishes. *To die for*, he said.

Once we've polished off the food, and the whole carafe of wine, Marcus suggests we go to a late-night café by the sea. The views are great, apparently, when it's light enough to see.

'Sounds like a plan.' I'm drunk on the wine, and excitement, and it feels great. I've been devoid of male company for so long that I'd go anywhere with this guy. Also, not a small part of me misses the devil-may-care-millionaire lifestyle.

We end up in a very bijou café, swing-a-cat bijou, but one which faces right out to sea. Lights twinkle all around the harbour like Christmas illuminations. I must be easy to please, as it feels like I've arrived in paradise.

It's only when he orders another carafe of wine to complement our cortados that I become even more relaxed and loose-tongued.

'What about Gabby? Where does she come from?'

I doubt he'll think I'm jealous, as he doesn't strike me as the type of guy who would go for tattoos and nose piercings. Not to mention the pink and purple frizzy hair, but I'm intrigued by their friendship.

'Gabby? No idea.'

He glugs quickly on the wine. If I hadn't just mentioned Gabby, I'd be grinning ear to ear. Gabby's like a thorn in my side.

'You seem pretty close?'

'She's okay. A bit too nosy for my liking.'

'Nosy? In what way?'

No doubt overdoing the interest in everything he says, as she's got to be smitten.

'Oh, everything. She asks constant questions. She even asked me the other day about you,' he says. 'On and on with the questioning.'

'Oh?' My heart starts to thump, and an uneasy feeling creeps in.

The lights might be twinkling, this guy drop-dead gorgeous, but I shiver.

'Where you came from. Why you left Marbella.'

My drink slips from my hand, and dribbles down my leggings. Marbella? How the hell does Gabby know I was in Marbella? No one on the resort knows that, except me. I've never so much as let slip that I even went there on holiday.

'Here. Take these.' He grins and hands me a couple of serviettes to sop up the spillage.

I wipe furiously at my leggings, and only stop scrubbing when he looks at me strangely.

'What?'

'Nothing.' But he's watching me intently.

It's as if he knows he's hit a nerve.

55

I decline Marcus's invitation to go back for a nightcap. An isolated finca in the middle of nowhere is the last thing I need.

We walk in silence to pick up the car. I stagger, he walks. I'm so desperate to get home, but dreading having to face Gabby the Hun. I'm praying she'll be asleep when I creep in. I'm now even more wary of her since Marcus told me she knew I'd been in Marbella, and that she's been asking questions about me. I can't rid myself of the rogue thought that she may somehow be connected to the past.

By the time we reach the resort, I've almost completely sobered up. Marcus kept the music on in the car, and we didn't talk much on the drive back. While he seems unfazed by the silence, I'm ready to scream.

'I enjoyed that. Maybe we can do it again sometime?' His eyes are all crinkly, flirtatious.

'Maybe.'

If I was playing hard to get, it would be working a treat. Problem is, I can't get past the fact Gabby knows I was in Marbella.

And another thing. Marcus has just told me another of my so-called maintenance clients, an Isabelle Montgomery (Phase 2, Las Colinas, five doors down from Avery) has also jumped ship. Right into Captain Hook's arms.

'I'll share the fees,' he says.

'You're all right.' I pout, flicking my hair defiantly. 'I'll manage.'

I will not manage, but there's no way I'll be beholden to this creep. Funny, how he's gone from hot to creepy in the blink of a throwaway suggestion.

'I'm sorry,' he says. 'I get you're disappointed.'

He drives slowly into the car park by the Spanish Village.

'Don't be. I'm a big girl.'

I sound like a spoilt brat, but it's the once-bitten thing again. I doubt I'll ever trust another guy as long as I live, even if he is as hot as Marcus. I've learnt my lesson where handsome cads are concerned.

Common sense over lust hormones is the way forward.

No jumping into bed with the first man who asks. It's Mum's voice keeping me grounded.

Marcus leans across to give me a light goodnight kiss on the cheek, and it's then I see Ms Bloody Rackham stroll past the kiosk and on up to the apartment. My apartment. She's holding something in her arms. No doubt the duplicitous furball.

I'm feeling really sad, and downcast, when Marcus drives off. Tomorrow, no doubt, I'll have a thousand regrets about going out with him at all, but more likely regrets about not going back to the desert.

I look up and watch Gabby open up the door on to the bijou balcony. My bijou balcony. She's still holding the furry traitor, but sets him gently down, and rubs him behind an ear before leaning on the railing.

I could cry at the sight. Not only have I lost my home, but I've now also lost my cat. Not to mention that the only eligible man for miles around is stealing my clients. This might not be his fault, but who knows? Perhaps he's deliberately targeting them.

All I want is to get my head down, sleep off what's threatening to be yet another whopper of a hangover. It'll be the last thing I need as I try to tackle my financial crisis.

At least Crystal is keen to see the penthouse, and if she buys it, it could help me back on my feet. I've no choice but to accept Marcus's offer of the half-share commission on the Pedersen sale, but after that I'll be standing on my own two feet.

I don't want to be beholden to any man.

56

HAYLEY

It only takes two days to get my 'in' with Jade Wiltshire.

Marcus confided how she's so desperate for money, having real difficulties keeping up payments on her apartment, that she might rent it out to help make ends meet.

Bingo! With Marcus's help, she's agreed to rent me her place in the New Year, for a couple of months. Until she gets herself sorted.

Meanwhile, I manage to avoid Avery and his girlfriend, although Marcus shared in confidence that Avery is looking to buy a villa on the resort. And Jade has a property on her books that's caught his eye.

Poor Jade. I doubt she knows that Avery is the brother of her ex-boyfriend, the guy who died on the roof terrace in Marbella. While Avery shared his suspicions with me regarding Jade's possible involvement in the death, I doubt very much he'll share them with Jade.

But I'm here for a story. Not to sort out their mess.

There's been nothing more from Teddy, and I relax, guessing that he's sorted out whatever his problems were. My plan is to speak to him over Christmas, and gently break it to him that we're over. If he hasn't already guessed. It's sad as we go way back, but for now I'm with Damon.

* * *

It's only a couple of days later, when I'm heading back to England for Christmas, that I start to freak out. As I'm about to board the plane, I get a new message.

> PLEASE DON'T IGNORE ME. I'M IN REAL DANGER. CALL ME… NOW!

The capital letters and lack of kisses make me come over nauseous. With damp fingers I pull up Teddy's number and press dial.

It rings several times and then cuts off. I try a couple more times, but it goes straight to voicemail.

I'm just about to panic even more when another text pings through.

> Ha ha Scrivens. I'm fine. Just wanted to check you were missing me. Catch up soon. Should be home for Christmas. Saving lots of money!

The red love heart emojis at the end help me breathe more easily.

It's out of character for Teddy to come up with freaky jokes. Especially as he's the one living with a murderer. Although the message has made me edgy, there's nothing more I can do now. I keep my reply simple.

> Take care. Catch up at Christmas.

57

I hurry through customs, beyond excited to catch up with Damon.

When I see him, my heart flips. He waves frantically and throws wide his arms. Although there's a moment's hesitation when he clocks my hair colour. I did send him a selfie, but he still looks shocked. Even more so when he sees the metal studs.

'Hayley?' He grimaces.

He zooms in for a bear hug, and clings to me for a couple of minutes as if I'm a life raft. He then hoists up my suitcase with the wonky wheels as if it's a feather. I might look like a punk rocker, but he looks like Elvis with his smooth skin and gelled hair. My pulse races in anticipation.

When we get in the car, and he starts the drive back to North London, it feels like we've been together forever. We chat about this and that, Christmas plans, visiting his widowed mum (whom I've just learnt about) and Mitzy, my cat.

'When do you go back to work? I'm assuming you've given up on the scoop.'

'What? No. It's getting really complicated, but I know I'm on to something big.'

I'm about to share how I've inveigled my way into Jade Wiltshire's apartment, when I sense the change in mood. The feelgood moment disintegrates, as Damon clams up and zips his lips into a thin line.

We head through Barnet, and on towards the Finchley Road in silence.

I finally break the impasse.

'Listen, Damon. I'm going back to Murcia once Christmas is over.'

I turn to look at him, but his eyes aren't blinking as he concentrates on the road. When I settle a hand on his thigh, he stiffens.

'You're going back without me?'

'You've got to work, haven't you? I'm going freelance a while longer.'

'Yes. I have rent to pay, don't forget.'

He threads his fingers reluctantly through mine, and steers with only a couple of fingers on the wheel.

'Listen, it'll be for three months tops.'

'Three months?' He now looks round, narrowly missing a cyclist in the process.

'I've so much to tell you. I need your input. There are seriously weird things afoot.'

He doesn't respond immediately, his attention back on the traffic, and it's only as we turn into our street that he opens up.

'Listen. There's been some really disturbing post. I didn't want to tell you, but you'll see it when you come in.'

'Post? What sort of post?'

He turns the engine off, and at the same time rain starts pelting on to the windscreen.

'Threats. Blood-smeared letters. Yes, real blood.'

What? What is he talking about? No one knows who I am and certainly not where I'm from.

'Addressed to me?'

'Yes. Addressed to you.'

* * *

I fling my bag and coat onto the sofa. Any excitement I might have had from getting home, even the idea of a passionate clinch with Damon, gets shunted to the background, as I grab the small pile of letters (three in total) typed in bold print.

We know your game… and we're watching you

Liar… keep your nose out of what doesn't concern you

Who else have you told? They're not safe either

My hands shake as I read the contents. When a red smear of what looks like dried blood comes off on my fingers, I make a dash for the bathroom.

This is all too much. I thought getting back home would give me time to regroup. Unwind. And prepare for the next few months. Teddy has just texted to say he's fine.

What the hell is going on? Has he let slip to Astrid who I really am? Although I haven't told Teddy that I'm planning on putting together a headline story, he might have guessed. He knows me pretty well.

And how does the sender of the letters know where I live? The postmarks are vague, but the stamps tell me they've come from Spain.

If I hadn't had the recent more upbeat text from Teddy, I don't know what I'd do. The letters must be from Astrid is all I can think of. She's the one person who has most to lose if I carry on digging.

Damon does his best to calm me down. I pace round the room while he tries to put my mind at rest.

'It's likely that Teddy let slip you're a reporter, and this is Astrid's way of warning you off.'

'What should I do?' My eyes plead with Damon.

'Don't go back. It's too dangerous. If Astrid is as crazy as you think, and if she really has killed before, you'd be mad to go back.'

Damon takes my hands, his eyes awash with concern.

He's right. I should throw in the towel, before it's too late.

'Teddy promised not to tell Astrid.'

'Can you trust him?' Damon takes his hands back, retracting the comfort.

'Yes. I do trust Teddy. Well, I did.'

I don't want to stoke the fire by telling Damon about the latest Teddy texts, as it'll make him doubly determined that I shouldn't go back to Spain.

'You need to forget all about your story. It can't be worth it. Who knows what might happen?'

Of course, I know he's right. But I'm not sure I can.

Damon leans over and pushes a purple strand of very brittle hair off my face.

'And maybe let your hair grow back?'

Although Damon tries to make light of the situation, make me smile, I feel uncomfortable. Teddy used to try to control me, tell me what to do, while he did as he pleased. He travelled the world, depending on me for everything, while I worked my butt off to keep things together.

I'm really fond of Damon, he could be my future, but he hasn't picked up on my determined streak. I'm not going to be scared off what is looking like a huge story, as it's all I've ever dreamed of.

'I'll grow my natural hair colour back, promise.'

'Great news. You know it makes sense. That means you'll not be going back?'

His face lights up and he lets out a deep breath.

'No, it doesn't mean that. I have to go back.'

58

Over the Christmas break, Damon refuses to talk any more about Spain, my story, or Teddy. Despite the uneasy impasse over me going back, we have a great time together.

It's only as the date of my return flight to Murcia looms closer that the festive mood subsides.

Damon grows sullen, and when I top up the pink and purple hair dye he knows he's lost the battle to make me stay.

I try to hide my anxiety by not talking much about my plans, and I certainly don't share that I got a couple of texts from Teddy over the last few weeks. The first one was a belated reply to a text asking how he was getting on.

> All good, sis. Weather still nice. Money rolling in. Probably won't make it home for Christmas, as I've got big plans here. Hope you don't mind.
> S xxxx

The fact he didn't get back to me straightaway made me guess all was okay, as he was in no hurry to get in touch. But I also felt tearful on reading it, sad that he seems to have moved even further away from me than I thought. I always assumed he wouldn't let me go without a fight.

A second text came through on Christmas morning, and again I didn't share with Damon, sensing that he puts a lot of the blame for what I'm doing on Teddy. He's suspicious, not convinced it's all my own idea. Despite my reassurances.

> Happy Christmas, sis. Have a great one. Missing you. S XXXX

It's only when I reread the texts the day before I'm due to fly back that I twig what's off about them.

It's the use of an S rather than a T to sign off. Teddy has always signed off to me with a T, never an S. He's Teddy. Never Stephen. I might be overacting, imagining things, and unwilling to admit that I'm no longer the most important thing in his life. But I'm now suspecting there's more to it.

At first I thought he used 'sis' in the messages as our private joke. Now I'm not so sure. What if someone is reading his messages? Keeping tabs on him.

Worse still. What if someone else is using his phone; pretending to be him.

59

On the morning of my departure, a glum Damon drives me in silence to Luton airport. He's like a petulant child who doesn't want to go back to school, and will fight to the bitter end to stay home.

He's been repeating on a loop that I'm not to go anywhere near Teddy. At first I was pleased he cared so much, but the warnings and his jealousy have become suffocating.

'Ignore Teddy. Stay clear. Understand?'

Damon keeps turning to look at me, white knuckles gripping the steering wheel.

'Watch the road!'

'I am watching the road. But tell me you won't see him. Please.'

When he pleads, doing the Mitzy-eye thing again, I soften.

'Loud and clear. Now stop worrying.'

Damon's dour mood is so at odds as to how he was at Christmas, once all talk of Spain was put to one side. His grim expression is now set in stone.

By the time we reach drop-off, I'm ready to say goodbye. I

love being with Damon, but the controlling vibe is getting worse. It's the last thing I need.

He hauls my two suitcases out of the boot and wheels them onto the pavement. I'll have to check the largest one into the hold, after all the Christmas presents he bought for me. Cats. Everything cats. Cat ornaments. Cat pictures. Cat cushion covers. And even a hefty cat doorstop.

I was chuffed when he presented me with the gifts, not because I'm a fan of cat memorabilia, but because he made an effort to embrace my plans for Spain.

'It'll give you an in with Jade,' he said, 'something in common. A cat fixation might help you bond, get her to trust you.'

'Wow. I hope she doesn't think I'm a weirdo.' I laughed, more concerned that my boyfriend was the weirdo. I was thrilled he'd made such an effort, but the amount of stuff he got me is well over the top. He looked really hurt when I suggested leaving some behind.

He cheered up when I smothered him in kisses. I think he's desperate for me to bond with Jade, so I'll get my story soonest and come back. He means well. Well, I think he does. But as we say goodbye, I'm more concerned that the brass doorstop will put me over the weight limit.

We kiss, hug tightly, and Damon wipes a hand across his cheeks.

'It's the cold. Makes my eyes water,' he says, slamming shut the car boot.

'It does, doesn't it?'

I take out a tissue, honk into it, and hover. For a brief second, I'm tempted not to go. To get back in the car and demand he drives me home.

Damon makes it easy for me as he opens the driver's door, and slips inside. Without further ado, he restarts the engine.

Through the open window he yells, 'I love you, Hayley Scrivens.'

'I love you too.'

But he's already driving off towards the exit, the window closed against the bitter winter chill.

I'm now on my own.

60

JADE

I climb the concrete stairwell to the apartment. The front door is prised ajar by the huge iron doorstop shaped like a cat.

'Yoo hoo. Out here,' Gabby yells from the balcony. So much for sneaking off into my cell and collapsing.

'Hi.' I wander out, and she hands me a steaming mug of something hot. 'Horlicks.'

It looks so inviting, but for all I know it's poisoned. She's really weird, in her oversized red and blue kimono. I've never actually seen her legs, calves, or thighs, but I imagine they're generous.

To cap it all, Gato is on her lap.

'Thanks. Maybe it'll help me sleep,' I say. Despite images of dying a slow painful poisoned death, I accept the mug.

Gato opens one eye, but closes it quickly, and is soon purring in seventh heaven.

'Did you have fun?'

'Yes, thanks.'

Here we go. She must have seen Marcus in the car dropping me off, so probably best not to pretend.

'Where did you go?'

Marcus is right. Nosy or what?

'Cartagena. I went with Marcus.'

'Oh. I thought you were going with a client?'

Why do I feel I have to justify whom I go with and where? She must have the hots for Marcus, and is likely checking out the competition to see if I'm interested.

'The client cancelled at the last minute. It was a spur of the moment thing with Marcus.'

'That was nice. He's handsome. Don't you think?'

Another question. She turns even a simple statement into one. It's so irritating.

At least the Horlicks tastes good, and the warm milk settles my insides. Gato looks so relaxed. I wouldn't be surprised if Gabby gave him some as well.

'He's all right if you like that sort of guy.' I'll not feed her any more on Marcus, deciding to stick to safer subjects. 'I see Gato is at home.'

'Yes, he's such a little cutie. Sorry, would you like him?'

'You're okay.' I wince as her slim feminine fingers rake down his coat. Gato's bald patches have nearly all gone now.

'Have you been selling properties long?'

The inquisition carries on. She seems relaxed, as if an agenda is the last thing on her mind, but who knows? She could be a really good actress.

She's now tickling Gato behind one ear, and his little tongue appears as he closes his eyes in ecstasy.

'Not that long.' I need to get to bed.

'Is this your first time on this resort?'

'Sorry?'

She's going to dig about Marbella, I know it.

'Yes. First time selling seriously.'

No point in lying outright, but hopefully she'll let up and I can finally crash out.

'Oh. I heard you'd been selling to millionaires in Marbella?'

She's watching me like a hawk. It's smoky dark on the balcony, and there's not another soul anywhere in sight. It's deathly quiet, apart from Gato's purr which sounds like thunder in the silence.

'Who told you that?' I narrow my eyes, but she doesn't seem to notice. She's on a mission.

'Not sure. I think it was Crystal.'

How the hell would Crystal know? Looks like the grapevine has done its job in telling everyone about my business.

I set the Horlicks mug down on the top of my glass-topped bistro table for two, and get up.

'If you don't mind, I think I'll turn in. I've a lot to do tomorrow.' This isn't a lie, as now I want to find out how Crystal knows I was in Marbella, and if it's true she told Gabby.

Crystal wants to view the penthouse in the morning, so perhaps I can ask her then. But the way I'm feeling right now, I'd rather forget Marbella altogether. If only people would stop reminding me.

I put my hand out to stroke Gato goodnight. The little sod hisses, before going back to sleep.

61

I'd forgotten how hard the mattress in the cell bedroom was. The main bedroom has the all-dancing, all-singing, made-for-comatose-slumber mattress. The mattress in the spare room, on the other hand, could be a medieval torture rack. I bought it in the bargain basement household shop, Pedro's, for the princely sum of 20 euros.

Despite the rack, I sleep like a log. And I only wake when my alarm goes off at 8 a.m. A straight eight hours' sleep for the first time in forever. And to make me feel even more refreshed, and hopeful, guess who is sleeping alongside me? Gato. As soon as my eyes open, he starts up the face licking. How do you remind a cat that the last contact it made was hissing at you with extended claws?

But for now, it feels a minor victory that he's back on side. There's no noise from the other side of the wall, so hopefully Ms Nosy Parker has gone out for the morning. Or better still, the week.

It's only when I go to the bathroom for a shower that my hair stands on end. She's left me a note, reminding me (as if I could forget) that the shower head spurts off to one side and leaves a puddle on the floor. Apparently there's a sponge under the sink. In that moment, my mind flits to Isaac. He was a neat freak who, if I so much as left a rogue drip anywhere in the bathroom, would lock me in my room for hours.

I tear the note up, hop in the shower, and am very tempted to leave a mess everywhere just to remind Madam that this is my bathroom. My shower. My faulty attachment. And I'll be responsible for my own property.

At least there's no other sign of life. The kitchen is spotless, except for the two Horlicks mugs from last night which are washed and upended on the draining board.

Gato's bowl is full of new tuna chunks, with a little bowl of water next to it. His spindly little legs follow me into the kitchen, and after a few rounds of threading himself through my legs, he starts slurping.

I try to creep very quietly out the front door, but not quietly enough. Gato instantly stops lapping and his soulful eyes are like a dagger to the heart.

'Back soon, little guy.'

Even with the front door closed behind me, I sense his eyes boring through the wood.

62

Thank goodness there's no sign of Marcus when I reach the office. Hola Sol is closed up, with a notice on the door saying he'll not be in till later. Likely scouring the resort, touting for paltry client pickings.

The thought that he might be doing a tour of my clients makes my blood boil. I really thought he was on my side. Last night was such fun until he mentioned how more of my clients had jumped right into his arms. For all I know, he could be pushing flyers through letter boxes. Could he really be that two-faced? I no longer know what to think.

Anyway, Crystal is my client. She's also promised to recommend my services round the resort. She feels bad for how Avery treated me, and having seen her bruises, I doubt she'll care too much if he objects to her viewing my properties. Maybe she'll not even tell him.

Yet deep down, I can't shake an uneasy feeling that flogging her an apartment without Avery's knowledge mightn't be the best idea. The last thing I need is to wind him up any more, but I'm so desperate for a sale that I'll have to take my chances.

I pick up the keys for the penthouse at Las Ramblas, leaving my office grilles in place, and decide to walk rather than take the car. When I pass the clubhouse there's no sign of Marcus's car, nor the black 4X4. I get more of a spring in my step when the sun starts thawing out my chilly early-morning bones. The temperature is definitely picking up, and the cloudless sky gives me a warm hug.

It's only as I approach Las Ramblas that I get edgy. Even the word *penthouse* brings me out in goosebumps, and the thought of the huge wrap-around roof terrace is making me dizzy. I still get nightmares imagining Isaac's body on the roof terrace.

Then I spot Crystal up ahead. She's wearing a red baseball hat (so much for camouflage!) and white capri pants. Huge sunglasses might hide her face, but her body is so long and gangly she'd be recognised from miles away.

'Jade, hi,' she says, in a whisper as I draw close. No idea why she whispers unless she's expecting Avery to jump out from behind a palm tree. There's not a soul in sight.

'Crystal,' I say, extending a hand before she has a chance to lean in for a more informal cheek-to-cheek kiss. Professional is my hat this morning.

'Is that it up there?' Her skeletal finger points. It's so long I think of ET.

'Yes, the one on the right that faces out towards the resort entrance.'

'Oh, I can't wait to get up there.' The whisper gets louder as her excitement bubbles.

It's my lucky day, as the bijou elevator is undergoing maintenance. I'm so not a fan of enclosed spaces. Claustrophobia is near the top of my phobia list, marginally under aviophobia... my fear of flying.

My book for quiz nerds has a whole section devoted to

phobias. By the time I genned up on the top twenty most common ones, I realised I'm a bit of a mess. Arachnophobia, fear of spiders, is on my list, but at least my nyctophobia, fear of the dark, that gripped in the aftermath of my Marbella nightmare is slowly abating. Sometimes when I have trouble sleeping, I recite the list.

Despite her height, Crystal is fit. She jogs the five floors in no time, while I've trouble keeping up. Once we're outside the apartment, she's buzzing with anticipation, jiggling from foot to foot.

When the key slips from my grasp a couple of times, she looks concerned.

'Are you okay?' she mumbles as if we're not totally alone.

'I'm fine. Sorry. My hands are just a bit sweaty.'

I'm certainly not going to mention the hangover.

I manage to open up the door to the penthouse and Crystal's attention is immediately grasped. 'Oh my God. Wow. Wow. Wow,' she says as she enters.

Bring back the whispering because her voice has risen like a million decibels.

'It's an amazing space, isn't it?'

The place is awesome. Gleaming cream marble tiles throughout. Cream sofas. Black appliances. Red canvas wall paintings. It was the original show home. The sort of place I'd love to own if it wasn't so high up with an isolated roof terrace. But Crystal wanders round as if in a trance.

'How much did you say it had been reduced?' Her eyes are out on stalks.

'By 20,000 euros. The owners are keen for a sale.'

'It's amazing. Would they accept an even lower offer?'

'Definitely worth a try. It's been on the market quite a while.'

'Can I see the roof terrace?'

The anxiety hits at such a rate of knots that I have to sit down.

'Are you sure you're okay? You don't look so good,' she asks, but she's not that worried. She can't hide her excitement as her eyes flick around the room.

'To be honest, I've got the start of a migraine. If it's okay, I'll stay here. You go on up and have a good look around.'

Without comment, she's soon skipping up the metal spiral staircase.

Then there's a dreadful silence.

I grip the table edge to try to stop the spinning, but my heart's in my mouth as I wait for her to reappear. I start counting down from 100. Close my eyes, and when I finally get to three, I hear her feet descend the stairwell.

'Jade. Jade. Jade. It's fantastic. I'll have it. Where do I sign?'

I manage to stand up, and break into a huge smile. This could be it.

'That's great news. Let's go back to the office, and we can go through all the details.'

'Sounds like a plan. Not sure how I'm going to tell Avery, but you know what? I might not tell him.'

All the whispering and screaming has been replaced by a weird, unhinged-sounding laugh. But who cares? This sale might be a lifesaver.

'You can tell me about Avery when we get back, and what you'd like me to tell him if he asks. Shall we go?'

'Of course I will. And you can tell me about Marbella.'

63

Why the hell has she just mentioned Marbella? Is she in cahoots with Gabby, trying to dig around in my past? She's giving me a very knowing expression, her eyes wide with interest.

I manage to side-track the subject by jangling keys loudly as I lock up, as I've no intention of sharing anything with Crystal other than details of the property she wants to buy.

We stroll back together, and twenty minutes later we're outside my office.

It's a relief that there's still no sign of the competition at Hola Sol, but a tad disappointing that I'll not be able to dangle my new client in Marcus's face. Especially as it's a woman. There'll be no mutual sharing of this commission.

Crystal helps me get the grilles off. Her arms might have the look of noodles, but she's as strong as an ox. She slides the grilles even more effortlessly than Marcus.

'Coffee? Tea? Or perhaps something stronger?' I ask.

I boot up the laptop while she pulls up a chair.

'Nothing for me, thanks. We can celebrate once it's all signed and sealed.'

'Sounds like a plan.'

Sounds bloody brilliant. This could really happen.

'The vendors like to be emailed, rather than phoned, so I'll do that now.'

'Great. The sooner the better.'

She puts forward her offer, then we go through what happens next. I recommend a local lawyer, and run through the community fees. I'm feeling ridiculously magnanimous, because I leave nothing out, and even share all the hidden extras.

But she doesn't seem fazed in the slightest. Funny, I had Avery down as a sugar daddy, as Crystal looks much younger. His swagger and neck-choking gold chains are aimed to impress, but it looks like she could be a lady of means herself. Either way, she'll be well rid of the creep.

'How did you get into property sales?' she asks once I've put the paperwork to one side.

'I'm pretty new to it.'

I stiffen. I don't want to have this conversation, but I need to be polite until the signatures are in place.

'You were in Marbella, I hear.'

Oh my God. She's not going to let it drop. She's looking at me funny, and for a minute I think she has a slight squint. One eye seems to be looking straight past me, the other one through me.

It could be my own discomfort, but Crystal seems less relaxed than she was five minutes ago. Suddenly a long couple of fingers tug out a couple of strands of hair.

When I grimace, she apologises. 'Sorry. A bad habit.'

She widens her enormous hands in surrender and tells me she won't do it again.

'I worked in Marbella for only a short time. But I fancied an apartment of my own, and couldn't afford the millionaire price tags.'

'Snap. Avery took me to Marbella, and we looked at properties.'

I come over queasy for the hundredth time in the last hour. The word *Marbella* has become a phobia all on its own.

'Oh.' I go for a wide-eyed interested look, but I don't want to hear any more. I'd rather hum and stick my fingers in my ears.

'We were recommended this resort by an agent. He told us Campo de Golf was the place to be.'

'There you are then. Written in the stars.' I now sound the loopy party, desperate to steer the conversation in any other direction than in the one it seems to be going.

'Carlos. Carlos... hmm.' She raises her eyes to the ceiling while she thinks. 'I can't remember his second name.'

'Fernandez?'

'Yes. That's it,' she whoops. 'He suggested we come and see you.'

That's how she knows I was in Marbella. The connection should make me feel easier, but it's making things worse. I get such a sinking feeling in my stomach. Why did Carlos have to mention that I'd worked with him? The thought that he and Crystal might have talked about me feels anything but random.

I worked with Carlos for less than a month, but within a day of arriving back in Marbella, I knew I couldn't stay. Too much history. I thought I could get over the Isaac saga, but the horrific images wouldn't go away. Still won't.

Carlos was okay. He was on my side, hated Isaac, and wasn't sorry what happened to him. Problem for me is that I guess Carlos might have suspected I was somehow involved in his death. He knows I conned Isaac out of £145,000, and got to keep it when the psycho got left for dead. I doubt Carlos shared this fact with Crystal and Avery, or with anyone for that matter, as he was the one who facilitated the con.

'That was nice of Carlos. I didn't realise. Avery never said.'

A few seconds pass, before she carries on. 'Anyway, you can now help get my property in the bag. Who needs men?'

I'd love to agree that she'd be well shot of Avery, but know to keep my business hat on.

'At least if you buy the penthouse, you'll have somewhere nice of your own.' Although we've been talking in muted voices up to this point, I now speak at the top of my voice as I've just spotted Marcus over Crystal's shoulder. He's jangling the keys to Hola Sol, but looking straight at us.

Hopefully he'll have heard the tail end of our conversation. With a healthy sale in the bag, we could get back on a level playing field.

64

Crystal finally gets up to leave.

'Let me know as soon as the owners get back.'

'Of course. Keep your phone on.'

'You bet,' she says, jiggling her mobile. 'How exciting.'

Five minutes after she's disappeared round the back of the kiosk, Marcus, Mr *Love Island* Looks, appears in the doorway.

'Well, that sounded like good news.'

'Sorry?' No harm in pretending that I don't know he overheard.

'A sale? The penthouse?'

'Were you eavesdropping?'

'Hard not to hear with the door wide open. Well, it sounded like good news.'

'Perhaps.' I stick my nose in the air. Chilled, so-not-bothered is the look I'm after.

'Congratulations.' He sticks his hands in the pockets of his shorts, and continues to lean against the door jamb. Could he look any hotter?

Butterflies start battering my insides (again).

'Thanks. It's not in the bag yet, but I think the owners will accept the offer.'

'That's great news.'

His smile looks genuine, and I'm tempted to jump up, do a jig and fling my arms around his neck.

'Hope so.'

'What say we go for another celebration drink this evening? I enjoyed our trip to Cartagena, and could do with the company. We could try somewhere new?'

'Oh? Lonely?'

My insides are gurgling with excitement. Perhaps I should give him a chance.

'Sort of.' He smiles with a wicked sparkle in his eyes. 'Shall I pick you up say around seven?'

'Why don't I meet you at the clubhouse again?'

I can't risk Gabby seeing him. Her less-than-sunny personality takes an even greater nosedive when she spots us together. And I can't face a new barrage of questions.

'Perfect.'

A couple of golfers, female, wander past the kiosk, and slow down by the window of Hola Sol.

Marcus doesn't delay, and is soon on his way to cut them off.

'Good morning, ladies. Can I help you?'

Creep.

As he ratchets up the sales patter, I start mulling over what to wear tonight. Perhaps I'll up the sexy look, as he deserves a chance. Who am I kidding? It's been so long since I was with a guy (really with a guy) that I deserve a chance. A girl has needs.

A sudden message pings on my phone, and jolts me out of my reverie.

> Everything okay? You're very quiet. Hope it's not a man? XXXX

I haven't even been on a date for I don't know how long, and as usual Mum's on it like a bonnet. It's as if she's spying on me, but it's hard not to smile.

> Couldn't be better. Will call tomorrow. XXXX

* * *

Today is looking like being the best day of the year. The sale is almost in the bag, as Crystal's offer has been accepted. She was over the moon, and is now bracing herself to tell Avery.

If she tells him tonight, as least I'll not be around. I'm beyond excited about going out with Marcus. Tonight feels like a real date, and the first one since... Isaac. The thought makes me squirm, but Isaac is history. This is a whole new chapter.

When I get back to the apartment to prepare for my date, there's no sign of Gabby. Heaven. Gato is slumped by the front door, replacing the heavy-duty brass doorstop that has been shifted behind the sofa.

'Gato. Come here, you.' I scoop him up and he licks me all over my face. If he was hoping for Gabby, you'd never know.

His bowl in the kitchen is empty, and he purrs round my ankles as I top it up. Soon he's lapping furiously, and the sight makes my heart sing. I can't wait until this is my flat again, and maybe this week I can brace myself to front up to Gabby about the future.

I then set to rifling my wardrobe for battle gear. I pull out my figure-hugging navy-blue dress, calf-length, with the silky feel and skinny shoulder straps. I float round the room (well, twirl round in the cubicle) and hug it to my body. With my spiky navy slingbacks, I'm ready for action.

For the first time in ages, I feel a real glimmer of hope. Like when I won the lottery, and knew it was time to have some fun.

65

I forget how much longer it takes to walk in heels, even kitten heels. By the time I get to the clubhouse it's 7.10.

There's no sign of Marcus in the foyer, so I wander over to the window of the Pro Shop and check my appearance in the glass. I tease my hair, flicking the blonde curls behind my ear. Then I spot Avery behind me.

Shit. Shit. Shit.

'Hello, Jade.'

Avery is the last person I want to see. In the reflection, I pick up his snarly bulldog expression.

'Avery. Hi.' I swivel round, and tweak my ankle in the process. I should probably have worn flats after all.

Looks like Crystal might have told him about the penthouse, as he launches straight into an attack.

'I hear you've been trying to sell one of your dingy apartments to my girlfriend.'

He dares stab a stubby finger against my breastbone.

I flick it away.

'Do you mind?'

'Yes, I do mind. Keep your bloody nose out of our affairs.'

'I'd be more than happy to, but Crystal is my client. Maybe you need to have it out with her.'

'I'm warning you. Keep out.' His eyes form menacing slits.

It's then I see Marcus standing by the entrance, watching us. So much for cool, calm, and collected. I'm now furious, and can feel my cheeks blaze with rage.

'Is everything okay here?' Marcus strolls over, and looks from Avery to me and back again.

'Everything is fine, Marcus. Just a little disagreement,' Avery says, patting Marcus on the back, before marching off towards the clubroom.

Marcus touches my arm.

'Are you all right? I saw that. What's the issue?'

'Can we get away from here, please? I'll tell you in the car.'

He takes my hand, and guides me out through the main door, and on towards the car park.

I have the most awful urge to cry. If this sale slips away, then I'm back to square one. Marcus might be hot, sexy, and who knows, a possible boyfriend, but if I can't pay my own way, I don't want to depend on any man. No matter how irresistible.

We set off in silence, drive past The Three Bulls, the tennis courts, and towards the kiosk. Only when we pass through the barrier do I let out all the pent-up air.

As if reading my thoughts, Marcus stretches out a tanned, strong hand, and rests it on my thigh. I tingle, but with my other hand gently lift it away.

Soon we're heading towards the beaches of Mazarrón. We drive up through the hills, and half an hour later we're on the sharp descent towards the coast. It feels so good to be off the resort, and out in the real world once again.

Marcus is now whistling, and I take back his hand and resettle it on my thigh.

'That's better,' he says, with the biggest wolfish grin ever.

You know what? He's right.

66

Of course being by the sea was going to be cold, but this isn't a mild sea breeze, more an Arctic assault.

As we walk along the front, the romance gets momentarily diluted by the windchill until Marcus strips off his linen jacket and throws it round my shoulders.

'What about you? Aren't you cold?' I ask.

'I'm fine.' Even though his arms are laced with goosebumps, he insists I keep it. He pulls it tight round my chest, kissing me lightly on the lips.

A strong scent of aftershave mingles with the salty tang of the sea. It's romantic to think it's from the sea, but more likely it's the smell of salt and vinegar from the sea bream baked in salt and the huge portion of chips we've just eaten. Marcus knows the best restaurants, that's for sure.

Now he's taking me to some tucked-away café-cum-bar off the beaten track. I'm not a fan of off the beaten track, but I'm feeling more confident with his jacket round me, and his hand gripping mine tightly. I snuggle up close against his body.

We head inland about a hundred metres, until we're

ensconced in a dimly lit café, oozing romance with an overkill of candles. But with Marcus beside me, it's soon up there with my ten favourite places in all the world.

'Coffee, young lady?'

He's soon motioning for the waiter, and despite my suggestion of cocktails, he orders cortados. We shared wine with supper, so I know I'll thank him in the morning.

'Well, Jade. Are you going to tell me where you've been all my life?'

A giggle swallows back a bout of hiccups.

'Where do you want me to start?'

Funny how quickly the coffee sobers me up. Not sure which are worse, the hiccups or the palpitations. I'd much prefer to ask Marcus the questions.

'At the beginning? How did you end up in Spain?'

It's so dimly lit, I can't make out his expression. He looks a bit eerie in the gloaming, his eyes masked, and he's withdrawn the comfort of his hand.

'It's a long story.'

'Try me.'

This is when I open up, and own up to the lottery win. Rather than telling him I won £20 million, as everyone in Marbella believed, I own up to a *sizeable sum*.

'I'm using my winnings wisely, investing in property, but want to keep on working. To keep me sane.'

My laugh bounces off the walls, which seem to be closing in. Who am I kidding? I'm far from sane, and working is sending me over the edge. I can't tell him I'm close to losing everything.

'Good for you. How come you came to Spain?'

He's watching me like a hawk. Does he know about Marbella? I need a few more cortados to gear up my mushy brain. How much do I tell him?

Five minutes ago he had the potential of a *Married at First Sight* candidate, but now I'm anxious that he might know more than he's letting on.

'I fancied a place in the sun. I mean, what Brit doesn't?'

Now a hiccup mingles with a burp, and a couple of blobs of coffee land on my dress. So much for sexy, romantic.

'I guess. That's more or less the reason I came here.'

'Oh?' I widen my eyes, trying to divert his attention from the coffee stains.

'Watched too many episodes of *Living the Dream*.'

He grins, a cat-that-got-the-cream sort of grin. When he slides his fingers across the table, takes mine in his, I don't resist.

'I think you're trying to act like a woman of mystery. Am I right?'

'Yep. Works every time.' Who am I kidding? Woman of mystery? A few months ago I fled Marbella, fearing for my life. I suppose being a suspect in a gruesome murder does hold some mystery, but enough said.

Once we've talked a bit about ourselves, holding a two-way mystery contest, we start gossiping about the others on the resort.

Crystal, Avery, and of course, Gabby Rackham.

'No idea where she came from,' Marcus says. 'She's even worse than you for not telling me anything.'

I giggle. Hiccup, giggle, burp. But the happy vibes are coming back. At least from what I'm picking up, there's no way he's romantically interested in Gabby.

'I think she has her eye on you,' I say.

'You could be right, but she's not my sort of girl.'

He leans across and pushes my wayward fringe back up over my forehead. Thank goodness it's dimly lit, as my face colours like a beetroot.

I look at my watch, and note it's nearly midnight.

'Oh, my goodness. Look at the time.'

'Golly, it is late,' he says. 'Maybe we should get going.'

I nod, and he gets the bill.

* * *

At least I'll not be going to bed drunk, as I'm sober as a judge by the time we get back. Okay, I weakened and have ended up back at the finca. The one plonked in the middle of the moon surface. But this time Marcus is with me, and the way I'm feeling, I could be in a five-star hotel. The isolated hovel couldn't feel more welcoming. Even if a wild boar, an Iberian lynx, or a poisonous snake invades the space, Marcus can look after me.

Did I ever feel this safe with Isaac? Maybe at the beginning, when he rescued me at Malaga airport... The thoughts start popping in and out as Marcus parks up and leads me towards the front door.

When I hover for a few seconds, he asks if I'm okay with this.

'I'm fine,' I say, anything but fine.

'Great. Let's get inside and have a nightcap.'

As he opens up, I follow.

A lamb to the slaughter.

67

Well, Marcus certainly hit the spot with the lovemaking. More than once, I might add. It's been so long, and he was so loving, and even hunkier in the flesh than under his bicep-bulging T-shirts, and chinos. This guy could be the real deal.

Afterwards, we fell asleep in minutes, his arms coiled round me like a python's.

Then, for some reason, I'm jolted awake from a deep slumber. As my eyes peel open, it takes a moment to work out where I am. I don't know what time it is, or how long I've been asleep.

I stretch out an arm along the sheets, feeling for warm flesh, but the bed is empty. Where the heck is Marcus? The place is in complete darkness, even without curtains on the windows. Outside is even darker than inside if that's possible. Visions of the moonscape pop into my mind, and I start to come over hot and clammy.

'Marcus? Are you there?'

I can't even find a light switch as there are no bedside lamps. The silence is so intense that soon I'm panicking. Am I locked in? Where the hell is Marcus? And why has he gone out?

I creep out of bed, no idea why I'm creeping, unless there's a slumbering wild animal in the shack, because there's no one for miles around. I eventually find a light switch, and when I turn it on, a single bulb flickers and emits a shadowy glow.

'Marcus? Marcus?' I wander round repeating his name, before I dare look out the front door (although it's round the back). I see the car parked to the side in a small rectangular bay which is clear of rocks and debris. I can't remember him leaving it there. Didn't he park off to the left? Perhaps I'm imagining things, as my mind is in overdrive. I'm tempted to grab my shoes, and make a run for it. Then I remember my spiky heels, and silky dress. The temperature inside is so cold, I dread how much worse it'll be out.

What was I thinking? I've made the exact same mistake all over again, ending up in a hunky man's home. A hunky man whom I hardly know.

I circle the lounge, round and round like a caged animal. Then suddenly I spot Marcus through the door, some twenty metres away from the finca, wandering across the moonscape with arms stretched out in front of him.

What the hell. He looks as if he's divining for water. What is he doing?

I slip my feet into a pair of oversized slippers, and dare step over the porch to follow him outside. It's small comfort that there are no snakes, wildebeest, or Iberian lynx in sight, as watching Marcus wander around in a trance is even freakier. He could be high on magic mushrooms, but he swore he doesn't do drugs. Who knows? I'm no longer sure who or what to believe. The only thing I do know is that my judgement is badly skewed.

I'm trembling as I take a few paces forward, picking my way cautiously over the pitted surface. When I'm only a couple of metres from him, I stop and watch. Then it hits me.

He's bloody sleepwalking. I cover my mouth with both hands, and exhale a few litres of pent-up air.

'Marcus?' This time I speak really quietly. I've heard it's very dangerous to disturb a sleepwalker. Not sure why, as I'm more scared of what he might do in his sleep. Perhaps he's a psychopath who only acts when under.

His arms are still outstretched, parallel with the ground, and he looks like a programmed robot with his arms pointing towards Mecca. Holy shit. What do I do now?

He wanders past me in a trance, and goes back inside. I don't know what's more unsettling, the barren wilderness, or the weirdo heading back towards the bedroom.

At least my quiz knowledge could be of help here because people who suffer from somnambulism (sleepwalking) shouldn't be woken when having an episode. So much for being saved from a rampaging bull.

An unexpected interaction could increase feelings of fear or anxiety. When startled the sleepwalker will act out in a manner like fight-or-flight response. They may lash out or fall, which could injure them or the person waking them.

Maybe being a quiz nerd isn't such a bad thing.

I creep quietly along behind Marcus, and watch him slide into bed. Funny, he stretches an arm along the empty half of the bed where I was sleeping, and says my name.

'Jade? Jade? Where are you?'

68

Marcus is soon in comatose-sleep mode, likely exhausted from all the walking, while I lie and stare up at the ceiling. Then I start to clock watch. The minutes tick by, then a couple of hours, and I must finally drop off sometime around 5 a.m.

When I hear the rattle of mugs, the jangle of keys, I jerk bolt upright. So much for not waking a somnambulist, as the moment my eyes open, I start panicking. I keep a pepper spray in my bag, but that's not much use as it's on the other side of the room.

'Morning, sleeping beauty.'

It's Marcus standing in the doorway, holding up a steaming mug of something. His beaming smile and relaxed stance make me less suspicious that it's laced with hemlock.

'Hi. What time is it?'

I stretch over for my phone, wondering why I haven't thought before now to input the number of the Spanish emergency services. It's the first thing I'll google when I'm back in Wi-Fi or roaming range.

'It's 8 a.m., sleepy head. Time to get up.'

He looks so fresh, cleanly shaven with the late-night stubble replaced by a baby-smooth complexion. He's dressed in beige chinos and a blue-striped shirt, which tell me he's ready for business.

He doesn't mention the sleepwalking, and I instantly doubt he has any recollection of the midnight stroll. I'm not sure whether to bring up the subject, but decide against it. I'm more eager to get away from here. It doesn't matter how hot this guy is, I've a panicky need to escape. How he manages to look so relaxed is anybody's guess, and for a minute I wonder if I might have dreamt the whole thing. My imagination is all over the place.

'Thanks. I could do with a hot drink.' I reach out and take the mug, but not before tugging the duvet round my chest. 'Have I got time for a quick shower?'

'Sure. Make yourself at home. I'll pop to the shop, pick up some bread and milk while you get dressed.'

'Great. I won't be long.'

'Neither will I.'

He leans over and kisses me gently on the lips. I cough as his aftershave catches in my throat. His eyes crinkle with concern.

'Okay?'

'Yep. Fine.'

How can I tell him I'm fine when the nightmares of moon-walking are clogging my brain? He retreats, and then I hear him unlock the front door.

I don't remember it being locked when I went outside in the early hours of the morning to follow him. Perhaps he re-locked it when he got up this morning.

The one thing I do remember, though, is the car. It was definitely parked to one side when I followed him outside in the middle of the night.

It's now directly by the front door.

69

It's 9 a.m. by the time we drive up through the resort. Rare rain clouds are gathering, and there's been talk of heavy downpours over the next twenty-four hours. When I climb out of the car, I put a hand up. Rain is plopping on to my silky dress, and my feet are frozen through.

'Are you okay? Need a jumper? Or umbrella?'

Marcus leans over into the back seat, and produces a bright red and blue golfing umbrella with *Campo de Golf* emblazoned in yellow.

'Don't worry. I'll make a dash for it.'

I'm shaking so badly, and need to get inside to warm up. It's not just the rain, but shock, and lack of sleep.

'Thanks for a lovely evening,' he says, eyes twinkling.

'Thanks.'

Water from my hair is dripping into my eyes, and there's a definite hint of tears joining the mix.

Marcus doesn't get out, as he's driving round to Phase 1 to check on some client properties. He says he won't be long, and after a light kiss on the lips, he turns the car back the way we came. I watch him drive off, before heading towards my apartment.

The kiosk isn't open yet. No sign of Seamus. Likely the forecast of rain has delayed his appearance. There's no sign of life anywhere, a bonus for me as I must look a mess. My silk dress is sticking to my legs, shoulders, chest, and stomach, and my hair is hanging like wet lettuce.

I walk as quickly as I can, my soles squelching in the rain. When I'm below the apartment, I look up, half-expecting to see Madam lounging on the balcony with a coffee in one hand, and a fag in the other. But there's no sign of her.

I'm dreading the Spanish inquisition when I appear, but I'm going to try to get a couple of hours' shuteye before I face work. No doubt she'll ask about Marcus, where we went, what we did, and start putting two and two together.

The stairwell is weirdly sticky underfoot, and I have to sidestep small clumps of mud that are caked in patches. Usually the stairs are spotless, like the rest of the resort. The community cleaners do a thorough job, helped by the fact there are so few people to mess things up.

The stairwell is also more echoey than usual. I look back over my shoulder, and wonder why the lower front door was already open. Gabby always makes sure it's locked at night, and I insist she remembers. Last thing I need is trying to make a bogus insurance claim.

It's only as I near the door to the apartment that my heart rate quickens. I slow down, put a steadying hand against the metal railing. Why is the door to the flat open? Perhaps Gabby is cleaning, and letting the air filter through, but usually she keeps the balcony door open, not the front one.

It isn't the cat doorstop holding it open either, rather a single brick. Then I see it. A trail of red treacle seeping towards me.

Gabby will have a right mess to clean up is my first thought.

'Gabby? Gabby? Yoo hoo.' My voice bounces off the floors, the ceilings, and rings in my ears. She's not around. There's nothing, no noise at all.

Something is up. Then I hear it. A low, continuous mewing sound coming from inside the flat. Gato. Then I see him, his little body stooped and trembling, as he appears in front of me. He's coated in the same red slime that covers the floor.

'Gato? What's up, little man?'

He collapses in a heap in front of me, willing me to pick him up.

I brace myself to look into the flat. It's the red. Everywhere is red. On the floor. Over the furniture. On the walls. I then spot the doorstop by a twisted body, which is also covered in red streaks. Oh my God.

Before I dare look at the body, I step backwards and retch over the railings. The silence is broken by the splat of vomit hitting the ground below.

At least my DNA won't be mixed up with the trail of blood.

70

HAYLEY

February

I've been back in Spain for little over a month, and still can't get anywhere near Jade. Even though I'm living in her apartment, she's deliberately avoiding me, and is like a whippet on a racetrack when I appear.

The place is so deserted, I feel like Jack Nicholson in *The Shining*. The isolation is about to tip me over the edge. I'm seriously thinking of throwing in the towel. That is until Marcus tells me that Avery and Crystal turned up on the resort less than an hour ago.

I hurry over to the clubhouse with my iPad, and settle in the corner with a cold beer. I'm hoping, as the couple have just got here, that the clubhouse will be their first port of call. Bingo! I'm spot on.

Half an hour is all it takes for Avery to appear followed by a very willowy Crystal. She's dressed as if for a heatwave, in a floaty opaque dress and open-toed sandals. She must be freezing, as

I'm shivering despite the hefty layers. Butterflies are soon pounding my insides.

I keep sneaking glances their way. While Avery orders from the bar, Crystal scans the room. Her eyes come to rest when she spots me. She squints as if trying to work out why I might be familiar.

No. No. No. She raises an enormous set of skeletal fingers, and waves. She mouths 'hello' at the same time.

How can she recognise me? I don't even recognise myself in the mirror.

I give the faintest nod, looking back down at my iPad, praying she doesn't poke Avery and point. It would be a disaster if he finds out who I am, especially now I have a chance of getting something.

My insides churn. I've no idea what to do next when the pair wander out onto the terrace. Should I follow them out, strike up a random conversation?

Problem is, Crystal might tell Avery that I look familiar. Even so, if they do question my appearance, they're unlikely to know I'm a reporter.

As I'm trying to decide what to do, Avery wanders back in. He holds a hand up over his eyes, like a sailor scouting for land, and lets his eyes roam the room. For a couple of seconds he stares my way, and screws up his eyes. I can hardly breathe.

When he finally turns and disappears back outside, the pent-up air explodes. There's no way he could have recognised me, could he?

I'm about to pack my iPad away and beat a hasty retreat when Crystal suddenly reappears on her own. Her arms are wrapped around her chest, presumably in an effort to keep warm. She looks like a walking cadaver.

Before I've even stood up, she's approaching my table.

'Hayley?' She squints up close, and whispers. 'Is that you?'

When I look confused, she carries on.

'I'm Crystal. Remember? We met at the pool party in Marbella?'

I still don't answer, no idea what to do next. If I was hoping Avery wouldn't recognise me, it looks as if his girlfriend has had no trouble.

She has a quick glance over her shoulder, before tapping me on the arm.

'Follow me. I'm off to the cloakroom,' she whispers. She waggles a finger for me to come after her, with a nervous glance over her shoulder.

When she disappears from view, I slide out of my seat with my own cursory glance toward the terrace, and head for the ladies'.

71

When I reach the cloakroom, Crystal is leaning her back against a basin.

'Crystal. How did you recognise me?'

It's my first question, as I'm totally shocked.

'I'm good with faces, and a memory like an elephant's.' She laughs, her voice shaky. Her alabaster skin has faint hues of blue from the cold, and goosebumps rampage along her arms. I'm tempted to offer up my jumper.

'You must be.' I glance at the mirror, horrified by my own appearance.

'Listen,' she says, 'I just wondered if you fancied having a coffee with me tomorrow. Avery is golfing and I could do with the company.'

I try not to sound over-enthusiastic, but Crystal could be the lead I need to move my story on.

'Sure. I'm around.'

'What say ten o'clock? Avery is teeing off early so we could meet up then.'

'Why not? Shall we meet here?'

'As good a place as any.'

'By the way, does Avery recognise me as the girl from the pool party?'

'Don't be silly. Avery's slow off the mark, and your new appearance wouldn't appeal to him.'

She gives a forced laugh. I'm not sure if she's telling the truth, but I've no choice but to let it go. Her next comment, though, throws me back into turmoil.

'I do know you're not an aspiring artist though.' She says this in a very low voice, and I look towards the door, petrified that Avery might appear. Or might be listening.

'It's just a hobby,' I say.

'I think reporting is your real job.'

How the heck can she know this? I told Astrid that I was a hairdresser. How does Crystal know I'm a reporter? My new profiles have me down as an artist.

'Don't worry. I'll not let on.' She taps a long finger against her nose. 'It'll be our little secret.'

'How did you find out?'

'Googling. I thought it was you on the resort when we first came to look round. Too tempting not to look you up.'

I throw a hand over my mouth, petrified my cover has been blown. If Crystal spreads the word, the game will be up. If Jade or Avery find out who I really am, then I've zero chance of writing any story.

'Don't worry. Your secret's safe with me.'

'Thanks.'

I nearly blurt out that I'm now going by the name of Gabby Rackham, but can't face any more questions tonight. Maybe tomorrow, I can tell her, but for now I need to get away.

'Listen, I'd better get back, as Avery will be wondering where I've got to. Till tomorrow. We can talk more then.'

There's a sudden movement outside the door, and I freeze when the door handle rattles.

'Crystal? Are you still in there? Who are you talking to?' Avery screeches, while I scuttle into a toilet cubicle and bolt the door. I'm shaking like a leaf.

I'm just in time because I hear him enter before Crystal has a chance to reply.

'Sorry. I didn't realise I'd been that long.' Crystal's voice is shaky.

'Well, hurry up.'

I hear Avery stomp off, followed by Crystal's almost silent tread.

My legs have turned to jelly. I'm not worried Crystal knows who I am, I'm more concerned Avery might have twigged. Or she might let slip.

He gives me seriously bad vibes.

72

I'm now excited and apprehensive in equal measure. Crystal could really help build my story. She's been to Marbella, knows Avery well, and has met Astrid. She might even know what's going on with Jade, and about where she fits into the whole saga. I'll need to stay sharp tomorrow when we meet up.

It's pitch black as I hurry away from the clubhouse. I'm desperate to get back to the apartment and lock the door. I'm definitely nervous after speaking to Crystal, as I certainly wasn't expecting the conversation we've just had.

As I climb the concrete stairwell to the apartment, my phone pings. It's like a scary boo in the dark. A message from Teddy.

> Hi, Hayley. I'm missing you. Are you missing me? Will be back home soon. Love you S XX

Relief at hearing from Teddy is short-lived when I notice he's signed off using an S again rather than a T. More weird is that he's added 'love you'. Teddy adds love heart emojis, never words to say he loves me.

My fingers are shaky as I respond.

> All good. Let me know your plans. XX

I keep my reply simple, as I'm more convinced than ever that this message hasn't come from Teddy. If someone else is pretending to be him, he might really be in danger.

I stop in my tracks and call his number. He should pick up, as he's just messaged. The phone rings a couple of times, and then gets cut off.

Before I open up the apartment, I quickly scroll through his previous messages, the ones where he was pleading for help. When I read them all again, I come over hot and clammy. What if Teddy really is in trouble? I've been so engrossed in my new life, and what's happening here on the resort, that I haven't given it enough thought. If I don't hear back from him, or speak to him in person in the next couple of days, I might have no choice but to go to Marbella and check he's okay.

Once inside the apartment, I slam the door and bolt it top and bottom. I pour myself a generous measure of whisky before opening up the laptop. Having just spoken to Crystal, I need to plan the questions to ask her, and things I urgently want to find out. She's likely my best chance to move things forward. So far everything else has led to a dead end.

I dim the lights in the lounge, and draw the blinds on to the balcony. In case anyone is looking up. While I wait for my laptop to boot up, I message Damon. At this particular moment, there's no one I'd rather see. If only he didn't keep pestering me with texts and calls about when I was coming home, I might be persuaded that he was 'the one'.

> How's things? Been really busy. Hope you're looking after Mitzy 😊 XX

He replies straightaway. I imagine the phone glued to his side as he flicks through channels. Just like Teddy.

> Mitzy grand. When are you coming back? You said 3 months. Lonely here 😔 XX

I'm about to put his mind at rest, tell him another month tops, when he sends a second text.

> BTW… another threatening letter came for you. I'll screenshot and send it over. You really need to get out of there. Sending it now XX

I watch the screen, my insides knotted and my hands shaking, as I wait for the screenshot.

> Keep out of things that don't concern you. You've been warned…

My insides turn to liquid. Damon has been telling me all along that I'm playing with fire. Maybe he's right, and I need to get back to England and forget all about a scoop. Everything is getting too weird, and it's surely not worth putting my life at risk. If someone involved in a murder knows I'm a reporter, I could be in grave danger.

> Thanks for sending. I'll not hang around much longer. Big kisses to Mitzy XX

I'm about to turn the phone off when another message pops up.

> Sorry I couldn't pick up. Astrid got me clearing up. It's been a busy day. Talk soon S XX

I reply with a single thumbs-up, and then turn off the phone.

I take a large slug of whisky, feeling more relieved to have heard back from Teddy, though still unnerved by the use of the new signoff. Hopefully he'll phone me back tomorrow when he can talk properly.

I open up a new document, and start typing questions I want to ask Crystal. Like does she know anything about the men in the black 4X4 that seems to be following Jade round the resort? How vindictive is Avery likely to be? Should Jade be really worried, and how much does Avery know about what happened to his brother? And does Jade know about Avery's connection to Marbella?

I'm assuming Avery shares what he knows with Crystal, but I might be wrong. I need to find out more about their relationship, to help me understand what's going on.

And with my concerns about Teddy, I need to ask Crystal more about Marbella. Especially about Astrid Olsen, Teddy's employer.

I knock back the rest of my whisky, praying that I'll get some sleep. My unease over Astrid is growing again. I want to forget how she made me feel when I was at her villa, but it's all coming back.

73

Even though I'm exhausted, I can't settle. My mind is in overdrive.

I decide to drive round the resort. The chances of being breathalysed are slimmer than meeting another vehicle.

I head round to Avery's villa, dreading to think what he'll have said to Jade when he found her staying there. From what Crystal implied, he's got a dreadful temper. Likely he threw Jade and all her stuff onto the street.

I park across the road from the villa, in a side street from where I have a good view of the front of the property. It's so dark this end of the resort that no one could see me even if they were looking out.

Through the front window I see Crystal moving around, and assume Avery is inside as well. It's then I spot the little grey cat that has been visiting Jade every night since she's been staying there. She's religious in feeding it. Even from where I'm sitting I can see its bony little body shaking in the cold night air.

It's been growing in confidence since it first appeared on

Jade's doorstep. But tonight it's hovering near the gate. My heart breaks from watching, and I think of Mitzy.

I get out of the car, slink across the road and take it by surprise. Before it shoots off, I scoop it up and wrap it in the folds of my enormous kaftan.

There aren't too many possibilities where Jade is likely to have gone. There's a chance she'll stay in her office, but I doubt it. She'll not want the love interest, Marcus, catching her sleeping rough. My best bet is that she'll opt for the Ropers' place on Phase 1. She'll want to keep clear of the community that houses Avery's villa so as not to stoke the fire.

I plop the little furry creature on the back seat, cocoon him in my jumper and head up towards Phase 1.

Bingo. Jade's car is directly outside the Ropers'.

I park out of sight of the villa, and walk the short distance up the front path with the cat nestled in my kaftan, and when I reach the door, I gently set him down. Luckily the door is ajar, and his meowing gets louder.

The sight of the cat breaks my heart, but I daren't look back. I say a little prayer that Jade will hear it, and as I'm about to get back in my car, I see her. I hunker down and watch her race onto the street to see if anyone is around.

* * *

I manage a few hours' fitful sleep, but get up early, my mind swirling with everything I need to do.

I head out on to the balcony, and spot Marcus opening up. It's only 8.30, much earlier for him than usual, and as luck would have it Seamus is already at the kiosk.

Once I pull on the baggy sweatpants and enormous Oxford

University sweatshirt, settling the camouflage sunglasses on my head, I set off to join them.

Marcus, as I hoped, offers to buy me coffee, and we sit together by the kiosk.

He's not as chatty as usual, so I dive straight in to the cat issue.

'There are a lot of stray cats on the resort,' I say.

'You could say that.'

'Does no one look after them? Rescue them?'

'Jade's the only one who seems to care about them.' His eyes soften.

'She's been looking after one while she stayed at Avery Knowles's villa. He's back on the resort, you know.'

'I know. I wonder where she slept last night?'

He looks round, up and down the plaza, and round the side of the kiosk. I assume keeping an eye out for Jade. He's definitely got her bad.

'I feel guilty living in her apartment, especially if she has nowhere to stay.'

'Listen, don't worry about Jade. I've got a spare room if she gets desperate.'

'But she'll want to bring the cat with her. I thought you said you were allergic?'

'I am. I nearly died once through my allergy. But I doubt Jade will be more worried about housing the cat than having a roof over her own head.'

'Maybe so.'

This is where I think I've got the better measure of Jade than he does. She'll be desperate to look after the cat, and not being able to house it at Marcus's could be a deal breaker.

74

Next thing is to get my head in gear for meeting up with Crystal.

First I decide to walk round the resort, and clear my head for what's to come. I take a detour via the Ropers' villa, and Jade seems to have already left. No doubt on her way to work.

It's then I notice Russell, the maintenance guy, wandering round the property.

'Hi. You're up early,' I say, pausing to speak to him.

'Hi. Yes, work to do. I'm installing security cameras for the owners.'

You've got to be kidding me. Looks as if Jade won't be staying here much longer. If I play my cards right, this could speed up getting her to move in with me.

I don't linger, but carry on towards the clubhouse. The place is as usual very quiet, and I find Crystal on the terrace when I get there. At least there's no sign of Avery.

She doesn't look as chipper as she did last night. Again she's dressed for the tropics, but I notice her eyes are red and puffy.

'Are you okay?' I ask, setting my coffee down beside hers, and taking a seat opposite.

'Not too bad. I didn't sleep so well.'

When I raise an eyebrow, she jumps straight in, and tells me how dreadful things are with Avery.

'He's hidden my passport, my bank cards, and even my phone. Can you believe it? He's paranoid I'll leave him.'

'Really?' I'm shocked, but all ears. I knew Avery was a nasty piece of work, but this could be on a whole new scale. I certainly wasn't expecting such an outpouring.

When she lifts up her coffee, long fingers wrapping round the whole expanse of cup, I notice red marks on her wrist. When I check the other wrist, there seems to be a matching set.

'Yes, he did this.' She holds her arms out, turns them over so I can get a proper look.

'Oh, that's dreadful.'

I'm not sure what I was expecting. Certainly not this. I thought she was after a casual chat, some female company, but she seems desperate to share.

'Avery is getting worse. He's always been controlling, but he's getting obsessive. And this stuff with Jade isn't helping.'

I sit up a bit straighter.

'Yes, I hear he caught her staying in his villa without telling him. Not very clever.'

'It's worse than that. He's really out to destroy her, and when I told him to calm down and leave her alone, he did this.'

She holds out her wrists again to emphasise the point.

'Destroy her? In what way?' My heart is beating faster. This is where I wish I had a hidden tape recorder.

'Not content with ruining her business, he's hired tough guys to tail her round the resort and threaten her.'

'That's a bit extreme.' My eyes stand out on stalks. 'Couldn't he just demand payment, with interest perhaps, for her stay?'

Crystal lets out an unsettling laugh, before tugging out a couple of random hairs. I flinch.

'Oh, that's not Avery's style. He really means to destroy her, and wants her to suffer in the process.'

At this point I wonder if Crystal is going to tell me that Avery is the brother of the guy who was murdered in Marbella. When she opens up without me having to pry, I feel the adrenaline pumping.

'He knows that Jade was the last person to see his brother alive. Between you and me, I think he's after her blood. Do you know, she conned his brother out of quite a lot of money?'

'Really?' I try the wide-eyed astonished look, as if I don't already know this.

'I thought, wearing your reporter's hat, you might have found this out?'

She smiles at me, with a gurgle of laughter.

'Yes, Avery did mention something like that when I met him,' I admit.

'Anyway. I'm worried for Jade. I'm worried for myself, but I'm more prepared for what Avery's capable of. I'm not sure she is. Maybe we can both look out for her?'

'She doesn't talk to me, avoids me as much as she can. I think she's really jealous I'm living in her apartment, even more so now that she's got nowhere else to live.'

'If I tell her what Avery is up to, and he finds out, I dread to think what he'd do to me. I plan on leaving him once I get my documents back, but until then I'd best keep away from Jade.'

There's a few moments silence, as we're both locked in our own thoughts.

'By the way,' she says, 'is your brother still living with Astrid Olsen?'

'Yes. Why?' I can hardly breathe. So much stuff is being thrown at me, but the dots aren't immediately connecting.

'She's a crazy bitch,' Crystal says. Although I agree with her, it's unnerving hearing her say it. Crystal looks so willowy, and fragile, that it's hard to imagine her bad-mouthing anyone. Well, anyone other than Avery.

'Do you think my brother could be in danger?'

'I wouldn't put it past her. Especially if she finds out he's related to a reporter. Astrid doesn't like to be double-crossed, that much I do know.'

Holy shit. The worries about Teddy come flooding back. If I can't speak to him over the phone soon, I'll have no choice but to go to Marbella. There's likely no one else looking out for him.

'And, if you can, I'd warn Jade to be on her guard,' Crystal says, staring at me intently.

75

The conversation with Crystal has ratcheted up the fear. The one thing it's confirmed is that I don't want to hang around here forever. If I don't make headway soon, I'll have to head back to the UK.

The good news though is that Jade finally agreed to move in with me, after a bit of cat shenanigans on my part. I admit leaving her cat outside Marcus's finca was a bit over the top, but it seems to have worked in highlighting that living with Marcus, even in the short term, isn't an option. She seems determined to keep the cat with her, and I couldn't help but sense Marcus's relief when she finally accepted my offer.

Teddy has responded to several more texts, telling me everything is fine, but I still can't get him to pick up when I call. I've decided to speak to Crystal again and ask whether she thinks I should head over to Marbella. The thing that worries me, really worries me, is that if I turn up and Teddy is in danger, I might also be in the firing line. The threatening letters that came to my flat, the ones that Damon has, aren't helping. It's as if I'm in someone's sights too.

Even if Jade is under threat from Avery, I might be in even greater danger from Astrid. Especially if she's found out I'm a reporter, and a reporter now working undercover in Murcia alongside Jade.

Damon is constantly at me to come home. He's picking up on how scared I am, but his endless reminding me of the threatening letters isn't helping. He's hell-bent on persuading me to come back.

From where I'm sitting, there's more than a kernel of doubt about returning. Whoever is sending those letters knows my UK address, but there's no evidence they know I'm here in Murcia. For now, I might be best to stay put.

* * *

Jade has now been staying with me in the apartment for the past couple of days, sleeping in what she calls 'the cell', and making me feel like a squatter who has illegally taken up ownership of her apartment. And she still won't talk to me.

Whenever I try to engage in conversation, she clams up. If I mention Marcus, try to draw her out, she clams up even more. I'm hoping she'll get more upbeat when things hot up with Marcus and, although I want to warn her about Avery, I've no idea how to warn her she might be in grave danger without blowing my cover. She knows he's after her, but has no idea of his real reasons.

I also know that Crystal is planning to put down a deposit on a penthouse apartment, and is buying through Jade. I have no idea why Crystal doesn't get as far away from Avery as possible, but who knows? Crystal is friendly, but definitely very weird. All I'm hoping is that if she does buy a property, it might mean a chance to get Jade to talk. I've got champagne on ice to share, and hopefully her tongue will loosen over a glass or two in celebration. I'm banking on it.

This afternoon, I'm meeting up again with Crystal, before getting off the resort for a rare trip into Cartagena to clear my head. I've booked a cheap Airbnb in the old town, as I intend to get drunk, and unwind. Try to forget everything, if only for a few hours. It won't be easy, but I need a break from looking at the four walls of the apartment.

Jade is going out with Marcus, likely not coming back if I've read the situation correctly. One day at a time is my new motto, and if I'm not going to be here much longer, I might as well make the most of it.

Before I head off, I feed Gato and lock him in the flat. He's fickle like his owner, and it's hard not to smile when he makes a beeline for my lap rather than Jade's. At least he's calmed down, and his purring brings comfort.

I lock up, and drive the short distance to the clubhouse. As I'm about to get out, I see Avery wander round the back of the car park. My first thought is at least he'll be out of Crystal's hair for a few hours.

Instead of going through the main entrance, I decide to follow Avery. I suddenly stop in my tracks, and duck behind a wall. Avery is standing alongside the black 4X4 that has been cruising round the resort, and talking to the driver. They shake hands, and Avery pats the guy on the back and hands over what looks like a bulging envelope.

Before Avery turns, I manage to slip off through the passageway that leads up to the clubhouse terrace. My heart pumps as I climb the stairs. It looks as if the guys in the black car might be in the employ of Avery. My first thought is that he might have hired them to keep tabs on Jade. But from their appearance, the guys aren't undercover detectives. They're tough, fierce, and sinister looking. Goodness knows what Avery has in mind.

I certainly wouldn't want to be in Jade's shoes, as she's likely their target.

76

When I reach the terrace, Crystal is sitting at a table that overlooks the small practice putting green.

'Hi. It's good to see you again. Cava?' She offers from a half-drunk bottle, her hand shaking as she lifts it up.

'No, thanks. I'll stick to water.' I set down my own half-drunk bottle of Evian water, and sit opposite.

Although I'm feeling anxious, the level having rocketed since I saw Avery in the car park, Crystal looks distraught. She fiddles with strands of hair between sips, and when she rests a hand on her throat, my eyes are drawn to a small but defined bruise on her neck.

'Oh, Crystal. Did Avery do that?' I point.

'Who else?' She sighs. 'Anyway, I'll soon be shot of him.'

'You're definitely going to leave? I thought I heard somewhere that you're thinking of buying an apartment on the resort?'

'I'd love to, but between you and me...' She looks around, leans in closer. 'It's the only way I can think of to get my passport back off Avery.'

'Oh. I did wonder why you'd want to buy an apartment on the same resort as him.'

'He's thrilled that I might have enough money to buy the penthouse. He's even suggested that this would allow him to sell the villa, and we could live there instead. Can you believe he thinks I'd want to stay with him?'

'So he'll give you back your documents to secure a new property.'

'Yes. Got it in one. Anyway, how's things your end?'

Where do I start?

'To be honest, I'm still really worried about Teddy. I'm thinking of going to Marbella to see if he's okay. What do you think?'

'When? When are you thinking of going?'

'Soon. Do you think I should?'

Her brow furrows. Strange she's asked *when* I'm thinking of going, as I'm more after advice if I should go at all.

'I'm more worried for you than your brother. I'm sure he'll be able to look after himself. Don't put yourself in danger for some man.' She leans across and puts a hand over mine.

I wonder if she might know he's not my brother, but an ex-boyfriend instead. If she googled properly, she likely found out more about me than she's letting on.

Although she's got a caring expression, I feel unsettled. She hasn't put my mind at rest by saying Teddy should be okay. Instead, I'm even more flustered, as I'm picking up her concern for my wellbeing. She really seems to believe I might be in danger.

We chat a while longer about this and that before I leave.

'It was lovely to chat. Stay safe,' Crystal says. 'By the way, whereabouts are you staying in Cartagena?'

I keep it vague, saying some random Airbnb in the old sector. It seems a strange parting question, but not as strange as her asking next when I'll be back. Before I can respond, she tugs out a strand of hair.

'I wish I could come too. And we could escape together,' she says.

77

Talking to Crystal hasn't helped. Her warnings about looking after myself, rather than Teddy, has made things worse. What if the black car has its sights on me? Avery has definitely hired them for some reason. What if they're after me, and not Jade?

As I set off for Cartagena, I'm more confused than ever. Crystal has made me question the sanity of going to Marbella. Now I've no idea what to do. My reporter logic isn't helping, because although I might have the bones of a great story, it's nowhere near the end. *The Murder on the Marbella Roof Terrace* feels more like just the beginning.

Also, I feel really sorry for Jade. She'll be thrilled that Crystal wants to buy the penthouse, but I dread how she'll feel when the sale falls through. I'm in a quandary whether I should tell her the truth, or let it play out.

Yet I reckon my allegiance must be to Crystal. Getting her passport back might be her only shot to escape from Avery. He's coming across as dangerously unhinged. The thought that he's hired professional hitmen makes things ten times worse.

Twenty-five minutes later, and I'm pulling up into the port.

Once I've parked, I get out my phone and google *cosy bars overlooking the harbour*. After a ten-minute walk, I'm sitting by the window of a bar called Hannibal's. Apparently Hannibal arrived in Cartagena to prepare for war, before travelling across the Alps with thirty-seven elephants in tow. Jade once shared this titbit from her encyclopaedic quiz trivia knowledge.

As the drink slips down, I slowly unwind. It's good to be off the resort. Maybe things will work out okay after all. I've got Damon waiting for me (with, okay, a bit too much pestering and eagerness for me to come home), and I've got the bones of a great story. As the Viña Sol slips hits the spot, I consider that I might soon have enough, if not for a prize-winning scoop, an attention-grabbing headline at least. The way I'm feeling, this might be a safer route. The threats and macabre goings-on are all too much. Part of me wonders whether I really should just walk away.

Anyway, time enough to decide where to go with it. For tonight, at least, I'm starting to feel more like my old, more positive self.

It's nearly eleven when I next check my phone. There are a series of texts from a number I don't recognise.

My heart speeds up, and a sharp pain shoots through me. My fingers are trembling so much, it's hard to scroll.

> You need to help me. I can't get out. Teddy
>
> PLEASE. Send help!
>
> She's crazy.
>
> She knows
>
> HELP

I stab at the phone, trying to call the number, again and

again, but there's no response. I send a message, not holding out hope for a reply.

I look round the bar, now packed with tourists and locals, but no one is looking my way. I don't know why I think someone might be, but I'm now dripping in perspiration and my guts are heaving. I flap a hand up and down in front of my face.

Teddy. He's in real trouble. Deep down I knew things weren't good, but was hoping from all the recent texts that it was just my imagination working overtime.

What if Teddy let slip to Astrid in a drunken moment that he overheard what she told the woman on the plane? The woman I'm now guessing was most likely Jade. And what if he let on that his sister also knows? If Astrid has found out I'm not his sister, but an old girlfriend, and a reporter, then I'm not sure which of us will be in the greatest danger.

I shake the bottle of Viña Sol... praying there's some left, so that I'm not too drunk to drive back. But it's empty. I can't risk getting in the car tonight.

So much for relaxing, letting go of the angst. I have to find out what's going on, and get help to Teddy.

We may be finished as a couple, but we go back a long way.

* * *

The cold sea air is biting, and it's hard to breathe as I walk back through the old town to my Airbnb.

I keep trying both Teddy's old number as well as the one that has just sent the messages. But there's nothing. Teddy's usual phone goes direct to voicemail, and the other number no longer seems to be in use.

I try to call Damon, but it's late and he doesn't pick up. I send an urgent message asking him to get back, but he'll likely not pick up till morning.

Everything will have to wait until tomorrow. Maybe Marcus can help, advise me what to do when I tell him my ex-boyfriend could be in real danger. It might be the time to tell him the whole story, the truth. Even if it jeopardises my chances of getting anything out of Jade. But none of that matters now if Teddy's life is in danger.

Someone must be able to help. There's also Crystal. When I show her the new messages, she might see why I'm so worried. Although she doesn't want me to put myself in danger, at least she already knows the whole story.

All of a sudden I freeze. The side alley leading to my accommodation is deserted, but I've a feeling I'm being followed. When I stop every few steps, I'm certain that footsteps behind pull up as well. I sober up pretty quickly, as my throat constricts and palpitations pound in my chest.

Who could be after me? I'm off the resort. Unless someone followed me here. But who? Why? The only person who knew I was coming was Crystal. And Damon, whom I texted earlier.

The lock on the apartment door is faulty, and for an awful moment I don't think I can open up. My head is spinning, and I'm scared I'm going to throw up.

I finally manage to turn the key, and once inside, I slam the door and pull across top and bottom bolts. I collapse against the door frame, and realise my whole body is convulsing.

It's nearly midnight. I pray for a few hours' sleep. But before I pull the duvet round, I send a last text to Crystal.

> Are you around in the morning? It's urgent. It's about my brother.

The message goes through, but ten minutes passes and it still goes unread.

I've no choice now but to wait until morning.

78

I manage a few hours of fitful sleep, but by 6 a.m. I'm wide awake. My head is thumping, along with my heart, and my mouth is sawdust dry. The first thing I do is grab my phone to check for messages. There's nothing more from Teddy, but there's one from Crystal sent just ten minutes ago.

> Of course. I'm not going anywhere. Text when and where to meet 😊

The message should make me feel better, but I don't think I could feel any worse. There's no noise anywhere, which makes my isolation feel even more sinister. Damon hasn't got back to my panicked texts, but how can he help when he's in England? He'll only tell me to forget about Teddy anyway.

After a mug of instant coffee, and a quick shower, I'm back on the motorway. For some reason I keep checking my rear-view mirror, an illogical fear that someone is on my tail. My pulse is racing, and I feel ill from both the hangover and the watery coffee.

When I come off the motorway and take the single dirt track that leads to the resort I see a large car on my bumper. It's the black 4X4 that's been stalking Jade round the resort. The one with the hard men that Avery organised to put the fear of God into her. I recognise the men through my mirror. What are they doing here at this hour? Oh my God. Has Crystal let slip to Avery what I'm up to? No. No. No. She said she wouldn't, but I no longer know who to believe. Are they coming after me now?

I try to quell the shaking in my body, gripping the steering wheel with white knuckles. I need to hold it together, and pray they drive past.

The car tailgates me as far as the roundabout by the resort entrance. Then it slows down, and pulls over into the side of the road.

I speed up, and careen through the security barrier which is already raised. It's only 7.30, and there's no sign of Santiago. Anyone could be coming and going.

I'm desperate to get to the apartment, and close the door against the world. I'm becoming more paranoid by the minute. Hopefully Jade will be asleep, although I'm praying she went back with Marcus, as she's the last thing I need right now. If I can get a couple of hours' shuteye before I meet up with Crystal, and plan a trip to Marbella, I'm hoping the paranoia will have lessened.

The resort is even more deserted than usual. There isn't even the sighting of a security guard. When I reach the Spanish Village, I park up and crawl out of the car. When a cat shoots past, I nearly jump out of my skin. I come over dizzy, and fall back against the car. Something is off kilter.

It's a sixth sense that someone is watching me. But who? Maybe the hard guys have driven the long way round the resort, and are heading my way? Perhaps they got here before me. The thought that they might have been on my tail all the way from Cartagena punches me in the gut. I've never felt more scared in my life.

Then suddenly the quiet is shattered by a bloodcurdling scream. Then by another. And another. And another...

79

Putting one foot in front of the other is really tough, as my legs have the consistency of noodles and it's hard to stay upright.

I throw my hands over my ears when the screaming starts up again. As I inch towards the apartment block, it gets louder.

Once through the heavy fire door, I cling to the railings and manage slowly to climb the stairs. Although the piercing screams have died down, I pick up the steady hum of a whimper. And it's coming from just outside the apartment.

The front door is thrown wide, and my eyes are drawn to a patch of red gunge by the entrance. It's then I hear a meowing sound from behind the door.

'Gabby?'

I nearly jump out of my skin when I hear the voice behind me. I swivel round, and then I see her. It's Jade, slumped in a heap in the corner opposite the entrance to the apartment.

'Jade? Oh my God. What's happened?'

I know I should look through the open door for myself but I'm petrified. I've never been more pleased to see anyone in my life. Even if it is Jade.

'They're dead. There's blood everywhere.'

I'm not sure I've heard correctly, as she's whispering and her head is hung between her knees. She's rocking from side to side.

'Who's dead?'

I put a shaky hand on her shoulder.

'I don't know. But I've never seen so much blood. I thought it was you.'

She turns her head to the side and heaves.

'Who? Who is it then? Who is dead?' I repeat.

She simply shakes her head.

It's then I see Gato cowering over the red gunge that has spilled out onto the landing. His little tongue is slurping greedily.

I put a hand round my throat and inch slowly forward until I reach the door. When I look inside, I throw my guts up, just as Gato shoots off down the stairs.

It takes me only a few seconds to see what's happened. Someone has been bludgeoned to death with my brass cat doorstop. The one Damon bought me for Christmas. His face pops into my head.

It takes a few seconds more to work out who the victim is.

'No. No. No,' I scream, frightened by my own howl.

The body, bludgeoned to death, is Teddy's. Although he's barely recognisable, with blood splattered all over his face and torso, and it's almost impossible to make out his features.

Through the coating of blood on his face, he has the look of a person long dead. There's no sign of his trademark freckles, and his lips are white, his hair long and straggly. An unkempt beard could have been stuck on.

I slump on the floor alongside him. I'm so numb, I can't cry. Worse still, I seem to have lost my voice. There's a faint shuffle of feet behind me.

'Who is it?' Jade asks.

'Teddy. It's Teddy.'

'Who's Teddy?'

'My boyfriend.'

If she'd asked me this yesterday, I'd have said my ex. But looking at Teddy now, all the memories flash in and out.

'Boyfriend? I didn't realise.'

She lays a hand on my shoulder. She has no idea who Teddy is. Or that he was staying with Astrid in Marbella. Or that he overheard the whole story Astrid told her on the plane back to Luton.

'There's a lot you don't know. Like the fact my name isn't Gabby. It's Hayley.'

She stares at me. The terror in her eyes mirrors my own.

Whatever she thinks, and whatever she wants to do, we're in as deep shit as each other.

80

I stay by Teddy's side as Jade goes back downstairs to call the police.

It's then I notice a mobile sticking out of Teddy's jacket pocket. I prise it out, wipe the screen with my sleeve, and slip it into my own zipped pocket. I need to see what's on it, find my own clues as to who might have killed him.

Suddenly it strikes like a thunderbolt that I'm going to be a prime suspect. If not *the* prime suspect. The body has been found in the apartment where I'm staying, but more importantly, as Teddy's ex-girlfriend, I'll be top of the list.

As soon as I get a moment, I'll stash the phone somewhere safe. It's likely the one he used to send the panicked messages last night. I can show the police the messages on my phone. That should be enough to lead them back to Marbella.

Hopefully the time of death will have been when I was in Cartagena. Thank God I was off the resort, and have enough of an alibi to have been nowhere near the crime scene.

I struggle up, and with a last glance back at Teddy, I slither across the bloodied slime, grabbing the door handle to steady myself. As I collapse in the corner at the top of the stairs, the world spins around me. I can hardly breathe.

But soon my mind goes into overdrive. Damon. I need to phone Damon. Maybe he can come and stay with me until I'm allowed to go. Who knows how long I'll be here if I'm a suspect?

Then I remember the letters sent to my flat in London, letters addressed to me, warning me to be careful. Damon could bring them with him. They'll show I was being threatened and might help clear my name.

As the clump of heavy boots sounds on the stairwell, I start to whistle, and rock from side to side. I must look really crazy, with my mad uncombed purple hair, and my clothes streaked in blood. I shouldn't have touched the body, but it was Teddy, and I had to say goodbye.

While I wait for the police to appear, I wonder how much Jade will work out. She has no idea what has been going on, and that I'm a reporter. Until now she'd never heard of Teddy, let alone my ex-boyfriend's connection to Marbella. And to Astrid Olsen.

Teddy must have done something really bad to piss Astrid off. I should have helped him. But it's now too late. The tears stream silently down my cheeks, and my body convulses in fear.

If Astrid had Teddy killed, who knows? I could be next.

81

JADE

I have no idea how I manage to get down the stairs. My hands are slimy, coated in traces of blood, and gripping the handrail is impossible.

My immediate thought is to call the police, but I can't remember the Spanish number. Then I spot Marcus walking towards me. He speeds up when he sees the state I'm in.

'Jade? What's wrong?'

I collapse into his arms, and point.

'Up there. You need to call the police.'

'Oh my God. Is it Gabby?'

'No, it's some guy. He's dead.'

Marcus takes me across to the kiosk, orders me to sit down, and races back up to the apartment.

I'm shaking like a leaf, no idea what to do. My mind is all over the place. And what the hell did Gabby mean that isn't her real name? She mentioned something about being called Hayley? I know she's in shock, but what was that all about?

Seamus turns up next, followed shortly after by an army of

police cars. All I can see is the blood. It was everywhere. I look down at my feet, and my shoes have a caking of red over them.

Despite the shock, it hits that I might be a suspect. It's my apartment, and I'd recently moved back in. My stuff is there, as well as Gabby's... Hayley's... whoever the hell she is.

I sit for what seems like an eternity outside the kiosk. Seamus forces me to drink a mug of sweet tea to cushion the shock. Although he's now looking more shocked than I must. He keeps asking what happened, but I've absolutely no clue.

Marcus reappears first from the apartment block, followed by Gabby being supported by two policewomen, one either side. As she's led off for questioning, a policeman tells me to go nowhere. He'll be back.

'Come and wait in my office,' Marcus says, taking my hand and leading the way.

When the door is closed behind us, I burst into tears, sobbing until I can no longer breathe. I can't comprehend what's just happened. Who is Teddy? Why was he killed? And why in my apartment? And where was Gabby at the time? Could she have killed her own boyfriend?

If she's been lying about her name, goodness knows what else she's been lying about.

82

It's now seven in the evening. Somehow I've held it together, and not been led away in handcuffs.

The police have been swarming like ants around the crime scene, and have questioned everyone in pidgin English, everyone being anyone they were able to track down. Even Santiago from the security hut was interrogated. We've all been instructed to stay put, and no one is to leave the resort. I'm surprised Gabby and I haven't been locked up in a cell, as we're the ones who found the body. I find it hard to think of her as Hayley, but that's now what the police are calling her.

Marcus hasn't left my side all day. But I'm now desperate for air, and to escape the claustrophobic confines of his office.

He reluctantly watches me leave, making me promise not to be too long.

I take the back route towards the clubhouse, the only place I can think of that I might find Hayley. If I'm feeling bad, she must be a dozen times worse, as the dead body was a boyfriend. Albeit one she's never mentioned.

The clubhouse is empty, but as soon as I step out on to the freezing cold terrace, I spot her at the far end, her head in her hands and slumped on the tabletop.

'Hayley?' I ask, the name feeling strange on my lips.

She manages to lift her head a couple of centimetres, and grunts.

'Are you okay?' I ask. Silly question, as she looks as if she's heading off to the gallows. Her face is red and swollen, her eyes puffy, and she's hard to recognise.

'Not really,' she says. Even the two words seem such an effort.

I pull out a seat, amazed how all of a sudden I'm the calm one.

'Who was Teddy?' I ask. 'Want to tell me about him? You said he was your boyfriend.'

I sound like a very professional policewoman, interrogating a traumatised witness. But I'm desperate to know what's going on, and Hayley, whoever she is, needs to talk.

When I pat her on the arm, she stiffens, and somehow manages to pull her head up from a slump position. She avoids eye contact, and starts mumbling.

'He was my ex-boyfriend.'

'Ex? Oh. I'm really sorry.'

She puts her palms over her eyes and face. Her fingers are so shapely, her nails painted a pale pink. Again I wonder why she doesn't make more of an effort with the rest of her appearance. Who the hell is she?

'Don't be. We were finished. It's a long story.'

'Try me.'

I stare at her, willing her to give me something. She takes forever to respond, as if she's trying to work out how much to tell me.

'He was working in Spain. My new boyfriend, Damon, tried to get me to come home. He said I was in danger.'

'You were in danger?' I start to come over clammy, waiting as if for some macabre punchline. Why would she have been in danger?

'Damon received letters to our flat in London, warning me that I should leave Spain. I wish I had left.'

She now starts to rock backwards and forwards.

'Why did he think you were in danger? Why were you being threatened?'

Her eyes look into mine, before she looks back down at the table. It's like getting blood from a stone. She doesn't want to talk, and is definitely hiding something.

'Will he come out to join you? It'll be tough on your own.'

'I hoped he would. I've asked him to come, bring the threatening letters with him. They might give clues as to who killed Teddy. But...'

'Go on.' I touch her arm again, but she pulls it away, and wraps both arms round her chest.

'He doesn't think it would be a good idea for him to get involved. But he'll be waiting for me.' She starts to cry again, tears flooding out through puffy slits. 'He was really jealous of Teddy.'

'Oh my God. Do you think he might have killed Teddy? Could he already be here in Spain?'

I'm now sitting bolt upright. This must be a lead for the police. A jealous lover, desperate to get rid of the competition. Perhaps Hayley was getting back together with her ex?

I'm waiting for her to carry on, but she's taking forever to form any words. She also seems to be having trouble breathing.

There's a moment's flicker behind her eyes, as if she's about to tell me something more – perhaps confirm my suggestion that

Damon might have murdered her ex – when the terrace door opens.

Avery Knowles appears, stares in our direction, and raises a hand in greeting. He's grinning from ear to ear, as if he's won some sort of contest.

83

I wait till he goes back inside, and then ask a catatonic Hayley if she'd like a stiff whisky. She manages a nod and a wan smile.

I breathe more easily, thinking Avery has gone, until I spot him by the exit talking to a golfer. He pokes his colleague and points my way, and then bursts out laughing. When he holds up his hand and waves at me, it's all I can do not to march across and punch his lights out. Although he's laughing, even from this distance, I sense menace in his slitty eyes and know I need to ignore him.

I turn my back, slump my elbows on the bar counter, and ask Javier for two large tumblers of whisky. I nearly jump out of my skin when a hand lands on my shoulder. A yelp escapes, at the thought that Avery is behind me.

'Jade. Are you okay? I heard what happened. It's so dreadful.'

Thank God it's Crystal.

'Sorry. I was miles away.'

'What a shock. Listen, I'll come out and join you. Give me a minute. Avery has gone, thank goodness,' she says.

I check the exit where Avery was standing, and breathe more easily when there's no sign of him.

'That would be good. Hayley's in a dreadful state.'

It takes a moment, but Crystal doesn't react when I use the name. Perhaps word has already travelled round the resort that the woman in my flat isn't all she seems. Anyway, it'll be good to have back-up when trying to cheer Hayley up. And back-up in trying to make her talk.

Crystal holds the terrace door open, while I carry the whisky tumblers. The terrace is dimly lit by candlelight, and large lanterns dotted round the place aim for a romantic vibe. But rather than romantic, the dull glow is like the set of a horror movie.

Hayley's face lights up a bit at the sight of Crystal, and we're soon circling the table like a coven of witches.

Crystal tries to cheer us both up, but is far from relaxed. She asks us both about what happened, what the police are saying, in between bouts of hair tugging. She manages to yank out a couple of clumps before I decide I can't take much more.

Strangely, Crystal seems much friendlier with Hayley than with me. It could be down to greater sympathy for someone whose ex-boyfriend has been murdered, but it feels more than that. It's as if they're good friends.

Before I've a chance to make my excuses, Crystal gets in first and says she had better get back to Avery.

'He doesn't like to be on his own too long.' She gives a wry smile.

I bet he doesn't. Why the heck does she stay with the guy? It's beyond me. I doubt after today, she'll want to go ahead with buying the penthouse. But for the moment Crystal's problems with Avery are the last thing on my mind.

She hugs me and Hayley in turn, Hayley getting a more

intense clinch, before leaving via the outside stairs rather than through the clubhouse.

'Did you see the bruises?'

It takes a second to realise the whisper has come from Hayley, although I know instantly what she's talking about. The marks around Crystal's neck and wrists couldn't be missed. They're the worst I've seen.

'Yes. They look dreadful. And what about the bruise on her cheek?'

'It's Avery. She's really scared of him,' she says. How she knows this makes me feel uneasy. I know Avery is a nasty piece of work, but it's as if Crystal has been confiding in Hayley. It's not that I need to be anyone's confidante, but theirs is an unlikely friendship.

'I don't get why she doesn't cover the marks up though. Do you?' I ask.

Hayley simply shrugs, before letting her head collapse once again on top of her arms.

84

When Marcus appears on the terrace, I don't think I've ever been more relieved to see anyone.

'Hi, ladies. You okay?'

He throws his arms wide to offer comfort hugs, and I know I shouldn't be, but I'm peeved when he embraces Hayley first. Likely she looks more vulnerable, and I have to remind myself that the bloodied corpse was her boyfriend. Current or ex, it doesn't really matter.

'Listen. I've got the car outside. What say we head over to my place, and get some shuteye.'

If he'd proposed marriage I couldn't have been more thrilled, except when I realise the offer is for both Hayley and me.

'We're not supposed to leave the resort,' she says, trying to snivel quietly.

'I've driven round the resort, and there's no sign of the police. The apartment is cordoned off, but that's about it. I doubt they'll be back until morning.'

'If you're sure, then I'm game.' More than game. Perhaps he can whisk me off to the airport for a quick getaway.

Hayley looks unsure, and I don't like to ask what her alternative sleeping arrangements might be. Crystal disappeared pretty sharpish, and it didn't look as if she offered Hayley a bed for the night. Likely Avery wouldn't have allowed it anyway.

She gives Marcus a strange look, and for a minute I think she's going to turn down his offer.

'Thanks,' she says. 'I've got nowhere else to go.'

'I slipped Santiago a few euros, plus a year's supply of tortilla chips. So he shouldn't be a problem,' Marcus says with a sheepish grin.

I could hug him, especially when Hayley manages a weak smile.

When I ask Marcus if he's seen Gato, and he tells me there's been no trace, Hayley offers to spend all of tomorrow trying to track him down.

'I'll have nothing else to do.'

The three of us creep down the back stairs, opting like Crystal did to avoid the clubhouse and make for the car park that way. Mine and Hayley's cars are still parked there, so it's unlikely anyone will suspect we've left the resort.

Marcus tells us to keep our heads down as we drive towards the exit. He slows as we near the security kiosk. Santiago pulls back the glass window, and has a quick word with Marcus.

'Be back no later than 7.30,' he says, before letting us through.

'Thanks.'

We drive the two kilometres to Marcus's isolated finca in silence, but it's such a relief to be off the resort that the desert landscape couldn't feel more inviting.

My mind is in overdrive from everything that's happened. Although being with Marcus feels safe, I'm not sure about Hayley. She sits in the front, and I gawp at her profile. Her weird hair. Her ugly clothes. And it dawns on me that this is all part of some manufactured disguise. It must be, and is likely linked to her going by a different name. She isn't Gabby, but Hayley. Who the hell is she?

Then I come over doubly nauseous when it crosses my mind that perhaps she's the one who murdered Teddy. Maybe the disguise is linked to his death. She says she was off the resort all night, and only got back when she found the body. Maybe she's lying? I've no idea what is going on, or what to believe.

I can't bear trying to prise anything more out of her. Not tonight. She's totally clammed up, and although I'm desperate to ask more questions, I'm sort of glad she's not talking. The events have been so chilling, I'm near to collapse from exhaustion.

When we arrive at the finca, Hayley looks all around, and hesitates before getting out. She gives Marcus another questioning look. What is her problem now?

When Marcus opens the passenger door, she tentatively steps out on to the pitted landscape. As Marcus strides ahead to open up, she walks hesitantly beside me.

He ignores our requests for more whisky, and insists instead on making us warm tea laden with sugar.

'Right, girls. You need a good night's sleep. You can have a bedroom each, and I'll sleep on the sofa.'

I'd prefer to snuggle up with Marcus, but romance is completely off the table. Even comfort hugs are a futile hope.

Hayley slumps on the sofa while Marcus goes outside to repark the car. I've still no idea why he does this; he's certainly got some weird traits. Hayley's eyes follow him, and I pick up her unease. What the heck is her problem with Marcus now?

To make small talk, I confide in her that Marcus is a somnambulist. Talking about anything other than murder seems like a good idea, to take her mind off events for even a few minutes. She's so traumatised that she looks like a bloodless corpse.

'What's that?' she asks.

'Marcus is a sleepwalker. I found out when I stayed here.'

'Really? That's a bit scary.' She shivers, her unease notching up a gear as her hands develop a steady tremor.

'It was. Hopefully he'll not wander into either of our bedrooms.'

I giggle, desperate to lighten the mood, but Hayley looks horrified.

'He'd bloody better not.'

Funny. I'm sort of hoping he does. As long as it's into my bedroom, and not Hayley's.

'Jade, I'm sorry about everything.'

'It's not your fault.'

It is so her fault, but now isn't the time to point fingers. She's in such a state, and I'm glad not to be in her shoes. Not knowing Teddy should surely put me in the clear as a suspect, but not so much her.

A few minutes before Marcus reappears, she takes a deep breath. My insides somersault, guessing she's about to say something important.

'It's probably not the time to worry you, but...'

'Yes?' I nod, willing her to hurry up. What the hell is she going to say? I sense it's not good news, for me at any rate.

'It's Avery.'

'What about Avery?'

'He's got it in for you. Just be careful.'

I let out a deep sigh. Is that it?

'I know he's pissed off that I stayed in his villa, and is trying to ruin my business. But I'm not going to give up.'

'It's more than that. Crystal says he's after your blood. He's really out to get you.' She emphasises the word *really*. 'The black 4X4 on the resort. They're Avery's men. Crystal is worried Avery might go too far to get revenge.'

'How the hell can he be so vindictive over a few weeks' illegal squatting in his villa? And what do you mean too far?'

I'm pretty snappy, fed up that Hayley has brought all this up now.

'It's just...'

'Just what?'

'I might be mad for thinking it... but.' She swallows hard, and I'm now doubly snappy. As if there isn't enough to worry about without her making it ten times worse.

I start counting down from 100 before she manages to spit it out.

'I wonder if the guys in the black car might be hired assassins.'

'Hired assassins?' You've got to be kidding me. 'Hired to kill me?' I burst out laughing.

But Hayley looks deadly serious. I know she's traumatised by what's happened, but it's as if she wants me to match her fear and misery. Bloody hell.

She simply nods, and starts to sniff.

'Maybe I shouldn't have said anything,' she adds. 'It's just Crystal emphasised that Avery can be really vindictive.'

She emphasises the word *really* for a second time.

I wish she hadn't told me her opinions. Now I'm doubly freaking. The first thing I'm wondering is why Crystal didn't warn me in such dramatic tones about her ghastly boyfriend. She and Hayley seem weirdly close.

I'm about to lose my rag, and yell at her to find out what else she knows. I'm definitely missing huge pieces of the puzzle. But hired assassins?

When I look towards the door of the finca, Marcus is standing there. Looks as if he might have heard our whole conversation. I know he dislikes Avery, warning me to keep well clear, but even from this distance I notice a pulse throbbing in his neck, and his clenched jaw. I know he's got my back, but he looks really angry. Hopefully he'll not punch Avery's lights out if he oversteps the mark.

Hayley has now completely clammed up, and won't be saying any more in front of Marcus. Instead she hauls herself up off the sofa.

Looks as if I'll not get anything more out of her tonight, and have no choice but to follow Marcus's orders when he tells us both to get to bed.

'You ladies need your sleep. Tomorrow will be a long day,' he says, looking from me to Hayley and back again. His usual soft expression has been replaced by a hard set to the mouth.

Poor Marcus. We're all he needs.

85

Soon the place is in silence. The finca has the atmosphere of a morgue, no sound coming from inside or out. Thankfully Marcus doesn't sleepwalk this time, although when he starts to mumble in his sleep, the noise gives me mild comfort. As I'm about to drift off, Hayley starts to snore. Large guttural grunts.

How the hell can they both sleep? I lie and ruminate, totally exhausted but unable to give in. Thoughts are rattling round and round in my head.

After everything that's happened, I know I need to give up my Spanish dream and get back to the UK. Losing all the money I got from Isaac (I still can't come to thinking of him as George Stubbs) seems a small price to pay for my safety. Fear is one thing, but dead bodies are something else entirely.

Hayley's theory about hired assassins is like something out of *Day of the Jackal*. I'd likely have laughed it off, if she hadn't been so intense with her warning.

If the police hadn't imprisoned us on the resort, I'd likely have booked the first flight back to the UK. But as the body was found in my apartment, I doubt I'll be booking a flight any time soon.

At least the Pedersens have paid their deposit (to Marcus, of course), and he's promised to pay half into my account in the morning.

I can't help the silent flood of tears when I go over it all. Who am I kidding? Crystal is unlikely to want to buy the penthouse now, after everything that's happened. Recalling her bruises reminds me how psycho Avery might actually be.

I go over a list of things I need to do in the short term before I can leave Spain. I've a leaden feeling in my stomach that it won't be so easy to leave everything behind. After what happened in Marbella, this was meant to be a fresh start. But death has followed me. Who's to say it won't come back to the UK? And who's to say I'll even make it that far?

I try and focus my thoughts to distract myself from the real or imagined threats, and work through the practicalities. I need to contact all my clients, again, and make sure their properties are shipshape. The place will soon get busier, and if I keep myself occupied, perhaps I can survive the next few weeks.

The only thing that will be hard to leave behind is Marcus. Another time, another place, he could have been my future.

My mind whirrs with everything. In the quiet of the finca, with miles of uninhabited landscape outside, the fear and paranoia grip. I suddenly remember Crystal telling me that she and Avery been told to seek me out, recommended by Carlos the property agent in Marbella. Teddy, Hayley's boyfriend, was working in Spain. She also knew that I was living in Marbella.

That's when it strikes with certainty. The link to everything must be Marbella.

The one thing I can think of that might tie us all together is Casa de Astrid.

Suddenly the night terrors are back, and it's as if I'm locked inside the villa with Isaac all over again.

86

We get up at the crack of dawn, none of us talking much, anxious to get back on the resort.

While Marcus pops out briefly to fill up with petrol, I'm left alone in the finca with Madam.

After I've showered, I find Hayley in the lounge scouring the titles on Marcus's DIY wooden bookshelf. Her fingers are trailing the titles.

'Have you seen these?' she asks without turning.

'What?'

My relief that she's moved on from hired assassins is short-lived.

'The titles. *Dead Man's Grip. Not Dead Yet. Want You Dead. Love You Dead. You Are Dead.*'

'Oh, he must be a fan of Peter James.'

'He seems to be a fan of death.'

You've got to be kidding me. Now it looks as if Hayley might have got Marcus down as a silent assassin. She's either suffering from hallucinatory PTSD, or she knows something about our host that I don't.

Her fingers trail the titles, and she counts the number with the word *dead* in them. Luckily, before she's a chance to offer up more macabre thoughts, there's the beep of a car horn.

We pile into the car, and Marcus drives us back to the resort and slowly past the security kiosk. Santiago gives us a wink and a thumbs-up, likely the most excitement he's had all year. Hayley and I keep our heads down until we roll up to the clubhouse.

'Can you drop us here?' I ask.

'Of course. I'll go and open up, and catch up with you later.' Marcus taps his strong hands on the steering wheel. I have the most dreadful urge to take one, silently cursing Hayley for being in the car. She hasn't spoken, or made the slightest sound since we left the finca, apart from an incessant bout of snivelling.

'Thanks,' Hayley says as she gets out, and turns to walk away from the clubhouse.

'Hayley. Can we talk?'

'What about?'

Is she kidding? Who might have killed her ex-boyfriend for a start. And who the hell is she? Why the disguise, which I'm now convinced is linked to the alias? Forget theories on hired assassins, I need her to start at the beginning.

'Everything. Who was Teddy, and why do you think he was killed? And who did it?'

I give her a stony stare, and her shoulders slump. She doesn't want to talk, but it's too late for that. I need answers, and fast. She's warned me about Avery and she can't simply walk away without telling me some more. If he's trying to have me killed, I need to know why.

'If you don't talk to me, you're on your own. No staying at Marcus's. Now are you coming or not?'

I lead the way, as she skulks along behind.

I order coffees and a couple of pastries while she heads

outside. We both need to eat, but looking at the pastries I suspect the birds will have a field day.

We sit in silence for a few minutes, and she's about to do the head-slumping on the table again, when I dive in.

'Hayley, who was Teddy? And where was he working before he came here to the resort?'

My hands can hardly grip the cup. I'm petrified of what she's going to tell me.

'He was staying in Marbella, and got himself into some sort of trouble.'

Shit. Shit. Shit. The word *Marbella* has it. I was right. Teddy. Avery. The murder. Did Avery murder Teddy? He was here on the resort when the body was found.

'Where was he staying?' My question comes out in a hoarse whisper. I know what she's going to say, and desperately want to clamp my hands over my ears.

'With a woman called Astrid. Astrid Olsen. He was working for her.'

This can't be happening. My past is back to haunt me. Astrid masterminded Isaac's death. Has she done the same to Teddy?

'Go on.' I give her daggers.

'I think she might have had him killed.' Hayley looks down at her feet.

'Why?' I'm screaming inside, but manage to keep my voice measured.

'I don't know. He messaged me he was in trouble, but I wasn't that worried. He's always been able to look after himself.'

I know she's leaving things out. Why? Why won't she tell me the whole story?

'Why did you call yourself Gabby? And are you in disguise?'

I throw my arms wide in a manner of disbelief.

'It's a long story. I'd rather not talk about it.'

'Try me.'

I'm not sure whether she's going to tell me any more, but when Crystal wanders up the stairs on to the terrace, she goes quiet and looks away. She tears the croissant into flaky pieces and lets them float to the ground.

It's like a soap opera. Crystal pats Hayley on the shoulder and asks how she's holding up. Certainly better than I am. Crystal doesn't seem bothered that I'm in the midst of a murder enquiry as well, as all her concern is for Hayley. Maybe she's helping Avery finish me off. But why? What the hell have I done?

I try to calm down, breathing slowly, closing my eyes between breaths.

When there's a lull in the muted conversation, I turn to Crystal.

'Crystal. Are you still interested in the apartment?'

It's worth a shot, although I'm no longer hopeful of anything. If she really wants to get away from Avery, why the heck would she wind him up by buying an apartment on this resort where he already owns a villa? Nothing stacks.

Funny, I've no idea where Crystal is from. I assume, from her accent, that she's English. But she could be from anywhere.

Asking the question about buying an apartment was really only something to say. A diversion from the leaden misery. But when Crystal gives a wan smile, a flicker of hope kicks in.

'Yes. Now more than ever.'

Really?

'Oh, that's great.' I sit up, and like Hayley, start breaking apart the flaky pastry.

'Why don't I pop by your office later?' she asks.

'Of course. I'll be at there all day unless the police take me away.'

I laugh nervously, while Hayley stares straight through me. I feel bad for having a hopeful moment, as her face is one of abject misery.

But I need to think of number one. With everything that's going on, the murder, the links to Marbella, imminent bankruptcy, psycho Avery Knowles, Crystal's interest in the penthouse might just be the fillip needed.

Also, if I can help Crystal, perhaps we can support each other. The more allies the better. She saved me once from the guys in the black car, so maybe she can help keep me safe from Avery.

87

Although I should be feeling more positive with the news that Crystal might buy the penthouse, I feel sick inside. Especially after Hayley's revelations about the macabre Marbella tie-up.

But while I'm stuck here, I need to try and make some money. Flogging the penthouse might keep me afloat until I can leave.

One day at a time. I can hear Mum's voice, her sage mantra.

As I walk past the kiosk my heart soars. Gato is outside my office door, snuggled up in an A4 cardboard box. The sort that holds six packs of copy paper. On the ground beside him is a bowl of water, and some tuna chunks.

'Couldn't let the little guy go hungry, could I?'

Marcus appears from inside Hola Sol, beaming from ear to ear. Could this guy get any better? He's risked asphyxiation to save my little man.

'Oh, thank you. Thank you.' I hunker down and lift Gato up. His purr breaks my heart, and I have trouble biting back my own tears.

'My pleasure. All okay?'

His sexy crinkly eyes are full of concern. I'm desperate to hug him, but Seamus is watching us as he sets up shop.

'Just had coffee with Hayley, and Crystal. If you think Hayley looks bad, you should see Crystal.'

'What's up with her?'

'Looks as if she's gone ten rounds with Mike Tyson.'

'No. You serious?'

'Deadly. It's that bloody Avery.'

He stiffens when I mention Avery. At least he's picking up what a psycho the guy is.

'Here, let me help.'

He brushes up close, and helps me get the grilles off. He starts to wheeze, and takes out an inhaler, closes his eyes, and squirts.

'That's better.' His wheeze slowly dissipates.

'Thanks. For Gato. For everything. Letting us stay at yours.'

'A pleasure. Maybe you can pay the rent in kind?'

His eyes twinkle with flirtation.

'We'll see about that. Listen, I need to get to work. Crystal is serious about buying the penthouse.'

'Really? I'm surprised she wants to buy on the same resort as her abusive boyfriend.'

The crinkle-flirty look has turned to one of bewilderment.

'You know what? I couldn't care less. All I want is the sale.'

I stick my nose in the air, lift up Gato's makeshift cardboard home, and follow the little guy inside. He's clinging seriously close to my legs, weaving in and out.

'Good luck. Catch up later.'

With that, Marcus disappears into his office. I watch his retreating back, and remember Hayley's unease around him, and her little throwaway comments. Makes me wonder if there might be another side to him, and I shiver, recalling Hayley reading out the titles on his bookshelf.

Everyone has read Peter James, haven't they? Even I've read a couple.

But the whole *Dead* Series?

* * *

The police come and go through the Spanish Village all day, questioning anyone they can find. Hayley gets another interrogation while sipping water at the kiosk. I'm not sure what else she can tell them. I'd love to listen in, as I'm certain she's holding stuff back. I watch from my office window. She's so distraught, and flustered, and starts to cry, hanging her head as if she's been told she's about to go down for murder.

Blue tape now rings the apartment block, and although the body has been taken away, forensics are still frantically looking for evidence. So far there has been no grapevine feedback of anything solid. The killer seems to have come and gone unnoticed.

I can't help wondering if they've questioned Avery at length. Knowing that he's got henchmen tailing me round the resort makes me wonder what else he's been up to. Did he have anything to do with Teddy's death? If Hayley thinks he might have hired someone to kill me, could the same person have killed Teddy? The thought makes me sick to the core.

I'd love to confide in Marcus, but still don't want to tell him about what happened in Marbella. Maybe one day, but then again maybe not. It's all too big a nightmare, and I doubt sharing my own macabre past would fuel romance. Also, a tiny part of me is shocked by Hayley's insinuations that Marcus might not be all he seems. But a killer? She's way off the mark.

She's likely jealous of our relationship, and the fact that I've hooked up with such a hot guy. Actually the only guy for miles around.

Just as Hayley manages to escape from questioning, and starts to head through the Spanish Village, no doubt to go on another extended power walk, Crystal appears. I nearly jump out of my skin.

'Hi,' she says, hovering over my desk. 'You got time to chat?'

Yes. Of course. All the time in the world. I need to cheer up and clinch this sale.

'Of course. Have a seat.'

Crystal launches straight in, asking if she can look over the apartment one more time tomorrow, and then she'll be ready to sign the paperwork. She wants to check fixtures, fittings, and take a few photographs to send back to family and friends.

Although I'm curious as to who these family and friends could be, I don't digress from the task in hand.

'Of course. What say nine o'clock? Then we can go and have a look.'

'Sounds like a plan. How exciting,' she squeals. I grimace as her long fingers toy with her hair, but the way I'm feeling now, she can tug out her whole head of hair.

Who knows? This sale might be my lifeline.

88

For a couple of hours after Crystal leaves, I get my head down and try to work. But visions of the murder scene keep popping in and out. All I can see is the blood, the red everywhere. And the smell is still clinging to my nostrils. I never knew death had a smell, but then I've never come face to face with it before. Although I know how Isaac died, how he was murdered, I was long gone before the body was discovered. I never saw his charred torso, but my imagination still runs wild with macabre imaginings.

I concentrate on simple tasks, bombarding prospective buyers with newsletters on available properties. Anything to keep occupied. When I start to hum, Gato gives me a strange look and restarts the purring. Despite everything, I can't swallow back the smile.

Around 4 p.m., I'm about to shut up shop and decamp to the clubhouse and wait for Marcus, when my eyes nearly pop out of their sockets.

Walking up to the kiosk are Avery and Crystal, hand in hand. She can't have forgiven the creep that easily, could she? I had her down as having a bit more substance. Avery has a broad grin plastered across his creepy face, and she's wearing sunglasses; no doubt to hide another black eye.

I stroke my hand across Gato's fur (he's pretty sneaky at getting up on to my lap and refusing to budge). I watch the two of them, although they'll not be able to see me as the office window is plastered with property details. There are so many choices on the resort that I could fill a hundred windows.

But I can see them.

Avery keeps leaning across the table to kiss her on the lips. They're like a couple of young lovers. They clink glasses as if they're celebrating something. It's the first time I've really looked at Avery for any length of time, but he's got a supercilious, superior thing going on, with the smug smile of a narcissist. For a fleeting moment, he reminds me of Isaac.

What is Crystal thinking of? Could she really be so in love with him that she'd sell her soul to the devil? The notion that Avery is back in favour makes me twitchy. I thought she wanted to buy the penthouse as a means of asserting her independence. Her independence away from that madman.

Their affectionate display is nauseous, and all I can imagine is that they're drunk. All forgiven in a haze of alcohol. What the heck does she see in him?

I start to feel panicky again, as if I'm missing something important. Gato's claws come out when I forget to skirt round the bald patch on his scalp. He hisses, and I bend and kiss the top of his head.

Five minutes pass, and Marcus appears in the doorway.

'Ready to pack up?'

'Yep. I'm ready.'

'Fancy a drink at The Three Bulls for a change before we head back?'

Sounds like a plan.

'What about Hayley?'

'We can pick her up afterwards. I've already texted her.'

He blushes. It'll be good to have some time together on our own. I shouldn't be mean, but Hayley's misery is infectious. And I don't want her ruining the good thing I have with Marcus with her crazy imaginings. I need a drink, and a bit of light relief.

* * *

Ten minutes later we're walking down the hill to The Three Bulls, and Marcus takes my hand. Funny, he's the one who brings the subject up.

'I see that creep Avery seems to be back in Crystal's good books.'

'Yep. I saw.'

'Is she still interested in the apartment?'

'I hope so. She says she'll be round in the morning to pick up the key, so I've got everything crossed.'

'So do I. For you.'

He slows his pace, swivels me round, and pulls me close.

I melt into him, and for a moment in time, things don't seem so bad. Maybe. Just maybe, things will work out.

'And I'm here for you. I'd do anything to keep you safe, you know that.'

If he'd said *I love you*, I couldn't be more thrilled. This guy is something else.

89

When we get back to the resort the following morning, Marcus drops Hayley at the clubhouse, while he and I stroll towards our offices. He whistles the whole way, and with the sun high in an azure-blue sky, it's hard to quell the optimism. I've got everything crossed that today Crystal will sign on the dotted line, and pay across her deposit. With money in the bank, I'll be able to rest more easily until I can get back to England.

Marcus boosts my spirits by suggesting I should start planning a refurb of my own apartment. After a professional clean, once the police have moved out, he'll help me pick some glossy new paint, and together we can get it back on the market. The word *together* is what lifts my spirits. He repeats again how confident he is it will sell; there's always someone after a bargain.

I hope he's right, but one thing's for certain, I'll not be living there again.

It's nearly nine by the time we cross the plaza. I grin when I see Gato, his nose pressed up against the glass of my office window.

The Girl on the Balcony

Marcus helps me to open up, and would you believe it? Gato, the little creep, makes a beeline for Marcus. Despite the wheezing, Marcus bends down and tickles him behind the ears. With his other hand, he produces an inhaler and clamps his lips round the mouthpiece. A few seconds in and the wheezing eases up.

'What's up with you?' he asks. 'Jealous?'

He's got that crinkly thing going on again, but it morphs into concern when I can't hold back a stream of tears.

'Come here.' He zooms in for a hug.

After an embrace that feels so good, he says he should open up, and tears himself away.

It's then I freeze, my previously relaxed body stiffening with rigor mortis. Over Marcus's shoulder I see none other than Avery Knowles heading my way.

'Jade. How are we this morning?'

Avery's teeth are small and uneven, but his smile is full of crocodile menace.

My skin prickles, and again I think of Isaac and his arrogant sneer. Nausea bites, not helped by an early overload of coffee, and my insides churn.

'Avery. How can I help you?'

I sit down behind my desk, desperate for a solid support.

What the heck does he want? I'm no longer looking after his villa, but he's here on a mission.

'Crystal. She tells me you're set on flogging her an apartment?'

He leans over the desk, and a waft of rancid breath hits me in the face.

'That's right.' Not that it's any of his bloody business.

'Well, I'm here to pick up the key. Crystal isn't feeling too well, and I'd like to see the apartment for myself. Give her my view on it. She's a bit gullible when it comes to investments. Know what I mean?' He taps the side of his nose and winks.

'Isn't she well? She was keen to see it for herself.'

'She's got a headache. A woman's thing.'

He gives me that smug narcissistic sneer again. Arrogant prick. I'm tempted to ask what he means by 'a woman's thing', and tell him men get headaches too. But I know to bite my tongue.

I'm gripped by the most dreadful fear as he stares down at me. Memories of the men in the black car, as well as Hayley's warning that he's out to get me, make my head spin. I'm scared I'm going to throw up.

I could refuse to show him the apartment, or even to give him the key, but something tells me that winding him up any more wouldn't be a wise move.

'Do you want me to show you round?'

The thought of the roof terrace is too much to take in, but I can always leave him to go up there on his own. The last thing I want is to go anywhere with this creep.

'No, you're okay. I can see you're busy.' He laughs and lets his eyes trawl the empty office.

I get up, and head for the property key box, and pick out one of the spares for the penthouse.

'Can you drop the key straight back, please?'

I hand it across, and he jiggles the key, tossing it up and down in the air.

'Of course, madam. Your wish is my command. Now tell me. Which apartment is it? I know it's the penthouse, but which block?'

I give him the details, willing him to leave the office. As he turns to leave, he adds a final comment.

'Wouldn't want to get locked out on a hot roof terrace, now would we? I must check out the door locks. Anyway, see you later.'

90

Once he's gone, I can't move. I'm shaking like a leaf.

His last comment tells me he knows what happened in Marbella. He's connected to everything that's going on. What has it all got to do with him?

I slump my head on top of my arms, aping Hayley's defeated pose. At this particular moment, my fear might top hers.

When Marcus appears in the doorway, his happy face morphs into one to match Gato's *about-to-be-abandoned* look.

'What's up? You look as if you've seen a ghost.'

'I'm okay. It's just Crystal isn't well, and Avery is going to check out the apartment for himself.'

Marcus has no idea about Marbella, and my past. I need to pull myself together before I blurt out the whole story. But I can't lose Marcus, he's the only good thing in this sorry mess.

'What's up with her?'

His tone is serious, and he looks rattled. Avery is getting to him. I guess he's only looking out for me, but he seems more wound up since he likely overheard Hayley talking about hired assassins.

I wish he hadn't asked what's up with Crystal. It's the very thing that's bothering me.

'A headache.'

'Oh. As long as you're okay,' he says.

'I'm fine,' I lie, anything but fine.

'Listen. I've got to head back to the finca, pick up some papers, but will be back in about an hour,' he says.

'No worries. See you later.'

He takes off in a hurry, but after he's gone, time drags. I clock watch, and shuffle papers round my desk. An hour passes, and there's still no sign of Avery. He should have been back with the key by now. Something tells me he's no intention of bringing it back any time soon. If at all.

Rather than hang around, I decide to go and find out where he's got to before I go crazy.

I pull on a pair of trainers, lock up shop, and head along the back route that leads to the Las Ramblas apartment block. I can be there in twenty minutes.

Not a single car passes me on the way, but it's only as I pass the car park for The Three Bulls that I notice the black 4X4 near the exit. I take an immediate right turn, and hunker down in the garden of an empty overgrown property. My heart is banging in my ribcage as I'm imaging the thugs have been lying in wait. Maybe today they're planning on killing me.

I make a snap decision: rather than carrying on down the main road towards Las Ramblas, I decide to access the block further down by skirting round the back of the properties on the other side of the road.

Once I reach my destination, I do a full 360 of the area, and am confident no one is on my tail.

I sneak round by the back entrance, knowing that Avery will have used the key I gave him to access the apartment from the front. My ears are pricked for the slightest noise, and as I climb the stairs up to the third floor, I keep pausing, listening for the faintest sound. But it's bizarrely quiet. Seeing the 4X4 has made things ten times worse, and has set my teeth on edge.

Something doesn't feel right. I can't put my finger on it. It's not only the lack of noise, but it's something else. As I draw closer to the apartment entrance, the silence becomes even more unsettling. Perhaps I was expecting to hear Avery stomping around from room to room, but there's nothing.

I freeze, fall back against a wall, when I hear a door down below open and close. The image of the bearded thugs sends me into palpitations. I've no idea what to do if they suddenly appear. I shouldn't have come alone, but it's too late for regrets.

Everything goes quiet again. My hands are shaking so badly that I drop the spare key a couple of times before managing to find purchase in the lock. But the door is already open, without a key lodged on the inside. Perhaps Avery has been and gone, and playing hardball by not locking up, and not giving me the key back. Maybe he didn't even look round.

I'm about to enter when I hear a noise coming from somewhere inside. I freeze, sensing I should turn round, and get the hell away from here, but I don't.

Instead I push open the door and step into the hall, dreading what I might find. Or what Avery might be planning if he's still here.

91

I leave the door ajar, scared to make a noise. If Avery comes at me, it'll be easier to escape.

I breathe more easily when I don't immediately hear any more noise. Perhaps I imagined the earlier sounds. I tiptoe into the living room, but there's no sign of anyone. Everything is untouched.

I let out a loud puff of air, wiping my damp forehead with the back of my hand.

Then I hear it. The scuffling noise again, and it's coming from overhead. I look at the winding staircase that leads to the roof terrace, and thrust a hand against a wall to steady myself. I'm swaying as if from seasickness.

I can't move. If Avery is up on the roof, I can't go up. His parting shot about getting locked on a hot roof terrace was a warning. Is he waiting for me to go up? He's been here long enough that he might have guessed I'd come to find him.

Suddenly, I pick up the merest hint of another voice. There's more than one person up there. I glance up in the vain hope of a clue. Who the hell is up there with him? Could Crystal have made it after all? Maybe her headache wasn't as bad as he made out? Oh my God. What if she's up there and he's going to punish her? It's obvious he beats her up, but what if her wanting to buy her own apartment has pushed him over the edge?

There's a lingering threat of danger all around, I can feel it. I've no choice. I'll have to face my demons, and climb the twisty staircase all the way to the top. I might be Crystal's only hope.

The stairwell spins like a merry-go-round as I gingerly negotiate the metal steps. When I finally reach the top, I close my eyes, stand very still and count to ten. The door out on to the terrace is closed, but there's a small window which lets me look out.

I press my nose up close. There are two people at the far end, standing near the maintenance gate which is wide open. How did they get it open? Only the community office staff hold keys to these gates.

Avery is easy to identify in his flowery shirt and straining shorts, but the other person is dressed head to toe in black. My first thought is that one of his henchmen has come up with him. But they're not talking, and Avery is standing very still. Even from this distance I sense his fear. The other person is threatening him.

Suddenly the person in black strikes Avery, karate-type blows. Sharp, and savage. I imagine the crack of bones. Avery slumps to the floor, averting his face from further attack. The assailant then drags Avery's weakened body towards the swing gate with what must be very strong arms. Avery's hairy stomach gapes over the top of his shorts which have ripped down the front.

The last I see of Avery is his body being hoisted up, and levered through the gate. A few seconds of silence feels like an eternity. Then the faintest thump breaks through, as the body must have hit the ground.

Suddenly my phone pings. Loud enough for the person to hear through the door. No. No. No. Damp fingers panic to turn it off. My knees give way, and I slither to the ground.

But before I collapse the killer turns my way. They might not have seen me, but I stare in disbelief, and know I need to get the hell away from here.

I manage to haul myself up, and race through the front door, down the stairs, and retrace my steps out the back way.

Thank God I'm wearing trainers. I run blindly, as if my life depends on it, sprinting across the grass towards the eighteenth hole of the golf course, in disbelief at the identity of the killer.

My mind is swirling. I start to recite wrestling holds, my quiz trivia knowledge invading my thoughts.

Leglocks. Toehold. Ankle lock. I've no idea which hold the assassin used, even if it was a wrestling move, but they certainly knew how to contain and control a body much heavier than their own. They knew what they were doing.

I've been wrong about a lot of things, but oh my God. I couldn't have been more wrong about this.

92

I can hardly breathe by the time I reach the clubhouse. I've no idea what to do next.

I manage to make it past the putting green to the shelter that houses faulty and uncharged golf buggies, and collapse in a dark corner.

The two murders – Hayley's ex-boyfriend's and Avery's – are connected, and I now know the link is Marbella. Avery knew about the roof terrace, and Teddy was working with Astrid. I'm still not sure why Avery was out to destroy me, but I'm now certain it had nothing to do with my living rent free in his villa.

I hang my head in a desperate bid to calm down. I should go straight to the police, but they'll likely link the two murders and I'll become a main suspect. Regardless of what I tell them. The first murder was in my apartment, the second in an apartment I'm flogging, and the one I've just been at. Thank God there's no CCTV around the resort. I'm praying no one saw me. I remember the black car, and start whimpering like a traumatised child.

Several minutes pass, and I clutch my stomach, which is churning like sour milk. I want to hide here forever. My mind is skittering in all directions. I need to come up with an alibi about where I was at the time of the murder. I wonder if the assassin has fled the scene, left the resort, or if they've gone back the way they must have come.

As my body convulses, and I rock from side to side, tears pour down my cheeks. My world is about to collapse, and I've absolutely no idea what to do.

'Jade?'

Holy shit. I smack my head back against the wall, rubbing at it furiously before I look up.

'Hayley?' My voice is a shaky whimper.

She bends down, a knee creaking in effort, and slips onto the floor beside me. When she opens her arms, I fall against her like a child to its mother.

'You're okay. Shhh.' She soothes down my hair and lets me cling to her. 'I saw what happened,' she says, whispering against my ear.

'You did?' I stare at her through a liquid haze.

'Yes. I was walking round by the tennis courts, and saw you march past.'

'And?'

I can hardly speak, my voice is shaking so badly.

'I followed you. I wanted to talk.'

Oh my God. What did she see? She wasn't on the roof terrace, so all she must have seen was the body catapulting over the side.

'Did you follow me to Las Ramblas?' I croak.

'Yes, I sat outside, waiting for you to come out. I knew you were showing Crystal round the apartment this morning.'

'Avery was looking round. Crystal wasn't feeling so good, so he went alone to have a look. He was ages, so I went to get the key back.'

My voice is so shaky, I've no idea how I manage to string the words together.

'Crystal wasn't well?' she asks.

'That's what Avery told me.'

Hayley falls silent, and I inch away from her comforting hold.

'What exactly did you see?' I ask.

'I saw Avery's body catapult off the roof. I assumed you were inside.'

'I didn't kill him, if that's what you're thinking.' My voice clears, and rises several decibels. Hayley can't think I killed him.

She goes really quiet, and moves further away. Can she really believe that I hurled Avery off the roof terrace? Oh my God.

The police will be here soon, and if Hayley tells her side of the story, recounting what she assumes has happened, then my life is over. It looks as if the girl on my balcony, the girl who has been irritating the hell out of me for months, might hold my future in her hands.

'Hayley. You need to listen to me. I know who did kill Avery though. I couldn't have done it, even if I wanted to. I wouldn't have had the strength to throw him over.'

'I noticed the maintenance gate on the terrace was ajar. You can see it from down below,' she says, staring at me.

She really thinks I might have killed him, somehow manoeuvring him near the open gate. She knows he was after my blood, warning me often enough, but how can she think I'm a cold-blooded murderer?

'You think I might have got him close to the edge and pushed him off? You've got to be kidding me.'

The way I feel right now I could kill bloody Hayley Scrivens, whoever the hell she is. But I seriously need to calm down. The only way out of this mess is to tell her exactly what did happen, and pray she believes me before the police get here.

Hayley doesn't speak for a minute, battling with her own thoughts.

'I wouldn't blame you if you did kill him, but...'

'But what?' I'm now screaming at her.

'If you didn't kill him, then who did?'

I take a deep breath, and tell her.

'Crystal killed him.'

93

'Crystal?'

'I watched the whole thing through the window in the door leading out onto the roof terrace.'

Her eyes pop out on stalks.

'Crystal? You've got to be kidding me.'

My voice speeds up, desperate to convince her I'm telling the truth.

'I saw her kill him. She knew what she was doing. I know all about wrestling holds. Quiz trivia.' I roll my eyes, sounding mad by imparting such a ridiculous piece of information at this point. 'She wrapped Avery in a lock, used her strength to contain him, and professionally tipped the body over the edge. You've got to believe me.'

Hayley stares at me, trying to digest what I've said, and, more importantly to work out if I'm telling the truth.

'Do you think she pre-planned the whole thing? His murder would then look like the revenge of an abused girlfriend. We all saw the bruises,' she says.

'Yes. Of course.' My heart races, praying this is what the

police will believe. 'We've seen the black eyes and bruises, and anyone else on the resort who met Crystal should be able to vouch for them... This is likely why she never covered them up.'

'You could be right. If she planned on killing him, then she's given herself a good reason.'

'You do believe me? Don't you?' I plead with my eyes, having learnt from Gato's sad endeavours. They're glazed from tears. 'I'd nothing to do with his death.'

'I think we both need to tell the whole truth about what happened today, and what we both saw. No more lies. As far as the police are concerned, you would have no reason to kill Avery.'

'I think Crystal might be a trained assassin. She knew what she was doing, and I suspect she planned the whole thing. Do you think she might have killed Teddy too?'

If Crystal did kill both men, then it should help keep Hayley in the clear. As well as me. Hayley and I need to be on the same side.

At this moment the wail of police sirens invades the peace of the resort. Hayley and I look at each other. I feel like I'm going to pass out, but Hayley looks even worse. Her mind is now also in turmoil with all the possibilities.

Before we stagger up, she grips my arm.

'I'm really sorry, Jade. I have so much to tell you, and can't hide it any longer. Let's meet up later on our own, as soon as we get the chance, and I'll start at the beginning.'

'What are you on about?'

Nausea grips my insides, petrified of what she's got left to tell me.

'Firstly, I'm not an artist. I'm a reporter. I came to Spain to get the full story on George Stubbs's death. Avery was his brother.'

Hayley manages to stand up first, and holds out a hand for

me to grip. I've no idea how I'll be able to walk anywhere. It's as if she's leading me on a death march to the gallows.

She squeezes my fingers, and leads me back up into the sunlight. The last thing she says before we go and face the music is, 'We'll stick together. Tell the truth about Avery's death today, and we can decide later on how much of everything else we share.'

I'm now completely unable to form any words, but divulging that Avery was George Stubbs's brother tells me I'm in much deeper than I thought possible.

It's all to do with Marbella, and Astrid Olsen. That's now clear. Maybe Hayley and I will need to keep a lot to ourselves. Because while Astrid Olsen is still alive, I don't think either of us will sleep easily again.

Looks like the girl on the balcony, more precisely the girl on *my* balcony, and I will need to work together.

94

It's late in the evening, and somehow Hayley and I have got through the day without either of us being thrown in prison. We both told the truth about what happened. Although Hayley didn't see Crystal hurl Avery off the roof, her account of Crystal's tales of abuse, along with the glaring black eyes, will hopefully be enough to save my skin.

Hayley found it hard to believe it was Crystal. I remember they seemed to have grown close, but at least for now, Hayley isn't going to offer the police any other possible suspects. Thank goodness.

From what has trickled through the grapevine round the resort, there have been no further sightings of Crystal, and no arrests made.

My head is still spinning with questions. Who murdered Teddy? Why did Crystal really murder Avery? Was Avery intent on killing me? And was it all to do with what happened to his brother, and my link to Marbella? Recall of the thugs in the 4X4 now makes more sense. They weren't trying to rough me up because of my squatting in Avery's villa. It was all somehow linked to his brother's death. But how?

When Hayley suggests we go for a walk, insisting she's desperate to talk to me, we set off towards the tennis courts, and settle side by side on a freezing bench. We're both shivering, a chill having settled in our bones.

Marcus wanted to come with us, the chaperone for two distressed ladies, but I assured him we needed time alone. Some time to put the world to rights. He has absolutely no idea what is really going on, and best it stays that way. Somehow I'll make it up to him if I manage to avoid capture.

I listen to Hayley's story, and how it started with what Teddy overheard on the plane. She thought she'd found her Pulitzer Prize-winning scoop, and was excited when her boyfriend moved in with Astrid Olsen as escort and general dogsbody.

'I guessed it was you that Astrid was talking to on the plane? You were sitting in the window seat. 2A I think it was.'

'Yes, that was me.'

'Did you have anything to do with her husband's death?'

'No,' I snap. She can't really think I did, can she? 'I was fleeing the villa at the time he got locked on the roof terrace. It had nothing to do with me.'

'Fleeing? What from?'

'From Isaac. That's what I knew him as, although his real name was George. He had locked me up, and I thought I'd never escape.'

'Why did he lock you up?'

I don't want to talk about it any more. She's too persistent, and it's all too much. So I keep it simple.

'It's a long story. He thought I'd conned him out of money, but I'd every intention of paying him back. In a nutshell, he was a psychopath. But I never killed him.'

Neither of us speaks for a couple of minutes, until I break the impasse with a question of my own.

'Why your disguise?' I ask. She's finally dressed in a pair of skinny jeans (surprisingly skinny legs considering my unkind images of horses' haunches under the bag-lady clothes).

She tells me next about meeting Avery, and needing a disguise when she came to Murcia, so that he wouldn't twig she was after information. When she repeats that he was Isaac's brother, and how he was coming to Murcia to find me, I can hardly breathe. Knowing this is one thing, but hearing it confirmed that I've been in the thick of everything is something else. Avery came to Murcia, not to find his dream home, but to track me down.

Hayley keeps patting my arm, and apologising. She's guilty of keeping secrets, trying to carve out a great story, but I can't blame her for where I sit in the sorry saga.

Once I hear Hayley's story, I still don't have answers to all my questions.

'It doesn't stack up. I get the link with Astrid, and why Avery might have it in for me when he thought I'd conned his brother out of money, and might even have been involved in his death. But if Astrid is at the root of things, then why kill Teddy? And why kill Avery? Do you really think Crystal just wanted to kill her abusive boyfriend?'

There's a long silence. A couple of residents walk past the padel courts, and onwards towards The Three Bulls. It's quiz night again. It seems a lifetime ago since I was queen of pub trivia. How can so much have happened in such a short space of time?

I'm about to think that we'll never get our answers, when Hayley produces a small phone from her very tight jeans.

'I've got all the answers here.'

Several more people wander past, and all of a sudden the resort seems to come to life. It's like inmates being let out on parole... one night only. I can see past Hayley's shoulder to the car park of The Three Bulls. It's rapidly filling up. When a large black people carrier drives past, I freeze. No. It can't be? Surely the thugs have gone? When I manage to read the tail end of the registration plate, I catch myself on.

'That car is a completely different model,' Hayley says, a grin in her voice.

Despite her duplicitousness, I have an overwhelming urge to hug her. But until she shares what she's got on the phone, I hold back.

'Teddy was locked in the villa with Astrid. She wouldn't let him out. Somehow he managed to escape, and make his way here. This is Teddy's,' she says. 'When I sat by his dead body, before the police arrived, I took the phone out of his pocket. It's a cheap burner.'

She holds up the tiny mobile, and opens it up.

Part of me is desperate to see what she's going to show me, and part of me wants to take the phone and hurl it across the tennis courts.

'Teddy composed an email he was going to send me. It never got sent, but it's saved as a draft.'

'Go on...'

'Read it for yourself.' She hands me the phone, and with a thrashing heart, I start to read.

Scrivens

I'm in dreadful danger. Astrid has locked me in the villa, and told me she'll never let me out again. I got drunk last night, and told her everything. I trusted her. She was kind, generous, and like the mother I never had.

I'm really sorry, but I let slip that you're a journalist, and she went crazy. When she learnt that I overheard everything on the plane, I thought she was going to kill me then and there. She took my phone after I sent you those panicked messages, and started messaging you herself. She had one of her staff tie me up, and padlock me to the bed. I really thought I was going to die.

She said she wouldn't come for you, that was all I cared about. But she did say she'd keep an eye on you.

Avery Knowles as you know is the brother of her dead husband. He is in danger too. He's heading to Murcia to track down Jade Wiltshire, I think with his own intention of killing her. But Astrid told me she intends to make him disappear. He started to blackmail her to keep his mouth shut about what happened to his brother. I've no idea how he knows Astrid masterminded his brother's death, but Avery is a nasty piece of work. Be careful of him.

I'm really sorry about everything. If I do manage to escape, I'll hitchhike to Murcia and we can leave Spain together.

Whatever happens, I pray you'll read this email.

I love you. Always your Teddy.

Hope to see you soon. XXXX

I hand Hayley back the phone, and it's now my turn to wrap my arms round her.

95

HAYLEY

I've never felt so alone. Jade and I have made a pact not to share with the police the whole story. With Crystal still out there, as well as Astrid, we know the need for silence. If Crystal was hired by Astrid to kill Teddy and Avery, goodness knows who might be next. Astrid would have good enough reason to take both Jade and me out. We both know too much.

I have a blockbuster story, without a doubt, one that could set me up for life. But at what cost? For now I've no choice but to keep quiet. But it won't stop me writing it. Who knows? In the future, when I'm back home, and things have settled down, I might take my chances. For now, it's all about survival.

Once we get back to the Spanish Village, Jade sets off to find Marcus. We'll be staying with him now until we can leave Spain. Funny, I really believed he might have killed Avery because of Jade. He's that smitten, and love can make you do funny things. But as Crystal seems to have disappeared without a trace, Jade is most likely telling the truth about what she saw.

I go through the clubhouse entrance, numb from shock and fear. There's a bustle of early-evening drinkers. Happy hour. No one looks my way, and I feel lonelier than I ever thought possible.

There's no one in the whole world now I can turn to. Apart from Damon. I've told no one else about the real reason I came to Spain, and was only going to share once I had my prize-winning scoop. It now looks as if that's never going to happen.

I go into a small meeting room near the cloakrooms. Thankfully it's empty, and I sit down and lift out my laptop from my rucksack.

It's hard to boot up as the Wi-Fi signal comes and goes, but I'm bracing myself to speak to Damon. After he said he didn't want to come out, or get involved after Teddy got killed, I've ignored all his calls. In some ways, I'm glad he didn't come. If he'd brought the threatening letters with him, who knows? They might have led the police too quickly back to Marbella, to Astrid, and goodness knows what else?

Both Jade and I know the need for caution, and have agreed not to offer up any information about Marbella. No doubt the police will sniff around Teddy's last-known whereabouts, and sooner or later question Astrid Olsen. But instinct tells us not to offer up any leads, and leave the dot joining to the police. There is nothing to prove Jade or I had anything to do with Teddy's death, and for now, that's all that matters.

The screen on my laptop finally comes to life, and when I press the WhatsApp video-call icon, the wait for Damon to pick up seems interminable.

His face looks like it belongs to a completely different person than the guy from Flatshare who became my lover.

'Scrivens. How are you? Why have you been ignoring me?'

His eyes are puffy, and in the background I see an array of empty beer bottles.

'Hi.' I've no idea where to start. What to tell him? Calling me Scrivens has put me on edge, as Teddy's face clouds the moment.

'Are you okay? You don't look so great,' he says.

He sticks his face closer to the screen as if to get a better look.

'Surviving. Just about. There's been so much going on. Another guy on the resort got killed earlier, but...'

'What?' He suddenly seems to waken up. 'You've got to be kidding me? Who? Why?'

'It's a long story. For another time. Everything's pretty shit. To be honest, I've been mad that you didn't come out after Teddy died.'

'Hang on. Just getting my beer...'

The screen flickers in and out as he moves away. When he sits down again, he glugs from a bottle stuck to his lips.

'Why didn't you come out?'

He carries on glugging.

'You have vital evidence that might have helped the police?'

I haven't known Damon that long. Not in the way I knew Teddy, but I'm a good judge of character. There's more to his behaviour than he's letting on. If he's got a new girlfriend, or worse still, one that's moved into my flat, he's dead meat. He's definitely not telling me everything.

'I've really missed you, Hayley. Honest. I need you home, and I really think we could have a future together.'

'You haven't answered my question?'

The seconds turn to minutes, and to what seems like hours, before he finally owns up.

'I'm really sorry. The letters, the threatening ones...?'

'Go on.'

'I wrote them myself. I made them up to get you to come home. I sensed you might be in danger, and you wouldn't listen to me. I couldn't bring them to Spain, as I might be arrested as a jealous lover.'

Oh my God. He made the letters up himself? I remember the smeared blood. The indecipherable postmarks. Holy shit.

Was this his way to prove that he cared? Really?

When I burst out laughing, more through hysteria than mirth, he stops glugging and sets the bottle down.

'Can you forgive me, Scrivens?' He makes puppy-dog eyes.

'Stop bloody calling me Scrivens. You know what?'

'What?' He looks like a burglar caught red-handed.

'Let me think about it. I'll be in Spain quite a while.'

'I really am sorry.'

'Just keep the flat tidy and look after Mitzy. Bye for now.'

As tears stream down my cheeks, I disconnect and look through the blank screen.

96

Somehow I get through the next few weeks. It feels good to lose the disguise, and I'm finding more people approaching to make casual conversations.

It might be my imagination, but Jade isn't so friendly now that my hair has grown back and I'm dressed in normal clothing. Marcus has to tone down interest in our conversations when Jade is around. It's hard not to be jealous of her as Marcus is a really cool guy. The finca is still pretty creepy at nighttime, and I have to cover my ears when the pair can't keep a lid on the lovemaking.

Damon messages regularly, and has tried to call several times. But I can't pick up. If he lied about the letters so easily, and wasn't there when I really needed him, how can I ever trust him again? I get why he did it, but a jealous, manipulating lover is the last thing I need.

Often, during the day, I stay at the finca. The police know where I am at all times, and have even popped out to see me in what Jade and I jokingly call *the desert*.

Today, the sun is shining high in the sky, and the heat has

finally broken through. It's scorching by midday, and I sit outside on the little patio, wearing a huge floppy hat, with my laptop for company. Marcus has finally had Wi-Fi installed, and so I can get work done.

I'm calling my thriller *What He Overheard*. Well, that's the working title of my no-holds-barred blockbuster. I'm tweaking locations, replacing Marbella with Monaco. Murcia for Provence, and so on. But I'm telling the whole story, and Teddy has been renamed Jackson.

Prologue

It all started with a conversation my boyfriend, Jackson, overheard on the plane…

It'll take me time to write, but in the desert I've got all the time in the world. It's my means of survival. Rather than pulling me back into the depths of madness, the task is keeping me sane.

When Marcus and Jade get back at the end of each day, my laptop is well hidden, and I'm either reading on my Kindle or watching Spanish television. My vocabulary is growing rapidly, and the plan is to take up Spanish classes when I finally get back to the UK.

* * *

Marcus and Jade are due back any minute. I've finished writing for now, and have promised to cook for us all this evening. That's another thing I'm getting better at. All things Spanish. Tonight it's seafood paella, laden with the most enormous prawns you've ever seen. Cooking is something else that takes my mind off things.

I pop into my bedroom to hide my laptop, and then dig out the burner phone of Teddy's that I found by his body. I often read through his last message to me, the email draft that never got sent. It brings him closer.

I keep the phone charged, and hidden behind a loose brick in my bedroom wall. Sitting on the edge of the bed, I wait for it to light up.

I sit up straighter when I notice there's a new message. What the hell. Who is messaging Teddy's burner phone? There's nothing else on it apart from the email that he never sent. No one else has the number. My first thought is that it's spam, a random rogue message from the network provider telling him the phone is out of credit.

It's only when I open the message and start reading that I come over dizzy. Nauseous. The salty smell of prawns coating my fingers makes me gag.

> Hayley. I hope you're well, holding up. Just be careful. Let the story go, and get back to England. While Astrid is still alive, you'll not be safe. Have a good life, and throw away the phone. Crystal

'Hello? Hayley?'

I nearly fall off the bed when I hear Jade's cheery voice in the background. I didn't hear the car pull up. Marcus will be parking it several times, as he's got a weird obsession about moving the car around. Even in his sleep.

With shaky fingers, I frantically secrete the phone back behind the loose brick.

'In here. Coming,' I yell.

'Hi. You okay?' Jade pokes her head round, making me jump again, and gives me a strange look as I hover by the wall.

'All good. Paella coming up.' I pick up a hairbrush from the small table below the brick, and drag it through my hair.

'Can't wait.'

When I hear Marcus come in, I know Jade's mind will have moved on. He's all she can think about.

* * *

The message from Crystal could be another chapter for my book. How did she get Teddy's burner phone number? Did she somehow get the phone to him?

Then I remember on the night Teddy died, as I hid the phone under the basin in the ladies' toilets, Crystal appeared a minute later. She must have seen me, and later lifted the phone out to get the number. There was no password on the phone, and enough charge to turn it on. That must be it, although it now seems so long ago.

Later, as I toss and turn in bed, I'm engulfed by fear. Maybe Crystal is really looking out for me, and warning me what might happen if I tell my story. If she is a hired assassin, goodness knows how far she'd go to keep me quiet.

But it'll not stop me writing my story, and maybe one day, when I'm old and grey, I'll be brave enough to tell all.

Tomorrow, one thing is certain. I'll be driving down to the coast, and chucking the burner phone into the sea.

Tying it to a brick if need be, to make sure the past sinks to the bottom of the ocean.

97

JADE

May – two months later

Hayley and I are finally given the all-clear to leave Spain, go home, or go wherever we want.

But for now, I'm going nowhere. Except back to Marcus's finca. He's been the best thing that's ever happened to me. Despite his cat allergy, he doesn't complain, keeping his distance from Gato when he can. That said, Gato is still a little creep, moseying between Marcus and me. He does slink away though when Marcus starts to wheeze, and the inhaler appears.

We've installed a cat flap in the office door, and Gato now comes and goes, but is always sitting up in his cosy new cat bed, watching for us in the mornings.

When I say Gato sleeps in the office, he sleeps in the far corner of what was once my office. In a little alcove behind a partition. Marcus and I joined forces, deciding to stop fighting for commissions, and installed an adjoining door between what were our separate premises. Gato seems to have worked out that he's to stay in my half of the new set-up.

We no longer fight for clients, or for commissions. Although I do take a back seat when a pretty woman wanders in. Marcus is still a bit of a slimeball when he's after a sale. He's the slickest real-estate agent ever, but at least I can keep an eye on him if the women get too familiar. We've reached a gentlemen's agreement that if schmoozing clients involves drinks and dining out, then we come as a pair.

I'm currently sitting at my desk, watching the world go by. The resort is busy at last, the warm weather finally here, and Seamus's kiosk has proven to be a little gold mine. Things are looking up, and I finally feel a glimmer of hope for the future.

Suddenly, Hayley approaches the kiosk, having completed her last wander round the resort. Since Avery's death, she's walked every day. Round and round. She's lost a load of weight, and gone back to a beautiful auburn hair tone. She could do with a new wardrobe, though, but I think her appearance is still the last thing on her mind.

She got rid of her creepy new flatmate-cum-boyfriend, Damon, telling him she didn't want anything more to do with him. After he owned up to concocting the phoney threatening letters, petrified she might tell the Spanish police about them, she knew she'd never trust him again.

Although we're *all girls together*, having stuck religiously to our stories, there's something about Hayley I don't quite trust. Marcus jokes I'm jealous of her, but it's not that. It's something more. My skin prickles whenever she appears.

Hopefully after today, I won't ever have to see her again.

She's standing by the kiosk, laughing with Seamus, and chatting merrily while he makes the coffees. He pops three takeaway cups into a holder, and gives her a handful of complimentary biscuits.

I watch through the window as she heads my way.

'*Hola*,' she says, stepping through the door. 'Coffees?'

She extracts the cups, and sets two down for Marcus and me.

'Thanks. Are you all packed up?' I ask.

'Yep. Off in an hour. Back to Blighty.'

'What's the weather like there?'

'Ghastly. Rain, rain, and more rain. At least everywhere should be green.'

'Pity you'll miss the sunshine.'

I look outside, relishing the heat streaming through the glass. This is more like it, the sight making my insides sing.

'I know, but I need to get back to work.'

My heart beats faster at the word *work*. I'll never forget she's a reporter, or that I fell for her phoney lines of being an aspiring artist.

'Have you decided what you're going to do?'

I ask the question even though I'm dreading the answer. What if she decides one day to tell her story?

Marcus is on a call, but I know he's listening. He's like Teddy must have been. With the hearing of a moth. Actually the hearing of the greater wax moth, the creature with the best hearing in the whole animal kingdom. I finger a copy of E. W. Egghead's latest volume which I keep on my desk. My fingers are damp as hell, anxiety making my whole body perspire.

'I'm not sure yet. I'm going back on the newspaper's payroll, and I'll see how things go from there.'

My relief is short-lived.

'In my spare time I might still write my thriller. *The Marbella Roof Terrace Murder*. Fact mingled with fiction.'

She must see my horrified expression because she laughs. The first laugh in months.

'You're not serious?'

'Ha ha. Only kidding.'

I wish I was convinced, but there's nothing more I can do. I know how scared she still is, and the fear is unlikely to leave her any time soon. With Astrid still alive, I doubt either of us will ever sleep soundly again.

I get up, go round to her side, and open my arms for a hug.

'You take care, and keep in touch.'

'Will do.'

Over her shoulder I see Marcus watching us. He winks. He's got my back.

I've never told him the whole story. Hayley and I made a pact to keep the details to ourselves. We've agreed never to tell anyone the whole story, and how we've worked out that Crystal likely killed Teddy as well as Avery.

The police, so far, haven't been able to trace Crystal. Presumably she was out of the country before they were on to her. Crystal Morrison wasn't her real name, but I suspect she has many aliases. And many passports. Hayley and I have nicknamed her The Vixen. The *She-Jackal*. It's our private joke.

The name Astrid Olsen has never been mentioned by the police, but Hayley and I suspect she may have hired Crystal on the dark web, possibly having no other link to the assassin.

With Astrid still alive, we know the need to hold tight on to our secrets. While she and Crystal are out there, no one is safe.

Hayley hugs Marcus next, and then picks Gato up. He licks her face, and his slithery tongue laps up the tears.

'Bye, little fellow.'

As she walks away, she calls over her shoulder. 'Keep in touch. *Hasta luego*. See you later.'

And with that she's gone.

Much as I like Hayley, truth is, I'm praying I won't ever see her again. Far too many bad memories.

She's one person I'll definitely be ghosting.

98

Once Hayley leaves, I decide to go for my own power walk, and soak up the rays. Today I'm ready to celebrate a whole new chapter.

As I stroll through the Spanish Village, and past my apartment, now devoid of crime-scene blue tape, I shiver. The place is on the market, but as yet there's been no interest. I no longer care if it never sells. Personally, I'd prefer the whole block to be pulled down.

I start taking photos as I walk round the resort, snapping the location of every new CCTV camera. There's been an overkill of installations since the gruesome murders, of which the smarmy sales agents avoid mention.

The resort is now really busy and as I walk, slowly, leisurely for the first time in ages, I remember why I fell in love with the place all those months ago.

It really is a little bit of heaven. I lift my sunglasses down from my head, tilt them over my eyes, and feel full of hope.

As I mosey down the long stretch towards the tennis and padel courts, my heart speeds up. I remember the black car that nearly ran me over. I feel panic when I remember how close I was to being bundled into the boot and taken away and chopped up. The nightmares keep me awake at night.

It was Crystal who came to my rescue. When she turned up, the Land Rover sped away. It was as if she knew they were around, and she was looking out for me.

I pass the fig trees. It's now time for the Brevas harvest. The first of two fig seasons. I smile, chuffed at my ever-growing knowledge of completely useless information. I hop over the kerb, and pick a handful of fruit to fill my rucksack. I sit down under a small pergola, glug at my water bottle, and chomp into the succulent figs.

I glance at my phone. There have been no pings, nothing to make me anxious, and I smile when I notice there's a message from Marcus.

Hopefully repeating that he's up for a huge celebration tonight, now that Ms Scrivens has left the country.

When I read the words, the world starts to spin, and a piece of fig lodges in the back of my throat.

> You'll not believe it. I think I've got us a buyer for Avery Knowles's villa already. Fill you in when you get back. XXXX

I should be pleased, more money in the account, but it's the mention of Avery's name that sets the panic off again. With all the villas on the whole resort, why would anyone want to buy the dead man's villa?

Also, it'll surely take forever for probate to be sorted in Spain. The buyer might have months to wait for completion.

Something feels off kilter.

I get up, and start to walk on, chucking a half-eaten fig over the fence. Then I send a brief message back.

> Great news. Who is the buyer?

I pause. Watch the screen as he types.

When he sends the message through, my legs buckle. This can't be happening.

> Someone from Norway called Astrid Olsen. Says you're old friends!

EPILOGUE
CRYSTAL

Ho Chi Minh City

I see her long before she sees me. I'm in disguise, my face matching one of my twenty passport aliases. My hair is shorn like a cadet's, and fake tattoos rampage up my neck. Unlikely she'll recognise me as the girl who posed as Avery Knowles's girlfriend on the day of the pool party. I was a random guest then of little interest to her.

She'd hired an unknown assassin from the dark web, and unbeknown to her I was already at work on the job. She only learnt later that Avery's new girlfriend, Crystal, was in fact her killer. Of course, she doesn't know my real name. No one does.

Meeting a client face to face is something I've never done before, but Astrid Olsen insisted as part of the deal. For £4 million, I agreed to take the risk. She paid a cool £2 million upfront, and the balance came through on the day I hurled Avery over the balcony.

I watch as she steps out into the road, across eight lanes of traffic. Even from inside the café the roar of mopeds and motorcycles screams through the glass. The roads in Ho Chi Minh City are like assassins in plain sight. To take them on, you need to be brave, but Astrid Olsen fears nothing. She walks with arrogance, not a care in the world. She doesn't even acknowledge the vehicles weaving this way and that, assuming they'll navigate round her.

We could have met up anywhere in the world. Astrid was travelling when I did the killings, and I suspect this is a modus operandi on her part, guaranteeing foolproof alibis.

She pushes open the heavy door, scans the room, and smiles in my direction. She must know it's me as all the other customers look like locals. Although I'm sitting down, my height could also be a clue. She'll not recognise me from the day of the pool party. Then I looked completely different. Feminine and frail, and clinging on to Avery.

She potters across to where I'm sitting by the window.

'Hello,' she says. 'Crystal?'

She's playing the game that Crystal is my real name.

'Astrid?'

'Who else?'

She's puffing heavily as she sits down.

'Would you like a drink?' I ask.

'Oh, yes, please. I doubt they do champagne, so a cappuccino should hit the spot.'

We could be old friends meeting for a catch-up.

All killers are deranged, psychopathic, but their public personas are multi-layered. Astrid is charming, relishing her role as chaotic millionaire benefactor. Looking at her, it's hard to believe she's left a trail of bodies in her wake. Yet I suspect she's proud of her legacy.

Am I mad? Probably, but who cares? I'm purely the paid tool

to get a job done. With villas in Spain, Switzerland, and France, money is my sole motivator.

'You got your money safely?' Astrid asks, slurping on the frothy coffee, and licking stubby fingers between mouthfuls.

'Yes, thank you.' I keep it brief.

I'm not sure at this point who should be more scared. I kill for money. She orders the hits. She'd be wise to fear me, and likewise, I should fear her. A few million and she could have me silently disappear. But in an instant, I could also make her disappear. That's how hired assassins work.

Both Astrid and I know the score.

'Okay, Crystal. Can I call you Crystal?' Astrid asks, beaming broadly and winking.

'Of course.'

'I want to tie down some loose ends. Avery and Stephen have both been dealt with? Right?'

She clasps her hands together.

'Yes.'

I wait for her to carry on as she asks the sort of questions that I normally get asked anonymously. But Astrid is looking in the whites of my eyes.

'What about the loose ends? Jade? Hayley? Damon? Anyone else?'

Astrid hums, clapping her hands in refrain.

'The men were the problem. They've been dealt with.'

'Ha ha. It usually is the men, isn't it?' She pauses a second. 'What about Jade? Do you think she can be trusted to keep her mouth shut? Tell me honestly.'

I like Jade. I don't like many people, but she's brave, unscrupulous. George Stubbs sealed her fate. She knows what happened to him, and that Astrid masterminded his murder, but she also knows when to keep her mouth shut. She was witness to Avery's death. I know she saw me throw him over the balcony. She saw my face, but gave me time to get away before she squealed.

'Leave her. You'll have no problems from Jade.'

'And Hayley?'

Do I tell her now that Hayley is a journalist, whose aim might still be to expose the whole sorry George Stubbs saga? Likely she already knows, as Stephen doubtless let too much slip. His treachery was probably what got him killed.

But you know what? It's not my problem. Hayley is okay too, and after today I'll be walking away from this job. Moving back to my base in Switzerland. Astrid Olsen will never find me again unless I want her to.

I never met Stephen before I smashed his skull open with the doorstop.

And as they say: Don't shoot the messenger.

* * *

MORE FROM DIANA WILKINSON

Another book from Diana Wilkinson, *The Girl in the Window*, is available to order now here:

https://mybook.to/GirlInWindowBackAd

ACKNOWLEDGEMENTS

As always, thank you to readers everywhere who pick up each new book in anticipation of getting lost inside the intrigue of someone else's story. Readers, you are an author's greatest prize.

I usually have a long list of people to thank when a book finally gets into print: early readers; friends and family members who encourage me along the way. As ever, I am grateful to you all, and trust by now you know who you are. Thank you.

But as with all my books, since I joined the Boldwood team, I have one stand-out person to thank. Emily Yau is the most amazing editor. This time round she did almost as much work as I did in writing *The Girl on the Balcony*. She has such a skill in picking out in detail how a book can be improved. Her suggestions always make sense, and getting this important book to print is testament to her perseverance and dedication. Thanks, Emily.

Boldwood Books are the most amazing publishers. I feel more than blessed to be in their fold. I would like to thank each and every member of the team for their tireless and professional efforts in getting authors' books out into the world.

Finally, the biggest thanks, as always, goes to Neil, my long-suffering husband who, every day, has to listen to the trials and tribulations of an aspiring author. And to James: still the most wonderful son in the world.

ABOUT THE AUTHOR

Diana Wilkinson is the number one bestselling author of psychological thrillers. Formerly an international professional tennis player, she hails from Belfast, but now lives in Hertfordshire.

Sign up to Diana Wilkinson's mailing list here for news, competitions and updates on future books.

Follow Diana on social media:

- X x.com/DiWilkinson2020
- facebook.com/DiKennett
- instagram.com/diddlers37

ALSO BY DIANA WILKINSON

One Down

Right Behind You

The Woman in My Home

You Are Mine

The Missing Guest

The Girl in Seat 2A

The Girl in the Window

The Girl on the Balcony

THE Murder LIST

**THE MURDER LIST IS A NEWSLETTER
DEDICATED TO SPINE-CHILLING
FICTION AND GRIPPING
PAGE-TURNERS!**

**SIGN UP TO MAKE SURE YOU'RE ON
OUR HIT LIST FOR EXCLUSIVE DEALS,
AUTHOR CONTENT, AND
COMPETITIONS.**

**SIGN UP TO OUR
NEWSLETTER**

BIT.LY/THEMURDERLISTNEWS

Boldwood

Boldwood Books is an award-winning fiction publishing company seeking out the best stories from around the world.

Find out more at www.boldwoodbooks.com

Join our reader community for brilliant books, competitions and offers!

Follow us
@BoldwoodBooks
@TheBoldBookClub

Sign up to our weekly deals newsletter

https://bit.ly/BoldwoodBNewsletter

Printed in Dunstable, United Kingdom